Ashes and Other Inheritances

A Small Town Best Friends Mystery Novel
with a Sweet Romance
Book Four of the Soul Sisterhood Series

Cori Wamsley

Aurora Corialis Publishing
Pittsburgh, PA

ASHES AND OTHER INHERITANCES
Copyright © 2026 By Cori Wamsley
All rights reserved. No part of this book may be used, reproduced, stored in a retrieval system, or transmitted by any means—electronic, mechanical, photocopy, microfilm, recording, or otherwise—without written permission from the publisher, except in the case of brief quotations embodied in critical articles or reviews.
For more information, address cori@auroracorialispublishing.com
This is a work of fiction. Names, characters, businesses, places, events, locales, and incidents are either the products of the author's imagination or used in a fictitious manner. Any resemblance to actual persons, living or dead, or actual events is purely coincidental.
Paperback ISBN: 978-1-958481-68-4
Ebook ISBN: 978-1-958481-69-1
Printed in the United States of America
Cover designed by Getcovers
Edited by Susan Helene Gottfried, West of Mars

Other Books by Cori Wamsley

Contemporary Fiction:

The Soul Sisterhood Series
    Braving the Shore
    The Treasures We Seek
    Good in Theory

Business:
    The SPARK Method: How to Write a Book for Your Business Fast

Children's:
    Monkey Mermaid Magic
    The Knight and the Ninjas

Anthologies:
    Twenty Won: 21 Female Entrepreneurs Share their Stories of Resilience During a Global Pandemic
    Living Kindly: Bold Conversations about the Power of Kindness

Praise for Ashes and Other Inheritances

"Haunting and beautiful. In this richly atmospheric tale of smoke and echoes, a century-old journal propels the heroine into an adventure of family mystery, tragic fire, and a town's dark secrets. On her journey of self-discovery, she finds these threads of forgotten life tangled in her own. This soulful novel makes you wonder if some flames are never truly extinguished."

~ Em S. A'cor

BookFest award-winning author of the Tweet Hearts series

"*Ashes and Other Inheritances* is a sweet, slightly spooky romance, as if Demi Moore, in the classic movie *Ghost*, meets *Antiques Roadshow*. Five stars!"

~ Ann Howley

Author of *The Memory of Cotton*

"Small town and international intrigue laced throughout a dynamite plot. An engaging, fun read that melds heart-warming romance with a fascinating mystery that transcends time. A page-turner sure to please!"

~ Cathy Corn

Author of The Lilith & the Fairies Romantic Suspense Series and The Lilly & Sophie Fairy Adventure Series

"*Ashes and Other Inheritances* captivated me from the first page to the last page. Whether you previously read any of the Soul Sisterhood series or not, you will enjoy learning about these characters and their lives. I could picture the small town because of the visual details Cori Wamsley described and could feel the love triangle that almost happened. I couldn't wait until all the pieces of the puzzle started to fit into an incredible, unique story that was unexpected but so exciting! Bravo Cori Wamsley for keeping my attention so I wanted to keep reading page after page."

~ Denise Ann Galloni

Leadership Consultant, Author, Speaker, and TV Host of *Empowering You*

"Every one of Cori Wamsley's books lights you up while fueling you with divine truth, all while being thoroughly entrenched in the story, wildly entertaining. They're the kind of heartwarming stories that have you curling up with a hot cup of tea, nestled in your favorite, cozy reading spot, chunky knitted blanket and all! You can't put them down! This one is no exception. I can't wait for everyone to read it."

~ Marta Sauret Greca

Bestselling Author of The Minimalist Method, Powerful Synergy, and Course Corrected | Speaker | Podcast Host | Financial Representative

"*Ashes and Other Inheritances* is a page-turning story that invites you on an enchanting mystery adventure. Teeming with culture, history, and a spiritual crossroads, the author crafts a sensory-rich atmosphere that deeply immerses you with each page.

"Morgan's journey not only guides her toward the correct path for her life but simultaneously unravels hidden truths that have remained buried in her quaint town. Her determination and growth make her a character you can't help but root for, and with romantic undertones and a backstory that tugs at your heartstrings, you won't be able to put this book down until you're finished."

~ Lexi Kingston

Author of *That Girl & This Guitar*

"Reading *Ashes and Other Inheritances* is like enjoying the perfect cannoli—well done at the edges, sweet at the center, and filled with a delicious story that lingers long after the last bite. By the final page, you will realize this story of mystery and love is yet another Cori Wamsley decadent treat. *Ashes and Other Inheritances* isn't just a book; it's a literary dessert you'll want to devour."

~ Dr. Shellie Hipsky

CEO of Inspiring lives, Executive Director of The Global Sisterhood Nonprofit, Editor-in-Chief of *Inspiring Lives Magazine*, and Bestselling Author

"I have loved every story in the Soul Sisterhood series, but *Ashes and Other Inheritances* takes the cake. Cori has such a gift for storytelling, and I love how seamlessly she intertwines mystery, intrigue, and romance. Her details are vivid, her characters unforgettable, and the story is an absolute joy to read. This book is fun, poignant, and kept me up far too late—I simply couldn't stop turning the pages!"

~Claudine François

Functional Health Practitioner and Author of *Your Midlife Body Code*

To every woman who has ever sifted through the ashes of what was and dared to build something new. This story is yours.

Chapter One

Some people say that life is a bowl of cherries, and they would be right in some respects. There are definitely pits. And a variety of sweet and sour moments.

But what I think they miss out on is the fact that you are literally comparing life to something that was once living and has been plucked from the living thing that nurtured it. It begins dying the moment that it becomes valuable to us. And if you don't eat the fruit, it rots.

Morbid, but *seize the freaking day*, right?

So I do. I always have. I've always sought the most flavorful, big moments. The moments that make us feel like we're truly living. The moments that leave us breathless because *that was a rush* ... or *we almost got caught* ... or *I just defined another epoch of living*.

I'm not an adrenaline junkie. But I love to feel alive.

"This is so close to perfection ..." I mutter to myself. I'm in Castel Gandolfo, a gorgeous town in Italy, south of Rome, with the man of my dreams. As in, he's in my dreams and not here in Italy with me physically.

I'm dreaming about him right now, as I'm gazing at the pristine lake from the porch of the villa, the sun angling off of the water, making it sparkle. I sip my cappuccino and let the flavor wash over me. Real Italian cappuccino, the bitterness of the roast mingling with sugary sweetness. Thinking about how wonderful it would be if he were here. But we broke up months ago. We had to.

I get this funny sinking feeling in my belly. Dread? Loneliness? A missed opportunity for joy? Or maybe it's something else.

Maybe I should have invited him to escape with me anyway. Just to see what he would say.

Unfortunately, this impulse hits when I'm halfway across the world from Mr. Gorgeous. I should have invited him to join me, and I am kicking myself for not thinking about it before.

Anyone have a time machine?

"You remind me of a painting." Interrupting my musings, Signore Zangari joins me on the porch and leans against the railing of his lovely home.

"Oh, I do?" I smile thoughtfully at my host, raising my eyebrows. "I didn't realize I was so picturesque."

He laughs. "No, you remind me of an *actual* painting. *Tè e Fantasticheria*."

"What does that mean?"

"Tea and Reverie."

"Beautiful." I sip my coffee.

He gestures to me and then out at our gorgeous view. "It's a painting of a woman standing on a porch and looking at Lago Albano, painted somewhere in this area well over a hundred years ago. It's quite famous in the region." Pulling out his phone, he calls up the image and shows me. A woman in the foreground gazes dreamily at the lake in the distance, a porcelain cup in her hand. Her hair hangs loosely around her shoulders and her blue-green dress sweeps to the right, as if she just entered the frame.

I glance from the painting to my coffee cup to the lake and back. "I don't see a resemblance."

Again, he chuckles. "You have the same faraway look. Like you are thinking of something magical that we can't see."

Now it's my turn to laugh. "You're reading my mind." We smile at each other, sip our drinks, and gaze back at the lake. But I refrain from telling him about my daydreams. They are like a delicious little burrito wrapped up in my mind, warm and welcoming. Or should it be a ravioli, since we're in Italy? "Is this painting at the papal palace? I'd love to see it while I'm here."

"Sadly, it has been missing for over a hundred years. There are rumors that it was smuggled to America." He points at his phone again. "This image was created from the artist's original sketches by someone who saw the painting and redid it by memory. That's all we have now." He points at the description on the Lazio Museum, Rome's website. "This painting is in Roma," he confirms.

"That's a shame." How sad that a piece of history went missing.

A beat later, Signore Zangari nods toward the worksite near the villa. "Progress is good, yes?"

"Yes, Baker & Willow will be pleased," I agree, pausing to inhale the aroma of my coffee. "Kenzi and I both are. And everything is on budget." I flew in to check the progress on the event center project being managed by the architectural firm I run finance for.

"We were certainly lucky that Kenzi attended our dig." He smiles. "Ottavia and I are so happy."

Signore Z wanted to open an event venue on their property, but as you would expect in the region around Rome, the ground was riddled with artifacts. In this case, a chunk of a house. We had to stop excavating and bring in a team to check it out.

Kenzi is one of our architects and had happened to volunteer for the archaeological dig at the Zangari villa. She struck a chord with Signore Z. By the time the dig wrapped up, Kenzi had inadvertently talked him into incorporating the beautiful ancient building into the new design. He and his wife, Ottavia, pitched her for the project. When all was said and done, Baker & Willow ended up taking it on, with Kenzi leading the whole thing.

Kenzi has flown back and forth several times to ensure that her design is coming to fruition properly, and as luck would have it, Baker & Willow decided to send me over before the next phase starts.

I didn't complain! A week in Italy in the fall—or, well, any time of year—is *fantastico*!

Smiling at Signore Z, I add, "I negotiated with a couple of the local vendors for different aspects of the project. We're getting tile from Caltagirone, which so perfectly coordinates with the ruins."

"I'm impressed. The most beautiful tile always comes from that city." He puts his hands in his pockets and smiles. "Baker & Willow has been spectacular. Only a few more months."

I nod, turning back to the lake. "I'm going to miss this place." I drape my carnation pink cashmere sweater over my arm and glance at my suitcases. Nico will be around with the car any minute to take me to my hotel. "Glad I get a day in town to explore before I head to Rome." And I'm thankful that the magic doesn't end here, today.

"You need to see the papal palace," Signore Z says. "I think you'll enjoy the gardens there." I did rather love the gardens at the villa, so he's probably right. I spent so much time sitting on a bench in the shade of the lemon trees crunching numbers that I will always associate the smell of lemons with spreadsheets.

A black sedan pulls into the drive, and I wrap the older man in a big hug. It's not very businesslike, but everyone from Baker & Willow has been staying at the villa, right beside the building site, so I feel like I'm leaving my uncle. I'll miss the big family-style dinners in the villa's dining room ... and someone else cooking for me for three meals a day. "I hope to be back again before we wrap up. You and Signora Z have been so kind, and you have such a beautiful home!"

"Ciao! We hope you come back, too." With a sly smile, he slips a long, narrow box into my open tote bag, and I just *know* that it's a gorgeous pair of handmade Italian loafers from his company, Pelletteria Zangari.

"Oh!" I want to rip into the box like it's my birthday. "Thank you!"

He laughs easily. "Wait till you get to your room." Then Nico loads my bags and whisks me down the road to Lago Albano Albergo.

Once I unpack in my room—and try on the chocolate brown loafers; YES!—I decide to sit on the balcony and enjoy the sunshine and an afternoon breeze: *il dolce far niente*. There really is so much sweetness in doing nothing! I pull out my crochet hook and work on another coffee cup koozie to drop off at the shop by my house. I've been selling them there for a couple years, and they're always a hit.

The air is fragrant, like there is a bakery nearby, and I make a note to check on that for the morning. The sky is Tiffany blue, and the view from the balcony shows me the entire town down into the valley. Catching myself halfway through an enormous exhale of pure bliss, I realize something: I'm on vacation alone in gorgeous Castel Gandolfo, Italy, and I'm sitting on my balcony crocheting? Maybe this is every little old lady's dream, and I'm just living it out a little early.

A lot early. Thirty-five is the new eighty-five, right?

And that's my cue to leave. Gotta grab life's sweet cherries.

Once I finish my current koozie, I snatch my crossbody and sweater and head downstairs, out into the open air. The road here is cobblestone, but they have a sidewalk, and it's fairly modern. I head down the road toward the palace. There are lots of little shops here, including that bakery I smelled earlier, so I browse the windows as I stroll by. They even have a yarn store!

I wonder if it's like Spin a Yarn back home—an adorable little bookshop, knitter's haven, and café. I was picking up yarn there last fall so I could make more koozies when I ran into Aaron coming out of the mini-market nearby with his arms loaded with bags. He stopped to say *hi*, and I was delighted. Our last breakup had been his doing.

Aaron is irresistible, and I wasn't seeing anyone. Next thing I knew, we were back together.

And apart a couple months after. And back together for a few weeks and then apart ... Actually, I haven't seen Aaron in several months now. Aside from the daydream at Villa Z. I wonder what he's doing ...

I've been peering into the yarn shop window as I reminisce, noting sweaters, vests, and scarves that are meant to lure people in, but I'll just stop there on the way back. As I turn to go—"Oh!" I just stepped backward on someone's foot. "So sorry! *Mi scuzi!*" I stutter-step like I'm walking on hot coals.

"Sorry, sorry, my fault," a man's voice says. "I was looking down." He shuffles a heavy bag, so I'm guessing he just exited the bookstore next door.

Then I look from the bag to the face. Wait. *Who did I just trample?* "Aaron?" *Who else looks like a blonde Henry Cavill?* "What are you doing here?" Dear God. I manifested my ex-boyfriend. I'm a wizard! It's Morgan Magic.

I should have that trademarked.

"Morgan? Morgan Sturm?" Aaron does a double take. "I'm on vacation. You too?"

"Actually, I was working till this morning; just clocked off. I'm here overseeing the numbers on a project." I smile, but I turn to go. I'm not about to bother him when he's on vacation. "It was nice seeing you. Enjoy your time here. It's truly gorgeous!"

"Yeah, same to you. It's good seeing you."

I flick my fingers warmly in a little wave. As I turn toward the palace, though, I notice that he's heading in the same direction. "Following me?"

Aaron chuckles. "I wanted to fit in the palace before dinner."

I bite my lip. Bad idea? Or okay? "I wouldn't mind the company, if you want to tag along." I don't have a fragile heart. I can handle hanging out with Aaron for the afternoon. I won't lust after him when we go back to our normal lives.

"I'm okay with it if you are." Aaron walks a few steps beside me. "Actually, when I was planning this trip, I kept thinking that it was totally up your alley."

A wave of warmth for this man works its way through my body, and I stuff it down and pretend I'm dead inside. But I can't. It's hard. I want to be here with him. He's right. "Yeah, this is absolutely my thing." Funny that we never planned a trip abroad together, but I guess we never were together long enough for our relationship to seem that stable. Claire once said it was like watching a ping-pong match. I'm guessing it's not because she found it boring.

As we enjoy the walk together, we end up falling back into a groove like we never broke up. And honestly, we wouldn't have if his job hadn't transferred him to the Charlotte office. At least, *I* don't think so.

We're talking and laughing, sharing our experiences over the past few days—he's been city hopping and landed here for the day. His plan is to take a high-speed train to Rome in the morning.

When we finally get to the palace, I drink in the opulence. The gardens here are so perfect that they must have someone employed full-time to manicure the topiaries, trimming a quarter inch of leaf here and there. Like obsessive perfection. We enter the building and do the tour. Then, we return to the garden. I'm in awe of the view across Lago Albano. The sky and sea are so blue that they don't seem real. The breeze carries an intoxicating scent of the nearby oleander and yellow may mingling with the musk of Aaron's cologne. *Magnifica*!

I squeeze his hand and look at him with wonder. "I can't believe we get to experience this together." My stomach gets tight as I recall the feeling of having his hand in mine but recognize that this is just a pretty fantasy. I'll be fine.

"This has been really nice. Feels like fate." Aaron wraps his arms around me in a huge hug and nuzzles that jaw into my tresses. It's a familiar move, but not too forward. "I missed you. Want to grab dinner before we head back to our rooms?"

"Sounds good," I murmur, my eyes half closed as I gaze at the sea and get drunk on this feeling.

He takes my hand, and we walk down Via Conciatore toward the restaurant that I found my first night here, Ristorante lo Rubino. The gnocchi was amazing, and I want Aaron to try it since this is his lone night in town.

We both order the gnocchi and side salad, along with the house wine. Funny thing about Italy: You just order house wine with every meal. It's totally normal. And cost-effective. I'm not one of those finance people obsessed with costs, but when special treats come in under budget, it warms the cockles of my heart.

As he walks me back to my hotel, our bellies a happy level of full, I notice a little shop that piques my interest. The centuries-old entry is flanked with huge picture windows full of antique knickknacks like pottery and a typewriter, books and doilies, jewelry and a barber's kit. I pause and eye up the *Sweeney Todd*-style knives and hum a little tune from the musical.

Aaron chuckles. "I was thinking the same thing." I smile up at him as my heart flutters. "You want to go in, right?"

"Yeah, let's check it out." I glance at the hours and pull him toward the ancient wooden door. "We have plenty of time before they close."

A tinkle of bells echoes through the shop as I shove the heavy door open. When we walk in, I'm hit with the stale smell of old paper and dusty desks, of centuries-old dirt in crevices and musty drawers that haven't been opened in years. The smell of the forgotten, of unknown mysteries.

The air in this store has a weight to it. I'm in a city where people have been living for thousands of years, in a building likely hundreds of years old, in a new-ish shop full of treasures untold from generations past. I see things that my grandmother and my great-grandmother would have used. A funny iron made of just iron—no electric cord. An inkwell. There's a card catalog ...

Okay, that's not cool. We had card catalogs when I was little. That's not an antique.

I'll let it go, though.

"Check this out," Aaron says.

I meander through the rest of the store to where he's standing in front of a painting of a woman wearing a dress that makes her look like an ostrich. I don't think the look is on purpose. "Weird."

"I kinda dig it." He puts his hands in the pockets of his jeans and cocks his head to the side.

"It would be awfully hard to get that in your suitcase."

"Good point." He takes a few steps and picks up something from a rolltop desk. "This, though, might be nice."

I peer over and see that he's holding a ceramic bowl with the Castel Gandolfo seal on it. The image of an angel standing on what looks like a castle reminds me of Castel Sant'Angelo, the building by the Vatican. "Neat. Is that a souvenir from the papal palace or something?"

"Shaving kit," Aaron says. He points at the brush that was lying beside it and then turns the bowl over. "Says it's from the 1890s. The price is good. I like it." He picks up the brush and smiles at me.

"You wanna grab the knives from the window to go with it?" I deadpan.

"Probably have a better shot of getting the ostrich lady on the plane than that."

I sing another familiar refrain from *Sweeney Todd*.

"I missed you," Aaron says softly. Which may sound like a strange thing to say to a woman singing a song about barber's knives, but really, this is part of my allure. He brushes his hand across my cheek, and my breath catches. "Did you find anything?"

"I might have," I whisper. *Trouble*.

The moment is broken by two men loudly exclaiming in Italian about the ostrich lady painting, gesticulating wildly. It is a cool painting. Even with the language barrier, I get it.

With a smile at Aaron, I turn and wander through the maze of trinkets, give the card catalog the stink eye, and find a stack of books. They're all in Italian, but they look so beautiful that I pick them up and browse anyway, enjoying the feel of the leather bindings and the brittle paper in my hands.

When we finally approach the cash register, I don't have anything, so I browse the rack of tourist pamphlets by the door while Aaron pays for the shaving kit. Then I spot one that looks amazing.

"Aaron!"

He startles, looks at me, and gestures *what* with his hands.

"We are so doing this." I hold up a brochure for skydiving in the countryside outside of Rome. God, what a rush that would be! And so beautiful! Since I'm going to Rome tomorrow anyway, I should book this so we can experience it together. Wow!

I skydived in several cities in the U.S., but I haven't done it in Europe yet. I love to stretch myself and see what else is possible. And I love being around people who do the same thing. But will Aaron actually jump out of a plane with me? Hmmm.

"You're awfully into risky activities for someone in finance." Aaron gives me a big cheeky grin, and I swoon. He finishes paying and wraps an arm around my waist as we leave.

"This would be a helluva way to see Italy, don't ya think?"

"And a helluva way to go out!" Aaron laughs and pulls me close enough that I get a strong whiff of his aftershave. "I'd rather not jump out of a perfectly good airplane."

"Spoilsport," I deadpan. Maybe I'll go alone. This looks freakin' amazing. What a way to get your blood pumping!

"If you're heading to Rome, we could meet up. Did you have plans yet?"

I shrug. "No real plans. Just two days in Rome to explore wherever. I've seen Castel Gandolfo all week, so I could easily join you, if you want me to tag along."

"I would love that," Aaron says. Then he gestures at the brochure I'm clutching. "How about a compromise on your idea? What about a hot air balloon ride? It's a little more my speed, and it's still an overhead view."

I give him a sideways glance. I get it. Not everyone is up for that adrenaline rush, but he does make a good suggestion for a substitute that we would both enjoy, rather than saying that I should go by myself while he does something he wants to do. I always loved that about him. He sought out things that would make us both happy. "I'll think on it."

"That sounds perfect." His stubble brushes my forehead as he plants a kiss there. Then he pushes back, looking startled. "Sorry, I got caught up in ... in us. How we used to be."

"Yeah ..." I sigh. I shouldn't get too caught up, though, so I jokingly rub my forehead where I feel like I got cactus-ed. "You gonna whip out that shaving kit when you get to your room? Getting a little stubbly there."

"I'm not actually going to use this, but yes, I plan on shaving in the morning before we go." His laugh floats down the alleyway.

Hand in hand, we proceed back to my hotel, and I buy my ticket for the high-speed train to Rome in the lounge area. It leaves at eight a.m.

"I am walking where Julius Caesar walked." I realize that I'm carrying myself regally as I step on the stone walkway of the Forum, the fabric of my straight-legged trousers swishing playfully with each step. That idea of the area's grand past floors me. Think of the people who have walked here. For millennia! Few things really put your tiny speck of time in the scope of the universe in perspective like walking somewhere of this magnitude.

"Someone bought a chicken over there," I continue. "And someone plotted revenge over there. And someone prayed to their gods in that little temple, asking for rain or forgiveness or maybe a better husband. Imagine what has happened here."

"And now it's a tourist venue," Aaron adds. "There are dudes along the street dressed as gladiators making bank off of taking pictures with vacationers. Caesar must be groaning as he looks down ... or maybe up ... at all of this."

I chuckle. "Too funny."

When we leave the Forum, we stop for fresh fruit at a little shop. Then we meander past the Colosseum and through the winding streets leading to the Parthenon.

"I think this is my favorite piazza." I pause to take in the view and again feel the ghosts of peoples past. Aaron squeezes my hand and grins in agreement. I gesture toward the ancient temple. "Want to go in?" When he nods, we cross and enter.

It's cooler than I expected, so I untie the sweater from my waist and slide my arms in. It's almost like being in a basement, but it's open and broad. So much stone. And the details in the walls ...

I think the neatest thing, though, is the oculus, the round opening at the very top of the dome that lets the light in. I always wonder about people building something like that, climbing their scaffoldings and ladders, adding concrete. I think it's concrete. And as old as this building is, everything surprisingly looks perfectly proportional. I'm just eyeballing it, but it looks like the aperture is flawlessly round.

"Come check out the statues," Aaron says, so I join him on a stroll around the walls.

Then I notice the angle of the light coming in through the oculus, hitting the wall like a spotlight. It has an artsy feeling to it, so I pause to take a picture. Maybe I'll frame that when I get home.

As we leave, I have a peaceful feeling. And then, I get excited. First, there's a pizza place across the piazza from us, so we could actually have pizza in the piazza, a tongue twister as well as a tongue pleaser. And second, there is a man near the alley, just barely in the piazza proper, stretching a sheet out on the ground. I wonder ...

"Aaron, let's see what's up over there." I nod toward the guy, who appears to be setting handbags out on the sheet.

"What's he up to?" Aaron squints in his direction. "Is he a street vendor?"

"I think he's one of the knock-off purse guys."

"Oh." Aaron looks around like he wants to escape. "I don't think they're allowed to do that here." He gestures low, but I see where he's pointing: across the piazza from the sheet guy, toward another alley. "See that guy?" I nod. "I think he's the lookout."

I glance from the lookout back across the square to the sheet guy. I see the lookout nod in his direction and walk down the alley away from the square. "That makes sense." But there's a little tingle of excitement in my stomach. "Let's just walk by, though. I wonder if he has any Divya Shanti." I love her designs!

"Is that a good idea?" But Aaron doesn't stop me. Instead, he follows as I drag him across the piazza.

"*Buon giorno*," I say, with a perfect accent, to the gentleman with the sheet of wares. I'm actually pretty proud of the accent that I've been working on since finding out about this trip. One of the Zangaris' daughters, Ella, said I nailed it. And she was thrilled when I told her she knew American slang better than I do.

"*Buon giorno, bella.* We have many different designer brands at special prices. Please take a look."

How is it that they always know I actually speak English? Do I look like a tourist? Eh. "*Grazie,*" I reply. My eye catches on a gorgeous colorblock bag in coffee, cream, and teal. I squat and tip the bag. As I thought, it's a Divya Shanti. The logo is a perfect replica, spelled right and everything. Dang, I'm good. "*Quanto costa?*" I ask as I check the zippers.

The man reaches over and tips a tag on the purse in his direction. It's orange. No number. "*Quaranta.*"

"Hmmm." I love this part. A little thrill ripples through my chest as I pull out my phone and punch a phrase into the translator. "*Ne prenderesti trenta.*" Thirty is reasonable, even though forty is also reasonable. Will he take it though …

Grinning, the man sizes me up, then he casts a nervous glance down the other alleyway. "*Trentacinque.*" The smile returns to his face, so I'm guessing there is no danger.

I can't complain about thirty-five, so I respond, "*Bene,*" and fish out my euros. Right as I hand him the money, though, the guy from the other alley swoops over and yells something in Italian that I don't have time to translate. They grab the corners of the sheet, and I think they are going to dash, so I snag the purse I just paid for, nod a thanks, and zip away from them down another alley, hoping I'm out of the way. Also hoping that Aaron is following suit.

A moment later, as I'm running hand in hand with him through the streets of Rome, I have to laugh.

Maybe the impulse to go back in time and call him was actually a little intuitive hit. Maybe it wasn't me saying, "I wish you were here," but rather a homing beacon picking up on his presence less than a mile from my location.

If you believe that sort of thing.

The sound of our pounding footsteps echoes off of the cold stone walls that line our path. The long cobblestone alley arcs to the left ahead of us, and Aaron and I slow to a jog to avoid implicating ourselves, hearts pounding.

I glance at him and smile. He grins back, a dimple showing near the corner of his full lips, close to that chiseled jaw I love so much, and though my heart is still hammering outrageously, it skips a beat as I gaze at my perfect match. When the whistle hits my eardrum again, I smile slyly. "This way," I whisper.

In the alley a couple minutes later, I might be walking now and acting casually, but my heart is pounding like I just told the school bully off. My hands are quivering at my sides, and I tighten my grip on the purse handle. In my head, I sing "Let it Be," by the Beatles, to bring my breathing back to normal, just like Dad used to sing to me when I was upset as a child.

Behind us, I hear running and then the metallic shrill of a whistle. I rip the tag from my purse and casually throw the bag over my arm like it's been there all day. I'm wearing a crossbody already, but I doubt anyone will pay attention. Glancing at Aaron, I point at the shop we're in front of. "Chocolate?" I ask. When he nods, I grab his hand, and we dash in.

"I feel like I should be a little scared, but honestly, I don't think we did anything wrong." Aaron looks perplexed.

I fan myself for a moment. Whew! "I bought a knock-off bag, so I kinda did." The thick smell of chocolate overwhelms me along with the adrenaline racing through my veins. That did scare me a little. I don't want to end up in Italian prison, and I don't know enough Italian without the translator app to talk my way out of anything. I pull my phone out, intending to panic-search how to say *lawyer*, just in case, but I decide I'm overreacting and slip it back into my bag.

I breathe in the thick, sweet air and feel a little bit high. The slow breathing calms me, though, and I remove my sweater to help cool down. "Let's taste some," I say. I saunter up to the counter, eyeing the dark chocolate with ingredients like sea salt, olive oil, and some words I can't guess at. "*Due, per favore.*" I rub the light brown circular birthmark on my wrist as I wait. It's a habit I've had since childhood, and it's oddly comforting. The birthmark is slightly raised, so I can barely feel the edges of it on my thumb.

With gloved fingers, a woman dressed in white hands us each a chocolate, and I indulge in a big bite. As the flavors play a symphony across my tongue, I feel a shiver work its way down my body. Maybe this has been too much for one day, but *wow*, it is worth it to feel so ... I don't know, immersed in life right now.

Frantically, I pull out my phone again and translate, "I'll take a half pound," so I can continue to enjoy this the rest of the trip. We leave the shop a short time later much calmer and with another happy little bag in my hand. Surely the danger has passed by now.

We continue down the alley, in the opposite direction of the piazza, when Aaron says, "You've really done well today." He nods toward my bags. "Chocolates and a purse. Isn't that every girl's fantasy?"

"And you," I say breathily. I don't know what made me say that. Then the look in his eye, and the smell of chocolate, and the experience a few minutes before, drive me to take his jaw in my hands and claim his lips with my own. He walks me a couple steps toward the nearby building and presses me against it as he deepens the kiss. I feel off-kilter for a moment and touch the wall, cold stone, pock-marked where the marble pieces were removed long ago. Then I return my hands to his scruff, and we kiss for another hot minute.

"You're trouble," Aaron says suddenly. He plants another kiss on my mouth and wraps his arm around my waist.

"No one is around, and I love it when you kiss me like I'm your mistress." Then a flush of heat works its way up my neck and across my face. We aren't really together. "Sorry. I shouldn't have done that."

"I don't mind."

We both laugh and continue on toward the next piazza, where an obelisk rises from a fountain in the center. I don't make any jokes here. Really.

Another cute antique store catches my eye as we stroll by. It has a bizarre alligator in the window wearing a summer hat, and its tail is painted black and white stripes. What other strange things will we find in there? Obviously, I need to check it out!

The store is full of fun little stuff like this. Tea cups with the faces of former popes. A metal school bus full of metal children that just look weird. *Did kids really play with that?* A stack of playbills from an old theater. A *wunderkammer* ... Oooh! A real *wunderkammer*!

A cabinet of wonders was a thing back in the fifteen and sixteen hundreds. They were glass-doored cabinets full of little treasures like old coins, odd bones and feathers, special rocks, sketches and paintings and diagrams ... almost an intersection of history, natural history, and myth.

I imagine the people of Rome would have loved the concept. Their emperors were big fans of this stuff a thousand years before *wunderkammers* came into vogue. Lena, one of the consulting archaeologists on the project at the Zangari villa, told me about one of the emperors having a skeleton of a griffin—obviously, not a real one—in his estate. She said that they found it when they were examining the dig site, which I'm sure was an incredible surprise!

This particular *wunderkammer* is about my height, with a curved top and floral carvings along the thick wood supporting the doors. I'm guessing it's oak. The stain allows the wood grain to show through, and I imagine I see faces in the darker sections, moaning and screaming as if they are trapped within the planks.

I stare into the cabinet before me, wondering who else thought the things inside were special enough to put on display. I eye up the framed collection of local insects, each run through with a straight pin to hold them in place, and shudder. Humans can be so disturbing in their fascination with the world around them.

"Find anything interesting?" Aaron wanders over to the *wunderkammer* and wraps his arms around me.

I hum in response. "Not really. Just thinking about all the stuff in this cabinet. These are all someone's treasures. Isn't that neat to think about?"

He nods. "I see what you're getting at, but they all have price tags. I bet the shop owner put them there because they didn't have a better space for them, not because they were the collection originally housed in this piece."

"You're probably right." I move toward the front of the store, grabbing Aaron's hand in mine. Pausing by the cash register, I peruse the knickknacks that cover half the checkout counter.

Pens, bookmarks, local candy bars ... journals ...

I'm not really a journal person. Journaling doesn't have that *joie de vivre* that I believe all acts should have. Why would I be sitting around *writing* about what I've done when I can be out *doing*? And so many journals from back in the day are incredibly dull. I read my great-grandfather's from about one hundred years ago, and it carries all the details of the feed and seed that he used on the farm, along with any other purchases he made. It was about as exciting as the reports I usually have to generate for work—I love what I do, but recording all the transactions ... eye roll. And I certainly hope no one is sitting around reading that a hundred years from now and judging me for it.

But journals ... right now, I'm strangely attracted to one that looks like an old book. It has a red leather cover, aged to look like it's been around a long time. It looks like oil from someone's hand has darkened the cover, particularly around the edges, where they would have thumbed across and opened it wide. The richness of the red calls to me, fading from poppy to oxblood at the corners. And then, I notice that the letter M is burned into the cover near the top center. M for Morgan, of course.

Why are women suckers for stuff with their initials on it?

I pick it up and turn it over in my hands. It feels *right*, if that makes sense. It feels like it's already mine.

It feels like I'm probably still drunk from kissing Aaron and eating that chocolate and running from the Italian cops. Maybe I'm just loving everything and everyone right now.

But I'm still not putting the journal down.

"Did you want to get that?" Aaron asks.

I bite my lip, glance at his eyes, and then look back at the journal. I flip it open, and the pages are even the right yellowy shade of white, with that brownish edging detail. I think I need it. "Yeah, I'm getting this."

"I'd like to get it for you," Aaron says. He holds out his hand for the diary and then smiles at the cashier. "*Prendo questo.*"

"Thank you," I say as I snake my arms around him.

One day left on this dream vacation, but how could it top today? I place the package inside my new purse and link my arm in Aaron's as we leave the store.

"Now," I say, "how about that pizza in the piazza?"

Chapter Two

The taxi ride to the airport has to be one of the most uncomfortable of my life, in stark contrast to our experience in the hot air balloon yesterday afternoon.

Bouncing along in the car, I reminisce about the gentle way we floated across the sky, gazing into the distance at Rome proper. We were far enough away that it almost didn't seem real. You could ignore the roads and anything modern and just focus on the ancient city looming in the distance. I felt like I had traveled back in time. The view was absolutely breathtaking, and the company was, well, magical. Just being in Aaron's presence has always felt ... inspiring to me. He's always fired me up, always made me feel this quake of unrest like we would run off and do something big together.

Yeah, we used to argue a good bit, but it was always about the things that we were really passionate about. Like the way he made spaghetti—breaking the pasta in half before dropping it into the pot is offensive, even if I'm not Italian. Or the way I insisted on keeping my entire collection of Margot Ashford novels on the nightstand. Or the way he refused to iron his shirts because he liked the way they made him look "roguish." His word. Or the way I couldn't let him just have five minutes of peace when he got home at the end of work because I wanted to be by his side and see how his day went. I wanted to talk. I thought that was a normal thing.

I glance at Aaron and then return to the memory of the hot air balloon, the joyous globe that felt like it symbolized our relationship: perfect on the outside, kept afloat by a lot of heat, and ultimately not lasting that long.

God, I was going to miss him.

After three glorious days with Aaron, I know we're done. I knew it was coming, but I'm still crushed. I kinda let myself fall back into this. I love everything about him, but I already said I wasn't moving to Charlotte, North Carolina. And he couldn't stay in Pittsburgh. He wanted to be closer to family. I didn't want to move somewhere that warm. I still have Seattle in my blood, and Pittsburgh gives me the gloom and rain that I need.

Maybe I'm part vampire or something.

Daydreaming and continuing to hang out aren't going to change things. And flying back and forth between our two cities would be a pain in the butt. And to what end? If neither of us will move, then we just fly back and forth forever?

As these thoughts are playing out in my head, I look over at him again. He gets me. He always has. But when both people in a relationship are a lot ... I'm not sure that's a recipe for success.

I feel like I'm always running *to* him or *away* from him. Why?

It's like there's something I have to escape ... my mouth probably. Definitely.

"What's up?" Aaron says. He quirks his brow and gives me a half smile.

We round a curve way too fast, and the seatbelt pulls across my belly and shoulder. I brush my hand through the air, chasing away the cobwebs of our travels. "The driving is a little nutty," I whisper.

"Agreed." He smiles and pats my hand, but then he withdraws his to his lap. I guess he's thinking the same thing I was. It's better to start separating now.

At the airport, we finally find the bus to the American terminal and hop on. We're side by side, but Aaron already feels like he's a million miles away.

In the terminal, we grab a glass of wine and charcuterie as I wait for the inevitable. Then, Aaron stands and lets out a long sigh, stretching his back. He grabs his suitcase and looks at me, cocking his head the way a dog would, the way he always does. He kinda looks like a golden retriever right now.

"You sound like an old man," I say. Not going to tell him he looks like a dog.

"And you ... what can I say?" Aaron gives me a half smile. "Thanks for making this such a memorable trip." Then he clears his throat like I'm going to get a scolding. "I guess I should have been more careful. It's hard not to fall back to our old habits. I'm going to be lonely without you in Charlotte."

"I'll miss you too. Not that I'm one to be careful either."

"I always thought your adventurous side was the most fun." He gives a dry laugh and parts his lips to say something.

"Flight 159 to New York City, boarding at gate 10." The intercom ruins my life.

"We'll always have Rome," I joke. My eyes are welling with tears, despite my attempts to be tough.

With one hand holding his suitcase, Aaron gives me an awkward side hug. "I'm glad we got to do this, but leaving you is always hard."

I sniff loudly. *Jerk.* He knows I have a no crying policy. "What can I say? All the boys tell me that."

"You're not as tough as you try to be." He touches my chin. "Now, don't miss that plane."

We have two pieces of chocolate left, which we were saving for the airport. The best way to say *arrivederci* is to consume Italian chocolate. It's a rule. "Here ya go," I whisper. I hand him a small wrapped treasure, squeeze his hand, and pop my little cocoa delight in my mouth so I have something else to focus on. Then I walk away, my legs trudging forward like I'm trying to escape a vacuum.

"This was the longest freaking day," I mutter. Dragging my suitcase to the car feels like I'm lugging a semi.

Claire raises her eyebrows as she tosses my carry-on in the trunk of her SUV. "Here; I'll take pity on you." She grabs my checked bag with both hands and, with effort, boosts it in beside the carry-on. "What did you bring home from Italy? A dead body?"

"Yeah, the catacombs were having a sale."

"You're disturbed."

"I'm exhausted and heartbroken. There's a difference." I fill her in on the happenings of the last couple days.

"Shut up," she whispers. "I hate to say this again, but you know it's called a *breakup* because—"

"Stop. Yes. I know. *It's broken*." Read the book. Watched the movie. Learned the lesson many, many times. Maybe I need the t-shirt so I actually remember it. "Let's talk about you."

"I don't date."

"It's refreshing to hear people say that." For a moment, I enjoy the view of the sky, as gray as my mood, and the naked trees we zip past on the highway, as dead as my desire to listen to anyone's love story. "What did you do while I was gone? I feel like it's been a century."

"I worked. Helped Mom around the house. Visited Shannon and her family. Reaffirmed that I don't want kids."

"That will do it. Your nieces and nephews are cute, but five is a lot." We both nod, and then I chuckle. I'm the middle child of five. I was the *a lot* part of that crew. I know what it's like! We turn off the interstate, and I watch the stately old buildings on Main Street out my window for a moment. "It's weird being back. I miss my apartment, but I also miss the villa."

"Oh, I'm sure. I loved the pictures you sent me. That view is gorgeous. I don't think I would have left the porch ... unless I was making a trip to the kitchen."

"Yeah, the food was fantastic. And they took care of Kenzi the whole time. Same meals but safe for her."

"Good for them. I'm sure it's hard being celiac there."

"Probably easier than it is here," I snark. From the stories Kenzi has told me, it's easier there.

Once we've lugged the luggage inside and up the stairs to my apartment door, I don't have much left in me, and Claire gives me a quick hug before I drag the suitcases inside. Five minutes later, I completely crash out on my bed and wake up clueless at 5 a.m. It's dark, and sadly, I can't smell anything baking like I would at the villa. Now I'm really disappointed to be home. Maybe Claire's mom will at least get up and make coffee in a little bit. That's the literal perk of living in the upstairs apartment of your bestie's house: Her mom shares coffee. And sometimes dinner. And I'm a shameless mooch.

The house is a large, lovely Victorian two-story brick from the 1880s in the middle of Hawthorne, Pa., walking distance to everything on the main drag. It's in a beautiful neighborhood full of similar big, old homes, likely where the elite lived in that time. Kenzi talked my ear off about it when she found out I was taking the apartment. I suppose architects are fans of architecture. Who knew?

Claire and Logan—her brother and Kenzi's boyfriend—grew up here, and Claire moved back in to help her mom when she was older. They both live on the main floor. When I started at Baker & Willow, I lived an hour away, so I was pretty serious about hunting down a new apartment. Logan, who I work with, mentioned that they were looking for a renter for upstairs. Claire and I became fast friends, and I adore her mom, so it all works out pretty well. Logan is probably tired of me popping into his office to say, "Your mom said *hi*," but I'm definitely not. It always makes *me* laugh, even if no one else does. And isn't that the point?

Plus, I truly love this house and this neighborhood, so I've stayed much longer than I originally planned. I feel like I live with family. The house feels so incredibly homey. I can't explain it. It's just right. And I haven't found a house for sale that has that same character and feel, though I've looked for a while. Eventually, I'll get a house, but I'm not in any hurry.

I yawn and roll my neck. Jet lag is a strange beast, and though my body feels well rested, my brain is a little foggy. And it's five freakin' a.m. No one should be awake right now.

Finally, I sit up and stretch the many-hour plane rides out of my limbs and twist my back around. Not feeling very human yet. I sniff the air and regret it. I'll need to wash my sheets later. I keep getting whiffs of bad breath from the dude beside me on the plane eating Cheetos. Finally, I decide to shower (that might help) and put on something that doesn't smell like an airport.

After my shower, I don a cozy sweater and pants set the color of a pine tree before I realize (sob!) this is the one that Aaron always said was his favorite because it brings out the acid green flecks in my eyes. I'm not crying in my apartment all by myself over a man who left months ago. I'm just not. Instead, I focus on the things I love here. Like the creak of that one floorboard smack in the middle of the room that sounds like every stately older home with little ghosties traipsing about in it. I usually avoid that board so I don't creep myself out, but I stroll right across it to mentally bring me back to my space as I approach the kitchen. Flinging open the fridge, I realize that it will be empty and frown. Then I double-blink because it is not, in fact, empty. "Oh, Claire. You're the best." She got me a few staples. What a great friend! I snag a raspberry yogurt and sit down at the desk by the picture window looking out over the street. The stained-glass panes above the window turn the dim light dancing across the floor into the reflection of a disco ball.

The sky is that hazy steel gray that assures me we won't be seeing the sun. A deliciously dreary fall day, contrasting with the party light in my room. As I'm enjoying the last bites of the yogurt, I pop open my new purse and dig out the journal.

Again, I'm struck by wonder. Mostly, wondering why I felt so compelled to buy this thing. Sure, it's pretty, it's shiny, it has my initial on it, and I was on vacation. BUT, and this is important, *I don't journal*. What need is this filling?

"Maybe my brain was trying to tell me it's time to start ..." I say aloud. A friend gave me one of those gold pens with a big fancy plastic jewel on top as part of my birthday present a few weeks ago, and it's been lying on my desk ever since, so I pick it up and stare at the first page of the journal. "What do people write in these things? Dear diary? Is that necessary?" Talking to myself AND starting to write a book about my thoughts that no one will ever read. Those are the hallmarks of total sanity.

Maybe I should start working out my feelings around Aaron. There won't be any reason to bounce back to him now, so I've got to stop thinking about him.

I know I'm overjudging what to write here—no one is going to read it!—so finally, I just groan and write the first thing that comes to mind: "I vow to leave the past in the past." There. Done. I journaled. Now I'm improving my mental health ... or something. Closing the book, I decide to start on my standard Saturday tasks of cleaning my apartment, visiting the library, and bugging Claire and Mama Oliver. That last part is my favorite.

———

My apartment is completely clean by eight a.m.

I debate about reading the latest Margot Ashford novel—it arrived while I was gone and is sitting on my desk, still in its beige envelope from the bookshop—when I hear the faint murmur of living souls in the main part of the house. Time to go hang.

I grab my new purse because I know that Eloise, aka Mama Oliver, will love it, and head back down the stairs.

We've gotten into the habit of leaving the door at the top of the stairs to my apartment and the door off of the mud room that leads to the main floor unlocked because, let's face it, I'm an awesome tenant, and who wouldn't want me slinking in to nibble and nosh with them or watch TV with them or catch up on local gossip?

They don't mind. At least, they haven't said that they do.

I gently knock on the doorframe into their main living area and poke my head in. "Mama O.!"

I can see Eloise in the kitchen in the far corner. A broad grin spreads across her face. "You're up early! I thought you'd sleep till noon."

"Ah, the other way around." I make a circle with my hand. "I'm used to getting up earlier than you, so I crashed out as soon as I got home and woke up before the roosters."

Cackling, Eloise picks up a muffin tin with batter wobbling delightfully. "Give me about twenty minutes, and you can join us for breakfast."

Claire enters in her pajamas, and I surprise her with a high-five. "Your mom made us muffins."

She looks at me bleary-eyed and adjusts her glasses. "Who are you?" she snarks. Her shirt says it all, *No talky till coffee*.

I chuckle and pull out mugs while Claire starts the coffee maker. "I missed you guys. Thought I'd pop in."

"You know I never mind that." Eloise pulls a bin of strawberries from the fridge, so I set some plates on the table. "What do you have there?" She gestures to my new fake Divya bag, which I set on the counter, so I give them the short version of what happened and how I acquired it.

"I don't think you can go anywhere without getting into some sort of trouble," Claire announces.

"True," I mutter, trying to keep my mind from drifting back to Aaron. *I vow to leave the past in the past.* "If it matters, I was thinking about doing some sweet, innocent, normal things today." Eyebrows raise. *Really?* "I was going to walk down to Main Street and have a look around. It was so nice to just stroll through the stores in Italy and enjoy the day. I'm really itching to do that here."

"That sounds really nice." Claire pulls the muffins out of the oven and turns off the heat. "I haven't walked around here in a while. There's a little antique store that went in a few months ago, and I didn't get a chance to stop in yet."

"Oh, that's my jam." I know, I'm not old enough for antique stores to be my jam, but I'm just that cool. "Let's check it out. Eloise?"

"I would love to, but I promised Shannon I'd watch the girls while she and Nathan take the boys to their hockey practice."

"You know they'll make you watch that princess movie again." Claire laughs.

"Every time I've been there for the past month, I've watched *that princess movie* again," Eloise shrugs. "It could be worse."

"Have fun with that!" I grin and pop a strawberry in my mouth.

A short time later, Claire and I decide to walk the two blocks to Main Street. It's in the high forties, so not too bad. A little windy. I put on my camel wool coat and my *tré chic* little red beret to stay warm and keep my hair from flipping everywhere. Claire's messy blonde bun does the trick for her hair, and she dons her navy wool coat, as well. I swing my new bag onto my arm with glee. No doubt we look sleek and sophisticated. Maybe a little overdressed, but it's fun.

Down the steps and onto the sidewalk. We pass the row of beautiful homes I'm honored to live by: grand entrances, big porches with roofs, antique wooden front doors, wrought iron fences, rich colors. As I'm admiring them, I ask, "Is it weird living in the same town you grew up in?"

Tipping her head back and forth a couple times as she debates, Claire finally answers. "Not really. A lot of people have left, so I don't run into many people I know from back in the day. Mom still has some friends around from when she was growing up, but it was different then. A lot of people still stayed where they grew up and had their families. Not that I would mind either way. I liked a lot of people I went to school with."

"Mmmm." Main Street looms ahead, and we pause at the stoplight to wait for traffic to stop. "I wonder if I would have liked it as much if I grew up here. I definitely like the old buildings." Then I laugh as I eye up the storefronts. "It's funny that I just called them old when I was in Rome a couple days ago."

Claire lets out a cackle. "It's all relative."

"Buildings from this era are neat, though. You know, a lot of people don't look up when they walk around, but they really should. There are such beautiful sculptures and little details on the tops of the buildings on main streets, but most people never notice them. There's another town near here where they have this lovely sculpture of an owl perched near the top of the building, and no one knows about it. It's only a three-story building, too."

"You know it's a lot safer for people to look straight ahead when they're walking. Looking up is a great way to trip and bust your teeth out."

"This is why I don't hang out with people in the medical profession very often." Claire is a nurse practitioner, and she enjoys finding ways to ruin my fun by talking about the dangers of breaking bones, puncturing something, and getting colon cancer. I love her, but yeesh. "Hey, since you grew up here, do you know anything cool about the history of the town? Anything about the buildings?"

Claire furrows her brow as she thinks. "Not really. I remember a couple stores that used to be here when I was little. A lot has changed, but there isn't anything really interesting or memorable."

"That's sad. Really? Nothing cool? No stories about haunted shops or notorious townsfolk?"

Laughing, Claire adjusts her purse and nods that we should cross the street. "Honestly, no. There's not much to talk about. A couple famous people grew up here. We have the Lyons Coffee family."

They own a lot of buildings in town, so their name is on everything. Plus, their *Wake Up and Roar* motto is pretty catchy, so obviously, I know about them.

"Snowbird Ice Cream has been around since Mom was little." She gestures down the street. "She knew the owner, but they sold it to someone else when I was in high school. I used to work there. And Logan did too. Shannon didn't want to work in food, so she was at a little clothing shop called Fads on the corner down there. Is that the kind of story you were looking for?" Claire smirks, clearly recognizing that it's mundane.

I'm a little disappointed, but not everything can be a fascinating legend of wonder. Every town doesn't have a crazy tale about the emperor being murdered there ... which was turned into a play that we still read centuries later. *E tu Brutè?* "Sure. It's interesting to find out what you used to do. Where did you go to school?"

Claire points down a street at the elementary school and mentions that she used to babysit a couple kids on the next block.

"So where is this little antique shop you were talking about?" We've walked past a bookstore, a hair salon, and a couple small restaurants already.

"Just ahead; it's on the corner of Main and Carriage Row." She gestures at the building, and I finally spot the sign: Gisela's Wunderkammer—Antiques and Fantastic Finds.

"Huh, *wunderkammer* ..." I was just looking at one of those in Rome. Nifty coincidence.

A light is on inside, but the window still seems dark. Probably a trick of the midmorning cloudiness. The contrast between this shop and the ones in Rome is stark: a gap of hundreds of years in the architecture, though the items inside are probably from the same eras, just different locales of origin.

The tinkle of a bell announces our entrance and a gust of cool air follows us in. A woman in her thirties or forties smiles at us from behind an antique glass sideboard bearing a modern digital screen checkout station. "Good morning!" she says. She pulls a bulky beige cardigan tighter around her maroon floral dress. "Have a look around."

I nod. "Thank you." Then Claire and I meander through the tightly packed store.

A strange sense of *déjà vu* or maybe nostalgia washes over me as I look around. "Are you sure we haven't been in here before?" I crinkle my mouth into a thoughtful pout.

Claire turns, holding a pair of salt and pepper shakers shaped like cows. "I've never been in here. Maybe you were here without me, though."

"Maybe ..." I'm not sure what this strange feeling is. I nod at what she's holding. "Those are cute, by the way."

"Yeah, I'd love a pair that's actually Salt-N-Pepa, though. I wonder if they make those."

I mimic a robotic voice. "Pop culture reference not found."

Claire gives me an exasperated look. "Come on."

I grin and respond, "I'm sure no one would have missed that opportunity. You might ask the owner if she's ever run across them."

Claire gives an approving look and puts the cows back.

I nod in appreciation of a frilly little pink tea set, and then I notice that there is a substantial collection of vintage clothes in a room just off the main room, set off by a huge doorway, almost like a wall was removed. Upon entering, I see designer items from at least twenty years ago, some older. I note some palazzo pants that look like a pair my mom wore in a picture from the '70s.

I move a beautiful purse and cough when a plume of dust tickles my throat. Instinctively, I grab my own bag, ready to pull out my inhaler, but the particles aren't enough to trigger an attack.

Tucked in a corner, the rack of furs calls my name. Long and short coats, different colors, some solid while others are patterned. I pause by one that seems to be rabbit fur, a soft dark blonde. With admiration, I gently stroke the sleeve.

Why does this look familiar? Did my grandmother have one like this? I strain to evoke some of the photos I saw of her from when she was younger, but I don't recall. Maybe I saw it in her closet when I was little. Whenever I visited, she used to show my sisters and me some of her favorite dresses and hats from her youth. And she had a box of costume jewelry that we would play with together, huge rings and clip-on earrings. Lavish necklaces and brooches.

"You like that one?" the woman from the desk asks. Her dress sways around her as she enters the room. She places a gentle hand on the arm of the coat and pets it as I had. "So soft ... a man brought this in recently. It belonged to his grandmother's sister. We have several items that belonged to her, since the family was finally ready to let go of them. There's a beautiful trunk over there." She gestures to a dark brown case on the floor. "And some lovely boots too." She points at the footwear, resting on a shelf. "The sister didn't have a family, so the gentleman who brought them in didn't have a direct connection. I wish he knew some of the stories around the pieces so I could share them. I love that about old things."

"Me too." I swear I've seen the items she points out before. "Did they have these on display somewhere before deciding to sell them?" Maybe that's it.

"Not that I know of," she responds. "He mentioned that they were just packed away with no one to enjoy them. That's why they brought them in."

"Huh." I shake the thought from my head. I was just in several antique stores in Italy, so it's probably all overlapping. Plus, though I'm curious about all the items she mentions, I'm distracted by her lovely voice. I don't recognize her accent. Maybe Eastern European? "Your store is pretty new. What brought you to Hawthorne?" I ask. Gently, I reach out and stroke the rabbit fur again, and a ripple of longing floats through me. Hmmm, I really want this, but I don't know where I would wear it.

"My grandmother, strangely enough. She had family that moved here from Germany during the war, and they built a life in Hawthorne. She inherited a big old house from them, one of the colonial revivals a few blocks from here. It's a lovely red-brick with an enormous wraparound porch. When I was little, my grandmother set it up as a rental with all the original furniture. I inherited the house when she died, but she said she didn't want me to be burdened by it. I started my shop a few months ago with the furniture from that house and some other items that I've been collecting from estate sales." The woman gestures around her. "And here we are."

"That's a cool story! Thank you for sharing!" I love hearing how people end up doing what they do. I resist the urge to continue interviewing her, though, and simply ask, "So you must be Gisela?"

"I am," she answers. She holds out her hand. "So nice to meet you."

We each introduce ourselves, but I want to finish poking around the store, so I suggest that we don't want to keep her from her work.

Claire and I notice several other interesting items ... a set of funny-looking old keys the color of rust ... a leather holster and a toy gun, probably from the 1950s ... some lacy handkerchiefs with colorful embroidered flowers. All beautiful and interesting, but not anything of note.

I approach a stately rolltop desk with ornate decorations along the top and flanking the drawers. "This is beautiful."

Claire hums in response. She's looking at some huge crocks in the corner. Like the kind you make sauerkraut in, not the shoes. They have small blue circular stamps on the front, probably a design from the company that owned them.

Turning back to the desk, I lift the lid and note the gleam of the polished wood. Someone cared for this desk. Appreciatively, I open and close a couple drawers, musing about the type of person who may have sat here. A man? A woman? Someone doing their bills? Someone writing a novel? Maybe someone who enjoyed writing letters to their friends at a lovely desk ...

A small metal bird is attached in the middle of the desk, close to where your eyes would rest if you were seated there. I touch the cold metal, admiring the detail work. It has a long beak, like a sparrow, and is perched on a piece of a branch with flowers like a dogwood.

I read a lot of mystery books when I was little, and this is just the sort of thing that would have opened a secret compartment in the desk in those, which I always thought was the neatest thing ever. They always found a pile of documents, like the deed to the house, or a missing key to a safe, or the lady of the house's jewelry squirreled away safely there. Or a finger.

My taste in books varied within the mystery genre.

"If only ..." I mutter with a smile, pressing gently on the little bird. When I hear a pop, I nearly jump out of my pants. Holy guacamole, I broke the desk.

I look around, but Claire is still enamored with the crocks, and Gisela is sorting through a box of something on the other end of the store. Neither of them heard it. As I glance back at the desk, though, I see that a panel along the back has slid down some. Crap.

Maneuvering it with my fingers, I struggle to push it back up so it connects with the piece above it. *I'm not buying a*—I pause to look at the price—*nine-hundred-dollar antique desk today!*

It's not working though, and I'm starting to overheat with panic. Suddenly, the panel slips farther, revealing a knob at the top. "Maybe it's supposed to open ..." I lean down to examine the opening and spot a place where the knob had fit neatly into the panel above. "Amazing."

Feeling gutsy now, I pinch the handle between my fingers and inch the panel down slowly. A thin cubby is revealed, and inside rests a book with a deep red cover.

I gasp and pull the book from its hiding place, wondering if it could be something really valuable, like a first edition Brontë or Emerson. Why else would someone hide it? It looks like it was handled a good bit, and the oils from someone's hand darkened the cover around the edges to crimson. No title on the cover or spine. Opening the book, I note the yellowed leaves and a name on the first page, Matilda Conrad, with the year 1910. A shiver works its way through my body. Flipping through a couple pages, it's clear that this was her diary.

I'm excited by the find, but I also know I should show it to the shop owner, in case she needs to contact the person who sold her the desk. It could be important to the family.

Approaching Gisela, I hold the diary up and smile. "I found this in the rolltop desk over there." When I explain how, she looks confused and then delighted. I hand her the diary.

"That's amazing! I didn't know there was a secret compartment. Please show me."

By this time, Claire has joined us. When I show them both the little bird and what it does, I can't believe my stroke of luck. I didn't actually break the desk!

"I'll reach out to the family to see if they want the diary," Gisela says. "Thank you for bringing this to me. I'm so impressed that you figured this out."

"Eh, I read, and I ... well, I guess I poke at furniture." She doesn't seem to get the joke, so I let it pass. "I'm glad I could help."

A few minutes later, Claire and I decide to head across the street to a little lunch spot that we haven't tried yet. Once we're outside, though, Claire realizes she left her scarf inside.

"I'll just grab it," she says, as she retreats through the door, jangling the bells.

Feeling pretty good about my find, I decide to check out the exterior of the building to see what hidden treasures it may have. Some of the best decorations are always at the top. I take a few steps away and look up. Sure enough, there is concrete sculpted as bunting and ivy scalloped around the top of the building. A crest in the middle shows the name Wilson and 1897, likely the original owner and the year it was built. Maybe I'll look that up later and see what I can find out about it. There have to be some interesting stories around here somewhere, even if Claire doesn't know them.

I inch my thick-soled boots back a bit toward the road and pull out my phone to take a picture. Now I'm debating, and I rock a bit on my heels. If I shoot from this angle, I can make it more artsy. What do I want? Artsy or just the facts? I gaze at the building as if it should have the answer.

Going for artsy, I step closer to the curb and tip my phone up. Unfortunately, I'm nearer to the street than I thought I was. With another step, I trip over the stoplight pole and end up coming down off the curb, landing in the street. I throw my arms out to stop my fall, but I miss grabbing the pole and the side of my skull bounces off the sidewalk.

Smooth move ...

Chapter Three

"Morgan?" Claire's voice pierces the air as bells crash against the shop door and tires screech in the street. My senses light up like warning lights on a car's dashboard.

Pain sears through the side of my head, my palms, and my right thigh. I see a flash of light and then the sidewalk swimming in my vision. My joints are on fire, which might explain why I smell smoke. Then, of all the things I can rationalize in that moment, I determine that the smoky smell is from cigarettes rather than burning flesh.

My mouth feels thick ... I taste iron and ash ... ah. I bit my tongue ... that's blood. My tongue throbs in response. And the other taste is dirt from the sidewalk that got kicked up when I took my colossal header. This flavor combo would get one star on *America's Favorite Baker*. Do not recommend.

When time starts moving again, I'm dragged onto the sidewalk from my half-dangling-in-the-street position by two arms, possibly attached to a person or people, and the motion shoots lightning through my skull. I mumble-gasp-grunt like the eloquent adult that I am.

"Morgan." Claire squats beside me. "Are you okay?" She starts in on protocol, checking my breathing, shining her phone light in my eyes—ow—and examining me for fractures.

"Is my bag scraped?" I slur, somehow still in the mood for a joke. I'm trying to maneuver my hands to pull at the strap, but my movements are so uncoordinated.

"It's fine," she replies dryly. All business. Not even a laugh? *You're not going to give me a laugh when I'm possibly concussed and making jokes?*

I let out a gigantic breath and start assessing my body myself. My ribs ache, but no actual pain. My arms and legs seem okay as I slowly adjust my position. My head is throbbing above my right ear. I can wiggle my toes. It seems that I'm fine aside from my head, so I push up onto my elbows.

I hear footsteps rapidly approaching behind me. "Should I call an ambulance?" It's a man's voice. He remains behind me, so I'm unable to see him.

"Maybe." Claire frowns at me, and even through my half-open eyes—even on a cloudy day, looking up is painful with all the light—I can see her hesitating.

So she thinks there's a chance I'll be okay. I take this as my cue to continue trying to sit up. She helps me to a seated position, and I feel the man step closer.

"Just to be safe?" he asks.

"She seems okay," Claire finally answers. "I'm a nurse practitioner, so I can take it from here. Thank you." I can hear a tiny smile of gratitude in her all-business voice, ensuring that the man knows she's not angry at him for offering help.

"Sure." But he doesn't seem to leave. "Do you want help getting her to the car?"

"No," I rasp. Darn dirt in my throat. I start to turn my head to face him, but it's still aching. So I pull my knees up and rest my forehead on them as I cough, arms wrapped around my legs. "I'll be okay. Thank you!" I call out, still gravelly. Then I start coughing. I flick my hand in the direction his voice came from to indicate that I don't need help. Nice of him, though.

"I'm right across the street if you guys need me," he replies. "I'll stay near the window. Just wave, and I'll see you."

We both call out discordant *thank yous*, and I assume he leaves.

"I fell off the sidewalk," I mutter.

"You're lucky that car didn't hit you," Claire huffs.

"Did I mess up my hair?" I immediately regret asking because I start coughing again. I fumble for my inhaler, just in case.

"You're something else."

When the coughing subsides, I jump right back in. "I'd rather be skydiving," I mutter.

"I think you're actually fine, but skydiving is off the table for a few days."

"I don't think I broke anything but my confidence in my photography skills."

"You were taking a picture when this happened?" Claire sounds shocked.

"Yeah, something normal." I finally raise my head, and though it aches, I don't feel dizzy or sick. "No broken bones?"

"None from what I could tell just checking you here," Claire responds. "But you're going to have some amazing bruises. Possibly a concussion."

"Oh good. Just what I was hoping for."

We sit in silence for a moment before Claire prods me. "How do you feel?"

"Okay-ish. Maybe we should go get lunch and then figure it out."

She looks me up and down, frowns. "I think we should get you checked for a concussion. Your head hit the sidewalk. Let's see if you can walk first before we decide how to get you to the hospital." Claire holds onto my elbows and gently helps bring me to a standing position.

"My head cushioned my fall." I'm not dizzy, so I take a couple steps. Thank God I wore chunky-soled boots instead of something wobbly. "Everything checks out. I am feeling a little nauseated now that the adrenaline has worn off, though."

Claire lets out a sigh. "I hate to be bossy, but we really are going to the emergency department."

"Maybe I'll feel better if I eat. Should we grab a sandwich first?" I gesture across the street at Hazel's. I'm actually not joking.

Claire gives me a look that any mom would be proud of, so I consent to getting checked out. She insists on holding onto my arm as we cross safely at the crosswalk and continue back to the house to get the car, but really, I'm fine aside from the throbbing in my head and a few aches. And of course, the slight queasiness.

I get my all-clear from the emergency room a short time later, and we finally get lunch. Yes, I'm glad I got checked out. It wouldn't be a good idea to walk around with a concussion, which I thankfully don't have. At the same time, I could have been reading. Or skydiving.

Once we're seated at Hazel's and have ordered, I pull a pill box from my purse—which somehow escaped the incident unscathed, by the way—and dump a handful of ibuprofen onto my placemat, pretending to contemplate them.

Claire grabs my hand. "Stop. How hard did you hit your head? Only four of those at a time. No more than thirty-two hundred milligrams a day. You'll kill yourself."

"You're just saying that." But I separate out a responsible dose and dump the rest back into the container, chuckling. I love messing with her.

"I'm not cleaning you up if you induce organ failure."

"Noted." I pop four into my mouth and wash them down with ice water.

"How's the pain?"

"Bearable. It's not great, though." I stir my water with the straw for a moment and look out the window at the spot where I attempted to breakdance ... or break my neck. "Who was the guy you were talking to earlier?"

"Guy?"

"On the street. He offered to call an ambulance. I couldn't see him. Did you know him?"

"No, just someone from the shop across from the antique store. It was nice of him to offer."

"I agree. Glad you were there, though."

"Maybe you should consider wearing bubble wrap."

"I'm not clumsy! It was an honest mistake. I was distracted trying to take a picture of the building. See." I pull out my phone and open the photo, which, I believe, is appropriately artsy. The building appears at an off-angle, the decorations at the top stretching across two thirds of the photo. I must have hit the button right before I fell.

"Good angle. I hope it was worth it."

"So worth it." I smirk.

Claire sniffs the air and a look of absolute delight crosses her face. "I wish I had asked her to add bacon to my sandwich. I didn't even think about it."

"That would be good with the smoked turkey." Just then, a server walks by with a tray laden with plates, one with pancakes and a heaping pile of bacon. "Oh! That's why you mentioned bacon." I sniff the air. "So weird. All I smell is cigarette smoke."

"You can't smell the bacon?"

I sniff again. "Maybe now?" I frown. "I smelled cigarettes when I fell too. I thought it was just exhaust and the dirty sidewalk."

"No one is smoking in here." Claire looks perplexed. "I hope you didn't mess something up."

I shake my head. "It's gone now. *Now* I smell bacon."

"Bizarre."

"Oh, no. Bacon smells amazing."

"Agreed."

Back in my apartment, I decide that relaxing the rest of the afternoon is a good idea, so I lie down on my bed and stare at the stamped pattern on the ceiling for a moment.

Maybe I should journal.

I grab the journal I bought in Rome and gently return to my bed. I normally flop, but I don't want to jar my precious brain. Again. Leaning against a cumulus-sized pile of pillows, I sit poised with the pen to my lip, mimicking a writerly pose. For a moment, I contemplate the words about to pour forth from my writing implement. Any minute now.

When nothing happens, I decide to jot down some notes from today. The Wunderkammer, the hidden drawer in the desk, my fall ... Flipping the journal closed, I peer at the cover. The same red. The same pattern of darker red from skin oil soaking in around the edges. The same yellowy pages. *Déjà vu* again? Or is this almost the same as the journal in the shop this morning?

That's interesting.

I'm starting to feel tired and take it as a signal from my body to sleep. I did have a bit of an ordeal. My eyelids droop, so I lean back on the pillows and close them.

When I open them again, the room seems foggy. Smoke? Or is my vision blurry? I'm seated at my desk, holding a pen in my left hand. *Why my left?* The other hand is pressed to a page, holding a journal open. The left and right pages are both blank. Curling my fingers into a fist, I notice the edges of the cover peeking out from behind the pages, a deep maroon. I suppose I decided to write in my journal again.

"How did I get here, though?" I must have been sleepwalking ... but I don't sleepwalk. Rubbing my eyes, I cough and then close the journal and peer at the cover. Was it upside down? Where's the M? I flip it over a couple times before I realize that the embossed letter isn't on the cover. Where did I get this?

So strange.

Standing, I pace the room for a moment before I realize that *this isn't my apartment.*

The walls are beige rather than pristine white. I'm in some sort of library or study, based on the shelves of books and the furniture. Did I somehow wander down the street and into one of the businesses? Maybe this is a room at the library that I haven't been in. Or the events room at the back of the book shop. I glance back at the desk. It's an open rolltop with beautiful carvings adorning the edges. I approach again and pick up the diary. It falls open to a page covered in writing.

Dear Diary,

Well, I suppose that's the proper way to start after all. I read it out loud.

I know I shouldn't have gone in there, but I did. And I shouldn't have stayed to listen to their conversation, but I just couldn't help it. I knew something was up, and my curiosity got the better of me. The man they call "Briggs" had something large covered up with a black cloth. Maybe it was a canvas? The other man nodded and said it would fetch them a good bit of money.

I didn't catch the rest. I was hiding in the shadows, and all I could think about was how I needed to cough. It's those cigarettes—Rosie keeps on telling me to quit, and maybe she's right. But they do calm me down, you know?

Anyway, I got out of there quickly so they wouldn't catch me. I won't breathe a word of this to Rosie. She'd give me an earful for snooping again, for sure.

So, dearest diary, you must keep this secret for me until I figure out what to do. I just know something's not right, but I—

Flipping to the next page, I see that it's blank. The writer stopped in the middle of their story. Turning the diary over in my hands, I ponder what this means before placing it on the desk again. Where did it come from? Who wrote this? What are they talking about?

Slowly, I approach the window and peer out. It's bright and sunny, not at all like when I fell asleep. The building across the street looks familiar, a brown brick five-story, likely a business building. There's a sign, but my vision blurs. I don't know what it says. I hope this isn't a latent effect of hitting my head. Everything starts going sepia-toned, like an old photo.

I need to get out of here. I don't even know where I am or how I walked here in my sleep!

Somewhere, a door closes. "Mattie?" a woman's voice calls from nearby. I don't recognize it.

Who's Mattie? I haven't met any Matties here. As my stomach flutters, I drop onto a fainting couch upholstered in velvety fabric and close my eyes.

When I open them again, I'm back on my bed. I take a long breath in through my nose and listen to the slight whistle it makes from stuffiness, taking in the realness of being here, now.

I must have hit my head harder than I thought.

The office lets me work from home the next day, so I don't need to drive and can be extra careful. I love that about Baker & Willow, among many, many other things.

I'm having a little trouble concentrating though. Yesterday was incredibly bizarre. I texted Claire about my dream last night, and she thought it was interesting. We agreed, though, that it was probably induced partially by jet lag, partially by banging my head. Still, I don't think I'll be writing in the diary today.

I'm not superstitious or anything. But if the journal has anything to do with that weird dream, well, I should just avoid it. I think most rational people would.

Around quitting time, I decide that I should get some fresh air, since it's pretty and sunny out. My vampire soul shrivels a little when I look out the window. *Ah! Sunlight! It burns!* But I know it will help me heal to enjoy the outdoors.

I change into leggings and a baggy aqua sweatshirt and pull on my favorite Seattle baseball hat to block the sun. Testing my balance on the stairs, I am assured that I really am fine, so I head out the front door and walk to Main Street for a stroll past the shops.

"Out for a walk?" An older gentleman is sitting on his porch as I stroll by. I nod, smile, and throw him a "yep" as I keep going. The people here are so friendly.

On Main Street, I cross to walk on the same side as Gisela's Wunderkammer, intending to admire all the wares in her window and the others down the block. But when I see where I fell yesterday, I remember the gentleman who offered to help. I should at least thank him. Maybe browse his shop too. That would be the nice thing to do. If I were him, I'd certainly wonder what happened to me, anyway.

And I always follow my impulses.

I glance across the street, where his shop must be, but that doesn't make any sense. When I fell, I had my back to him, so his shop has to be on the opposite corner or close to it. If Gisela's is here, and Hazel's is across the street that way, then that man had to come from across the street in the other direction for him to notice me on the sidewalk.

I know I look ridiculous as I'm miming my thoughts, pointing across the street in different directions, but it doesn't bother me in the least.

"Lost, dear?" an older woman asks.

I'm not sure how to answer. "I'm figuring it out. Just ... retracing my steps from yesterday. Thanks, though!"

She smiles brightly and enters Gisela's.

Finally, I decide to just try my luck. I cross the street to a brick building, much like many of the other buildings on Main Street. It has to be this particular business because the ones farther away wouldn't have a view of that corner.

This building has an entrance on the side facing me, with a huge sign above their window emblazoned WellSpring Robotics. A glance in the window on the other side of the door doesn't give me much to go on, thanks to the angle of the sun causing a lot of reflection. It's not a big display area like most of the other shops. I only see a couple potted plants and a miniature of a robot from some movie I can't recall off the top of my head. Pop culture reference not found for real this time. *Wait a sec.* Is this a shop or a business? I guess I'll have to find out. It's not somewhere I would normally go, so I get this little tingle of adventure in my gut. What am I going to find in here? Maybe some lovely massage chairs or fun little gadgets!

Half-jokingly—yes, a joke with myself—I touch the doorframe to ensure that this place is actually real, and it seems to be. I don't want any more bizarre sepia-toned dreams where nothing makes sense, so I thought it was pertinent since I was expecting a shop instead of a business. Maybe I'm overthinking. I check the hours and push the door open.

The room is divided into two sections. In the front, the walls are lined with displays of different assistance devices, each labeled to help shoppers find the right area. I spot prosthetics and some communication devices among the unfamiliar items on display. We convinced my mom a few years ago to get a speech-generating device for any emergencies, since she's deaf and not everyone knows American Sign Language. Farther along the wall is a futuristic-looking wheelchair and something else I can't quite explain, likely for mobility.

Suddenly, I'm only somewhat convinced this place is real.

"Welcome to WellSpring. Can I help you?"

I turn and see a woman in her early twenties with a round face and an eyebrow ring. She's wearing a lemon-colored button-up half tucked into navy pants. Her vibe says she's definitely cooler than me. I smile. Gotta love when people can truly be themselves at work.

"I'm not sure if I'm in the right place." How to begin? "Yesterday around lunchtime, I fell on that corner." I gesture across the street. "And a man came to see if I needed help. I was with a friend who is a nurse practitioner, so we were good. I wanted to thank the man for checking on me. I think he came from a business or shop over here. He said he would stay near the window in case we needed to flag him down." I think that makes sense. I raise my eyebrows in the hopes that she knows something of the story.

"Oh, yeah." She smiles. "You want the big guy. He told us what happened. I'll get him." The woman turns and enters the back half of the room, which is separated by a half wall with Plexiglas reaching from the top of the wall to the ceiling. I can see a handful of people back there, some at desks, some gathered around a table, pointing at something and talking.

The big guy? Does she mean the boss or an actual large dude? I watch as she approaches one of the men at the table. He has dark hair and a thick beard, and he looks nice in his olive Henley with slacks. He glances up at me and then resumes talking to the woman, so I casually browse the communications collection. I don't want to appear to be staring, but he doesn't seem to be larger than the average Joe. I'm guessing she meant boss.

When I hear footsteps, I smile as I turn to look at him. As I open my mouth, though, my voice catches. There is something so familiar here that my brain hiccups. I've seen those eyes, but it's been a long, long time. There are little crow's feet adorning them now and a couple strands of silver mingling with the brown in his beard and hair. The beard is entirely new, which is why it took a second for me to realize that it really is him.

Also, strangely enough, he looks happier. Healthier. Like a weight has been lifted. Also, like he's been lifting weights. He used to be wirier.

I'm glad to see him this way.

At that moment, I realize that he's staring, too. His brown eyes flicker from my face to my ball cap a couple times, like that's confirmation of what he's thinking. To be fair, you don't see many hats or shirts or really anything with "Seattle" emblazoned on them in this area. Kinda the wrong side of the country.

He breaks the silence first, a look of disbelief on his face. "Morgan?" That single word holds a lot of surprise. But he doesn't sound like he doesn't want to see me.

"Um, yeah. Beau. It's been a while." I'm not often at a loss for words, but this is ... wow. Never expected to run into this guy again. "I thought you were living in Cranberry still." Honestly, I haven't thought about him in a good ten years, and the last time was when we lived about forty-five minutes north.

Haven't thought about him often, I should say.

"I moved." It seems that he barely processed what I said enough to get two words out. He's still staring.

Blinking, I realize that I have absolutely no right to be here. "Look, I didn't mean to walk back into your life like this. I just wanted to say *thanks* for stopping yesterday to check on me. I didn't realize it was you. I couldn't see you," I assure him. "And your voice didn't register for some reason ... I guess you sound a little different, and well, I *had* just hit my head. So, I'm sorry to bother you, but I ... thank you."

"Yeah ..." Beau's eyebrows are cocked like I'm a mirage. Then he raises them. "That was you? You fell? Of course, yes. I didn't realize it either. I mean, all I had to go on was the hair, and it's ... shorter."

"Funny how a good haircut and a hat can disguise a person, huh?" This is a weird conversation. I clear my throat. "Anyway. Thank you. I don't want to interrupt your work. It looks like you're ... doing some really good things in the world." I gesture to the displays.

Beau takes a long breath in, and I'm sure it's from relief that I've changed the subject. He smiles cautiously. "We do. WellSpring has contracts with a lot of different companies in North America to create devices to help those with disabilities. We just filed a patent for an assistive robot that can carry out different kitchen tasks for those with reduced ability of their arms or hands. It will be really helpful for people with arthritis or nerve damage, muscle atrophy. Lots of different things. It can be hard for them to grasp a spoon and stir, for example. So this robot sits on a counter and ... I'm sorry. I'm boring you. You didn't come in here for this."

I hold in a laugh because, honestly, it was starting to sound like an elevator pitch, though fascinating all the same. "Hey, don't assume that you're boring me." I touch one of the communication devices, and I know he knows what I'm thinking. I glance up at him and truly see his heart. "This is really interesting. And I'm glad you finally got to do what you wanted to do. This was still a dream the last time we talked." I smile. "I'm happy for you."

"Thanks. It's been a ... a major uphill battle to get here."

Inwardly, I cringe. I remember the uphill battle. His sister, Rae, was a pharmacist who became addicted to her pain meds after sustaining an injury. She was struggling. Two young kids. Her husband left, never to be seen again. So she leaned on her family. Beau had the kids more than she did because she was spiraling. And that was while he was in grad school.

I look around the room at everything he's accomplished. "I guess things turned out okay." Looking back at his eyes, I sense an untold hurt there. "How's Rae?" I ask gently.

The tension in his jaw and the speed with which he looks away tells me part of the story before he even opens his mouth. "She's gone."

Acid curdles in my stomach as I think the worst but hope it's not true. "She ... she moved, too?"

A wrinkle appears like a lightning strike between Beau's eyebrows, and he looks anywhere but at me. "No." All the air leaves my body as I realize the truth.

I place my hand on my heart and then on his arm. "I'm so sorry to hear that." My voice is thick with emotion. I really didn't want that for Rae. I always hoped that she could pull through, especially for her children. I thought she would be fine after she got help. Somehow, I don't feel like I should ask for the rest of the story, though. It could have been anything. "Are the kids okay?"

"As okay as they can be. I'm taking care of them. I adopted them once I was able to. They're both at the high school here. That's why I moved. I didn't want them to leave the district since Emmett had started kindergarten here. They needed some stability."

That's right. I forgot that this is where Rae lived. "I'm glad you were able to do that for ... Emmett and Vivienne?"

"Yeah. That's them." I get a small smile for remembering their names. "And they are doing pretty well, considering. Both are playing soccer, doing great in school. Vivi just got her license."

I smile back, though I'm not sure what else there is to say.

"What have you been up to?" The stress has washed from his features, with the talk of his niece and nephew, though he still doesn't look happy, *per se*.

"I just got back from Italy." I brief him on my life with Baker & Willow, my recent trip sans Aaron stories, and in general how things are going. "And yesterday I hit my head, so I'm glad I remembered all of that!" A wry smile crosses my face.

That at least gets a chuckle.

"Well, I'm sure you're closing soon," I finally say. "I don't want to keep you any longer."

"Yeah, I should get back." He clears his throat. "We're working on a special set of arms for amputees to be able to drive. It's ... actually going pretty well. But we're on a deadline." Glancing back at the group huddled around the table, he nods to the woman in yellow who had greeted me. They must be waiting on him.

"It was nice seeing you." I really mean that. I smile and touch his arm, turning to leave.

"It was nice seeing you, too. I'm glad you're doing well." He pauses. "I worried about you."

Damnit, I'm not going to cry. No. I turn back for a moment and search his eyes. "I worried about you, too. Really. And I'm glad things are looking up."

When I get back outside, the sun is dipping low in the sky, so I cross the street again and take a brisk walk to clear my head, but instead, scenes from my life flash through. The before times. The unsteady times. The times I impulsively cut bangs after a breakup. The learning times.

My move across the country from Seattle to Pittsburgh and the couple years that followed was ... a learning time.

So was my transfer to a small college just east of Pittsburgh when we split up, so I could continue pursuing my degree in finance in a stress-free setting. My third college. After graduation, I hopped around every couple years, taking jobs here and there that were interesting, at first, but ultimately, they didn't scratch the itch.

I needed adventure. And time to grow my bangs out.

I own that I'm impulsive. It's that whole *grabbing the sweet cherries* thing. Which is sort of funny because I'm super precise when it comes to investments. That's the only area of my life where I'm supremely confident and accurate. It's called *finesse*. (I should breathe on my nails and shine them right now.)

Like when someone is lining up a shot in pool. Slow, steady, cool. That's me when I'm checking financial forecasts and working with trends. I love checking out new real estate for the investment portion of Baker & Willow. There are so many opportunities for building communities and helping the company make money. Ethically, of course. I don't do things any other way.

But outside of work, I need to get my blood pumping. Except ...

The steadiest I've ever been was when I was with Beau.

Chapter Four

The next morning, I recount my encounter with Beau as Claire and I are standing in line at Lyon's Den Coffee, where a huge *Wake up and Roar* poster of an intense lion sipping a latte adorns the wall behind the counter.

"It was ... weird. I don't know. I haven't seen him in so long." I pause, but Claire nods encouragingly. "I've thought about him ... on occasion, but seeing him in person really threw me. He looked different, but he seemed like he was, I don't know, calm?"

"He wasn't calm the last time you saw him?"

The years shimmy away from my memory and reveal the bits and pieces of my life with Beau that I still recall. It was well over a decade ago. "The look on his face when I walked away back then was pain. But he understood. I couldn't be there anymore. Sometimes you just have to stand up for yourself and the life that you hoped to live. That wasn't it." I frown. "And no, he wasn't calm that last year or so. He was under so much stress." And my gut clenches as I realize that I still feel guilty for leaving, for taking care of myself. I've told myself a million times that what I did was reasonable, that I tried, that most people would have left. But that doesn't stop the pain. I press it down in my mind and give a grim shrug.

Claire lets out a long breath. "You always seem to know what you want, even when it's tough. I admire that about you." We step forward in line as the person at the front finishes ordering.

"Thanks." I nod. "I try to."

"I don't know how you do it, to be honest. How do you always manage to be so ..." She flutters her hands in the air, as if calling the words in. "Supremely confident?"

I snort. "Is that what you call it?"

"Yeah. You always have this calm command of life. Don't you have a little voice in your head that tells you you're doing something wrong or that you aren't good enough or anything? You know, like normal people?"

I have to laugh at this. "Of course I do. His name is Bradley."

"Who's Bradley?" Kenzi looks like she just walked in on juicy gossip and wants the scoop as she and Logan step into line behind us.

"First things first." Claire holds up a single finger and then nods at her brother. "What are you doing here?"

"I dropped a lasagna off at Mom's," Logan replies smugly as Claire makes a mouth-watering face. "She said you guys were here, so we thought we'd get some coffee too."

Then Kenzi cuts to the important stuff. "Now, who's Bradley?"

I breathe deeply to nourish my ego as I'm about to reveal my number one life tip. "Bradley is my inner critic. He's a middle-management nobody who thinks he's special and micromanages everyone. Really, he has no power though. And, who actually goes by Bradley?" No one responds, so I keep going. Because I'm on a roll. "Only this guy. He thinks it makes him sound important. *I'm* not about to let Bradley mansplain my self-worth to me. When he starts talking, I just tell him to shut up." When I finish, I realize that my friends are all staring at me bug-eyed. "Thank you for coming to my TED Talk," I mutter. Somehow, I feel like one of those recipe bloggers, yammering on about some unrelated topic when you're just scrolling down their page for the recipe so you can make dinner.

That's not how it goes over, though.

Claire throws her hands up like she's been knocked backward. "How? What? Where did you come up with that?"

"That's really good!" Kenzi says. "I need to write that down. Maybe I'll name mine Kevin."

Logan scans the room, clearly hunting for an exit. "Who goes by Bradley?" he repeats, an amused look on his face.

"Right? Glad you like it. That's how I keep myself in check." Gotta have goals, baby. Keep going for those sweet cherries. It may sound a little odd or even harsh, but I'm not about to let myself keep myself from getting what I want. But then, that little finger of guilt about Beau pokes me again. Maybe I started putting up walls around his memory a while ago. Maybe it hardened me. Maybe I need more bricks.

When I place my order for a flat white, I step to the side to wait for my friends and find myself gazing at WellSpring across the street.

"Do you think he wanted to talk to you?" Claire nods toward the shop. "I mean, you were the one who left."

"I don't think he was opposed to it. He definitely looked surprised to see me again." My vision grows fuzzy as my focus shifts to the day I told him I couldn't do it anymore. I needed stability. And normalcy. And something of my own. I didn't want to keep sharing on the level that I had to share. "It wasn't his fault that I left." I rub at my wrist birthmark, just thinking. Trying to push the sorrows back down. *I don't cry, remember?* I have to keep reminding myself.

Kindly, Claire changes the subject. "What does he do at WellSpring again?"

I explain, but then my gaze catches on the sign. "Clever name for it. His last name is Blackwell."

"Mmmm, I do like that." Claire and I walk to the delivery counter to wait. "Here's what I don't get. Like I said, you are so supremely confident. You even left Beau—which had to be hard—because you knew you had to." She gives me a knowing look. "But then there's Aaron."

I roll my eyes. "Don't remind me."

"Really, though." Claire touches my arm. "Are we done fixating on him yet?"

She's right. And I think I am. But the thing is ... *Aaron*. I suppose he just felt like home after a while. And we kept getting thrown together. It felt like fate.

There was the time I was shooting tequila with friends and ended up too hammered to drive home. Aaron came to get me. And we ended up back together.

And that time when I decided that I could repaint my bedroom on my own and fell off the ladder. Aaron came to take me to the hospital. Sprained wrist. No fracture. But we ended up back together. Again.

And the time that I was stranded on the West End because the bridge was out (a boat hit it, and it was unstable). My GPS kept routing me back to the bridge. (I'm surprisingly terrible with this stuff.) Aaron happened to call, saying he missed me, and he pulled up a map on his computer, routed me to a burger place, and met me there. Bought me dinner! And we stayed together for a whole glorious month.

I cut my own bangs after we broke up that time.

I pause mid-reverie to respond. "Yes, I'm done." Then I frown.

I like to think that being with Aaron is always sweet cherries, but the pits come along, eventually. And when I'm *not* with Aaron, I hunt for other things that make me feel alive.

During an Aaron lull a couple years ago, I decided that I would start a side gig flipping houses. I did exactly one. And I made $1,000 for all my trouble.

When I started my job at Baker & Willow, again in the eye of the Aaron storm, I bought a fancy car, which happened to be front-wheel drive. I lived on a hill that was frequently icy then. And didn't put winter tires on. I totaled the car that winter. Not my brightest moment.

Impulsive. Alive. Heart-pounding—

"Why do you always go back?" Claire knows the stories.

I huff out a breath that flutters the curls around my face. "I feel ... restless." There is no good reason for that. I've always been loved, so it wasn't my upbringing. I was crushed on either side of the sister sandwich by two amazing beings. And my parents rock. And I always have friends, as evidenced by those joining me in the Lyon's Den this morning. My lioness heart purrs. Well, most of it anyway.

Claire pulls an innocent face. "Maybe you should journal about it some more." She knows my stance on journaling, especially after that funky dream.

And journaling isn't me anyway. I'm the *too loud*. The one who needs to one-up everyone. My memory drifts back to when I got a tattoo of a phoenix the moment I turned eighteen—yes, that day—because it was my *birthright* to get a tattoo as soon as I was of age. I once wore duct tape as a shirt when I went out clubbing in college. That would be college, take three.

I couldn't take all the drama with Beau. For all the love he gave ... I still couldn't. And he was practically split in half back then: half the Beau I loved, half the frazzled, stressed, angry ...

I feel like, sometimes, I seek drama out and then shove it away when it finds me.

The smell of cigarettes envelops me without warning, and I gag. "Do you smell that?"

"Coffee?" Kenzi asks as she approaches.

I wrinkle my nose so hard, it almost turns inside out. "No, it's cigarettes."

Claire gives me an incredulous look. "Cigarettes?" Then she chuckles. "You know, smelling cigarette smoke when no one is smoking is actually a sign of menopause."

I give her my death stare. "I will steal your soul and then set up a profile for you on every dating app."

"... and a sign of a stroke," she mutters. Then she meets my gaze as if I didn't hear her. "Okay, don't be so sensitive. We're the same age." Claire waves me away. She's not threatened. She knows I'm kidding ... sorta.

We are saved from fisticuffs by the barista calling our drink orders. We all grab our respective brews and walk outside.

Next door, Gisela appears at the entrance to flip the sign to Open. Seeing her gives me a little spurt of motivation.

"I'll catch up with you guys," I say. "I want to run in here and ask about that diary I found the other day. I wonder if Gisela found the owner. Heck, maybe she'll let me flip through it for a little inspiration, since I'm clueless about the whole journaling thing." That last bit gets some chuckles. They know I don't do anything that requires quiet focus besides crocheting and work.

Claire nods. "I'm curious, too. I'll come with you." She glances at her watch. "I have time."

The two of us enter Gisela's and approach the desk, where the owner is sorting a box of what looks like antique drawer knobs. "Welcome. Did something bring you back?" She smiles and places a hand on her hip, swishing her rust-colored skirt with the movement.

"Sort of. I was wondering if you located the owner of the red diary that we found in that desk." I point in the general direction.

"Yes. Matilda Conrad's family." Gisela sets the box down and leans on the counter. "They didn't want the diary back, so I've been debating what to do with it. Rosella was Matilda's sister, and it was her great-grandson who brought Matilda's things to us. They thought maybe a local museum would want the diary, but they weren't interested. I spoke with the Historical Society, but since she wasn't a person of note, they also turned it down."

Not a *person of note*. How sad. Is that how we're all written off when we're gone? I didn't think I'd end up with a Wikipedia page or anything, but still. "Could I see it?" I ask. "I was curious about it."

Gisela opens a drawer and hands me the journal. "Sure, take a look. I need to take care of a couple things, if you don't mind."

"Not at all."

Claire glances at her watch and then joins me in examining the diary. A yellowed old envelope is just inside, so I open it and find some newspaper clippings, not quite brittle, but I still handle with care. In the first, the picture shows two women in early 1900s dresses standing in front of a shop window. The name of the shop, Carriage Row Tailoring, adorns the window in block letters.

"That's this street." I point at the floor as I speak. "The shop must have been nearby." Then, I look at the framing and shape of the windows in the photo. "Actually, I think it's this shop."

Claire looks surprised. "Really? I didn't pay attention when we came in." We both look at the front windows. "They are the right shape."

I peer at the women in the picture. Are they friends? Sisters? Coworkers? It's hard to even see their faces due to the quality of the photo, but their dresses are fairly plain. They look young. The headline says, "Carriage Row Tailoring Opens on March 4, 1910." Skimming the article, I get the answer to my question: sisters. They opened the store together and specialized in custom designs. Readers were encouraged to book for their spring and summer weddings and special occasions.

I open the next newspaper clipping and see a photo of a building with fire damage, an old firetruck sitting in front, and a crowd of people. The article says that the Lantern Palace Theater, located on the second floor of the Morgan Building—ha! That's my name!—on Carriage Row, had caught fire when a spark from the projector lit on the film during a showing of Poe's *The Cask of Amontillado*. I didn't realize there was an adaptation of *Cask* that old! I may need to hunt it down and watch it. Maybe I'll look up where the Morgan Building was, too.

The article goes on to say that several people died from smoke inhalation, as it appears they got caught in the stairway, with too many people trying to escape at once. On top of that, the door at the bottom didn't open wide enough to let people out quickly. Apparently, the business had been cited before for the door opening in rather than out and also catching on the floor, making it difficult to pass through.

"Wow, this is awful," Claire says.

I nod and keep reading. Several deaths in the stairwell, three near the front row of seats, and one in the room where the film equipment was running. I summarize aloud, "Clyde Ganza was running the equipment, and it seems he tried to put the fire out on his own." I scan a bit. "A survivor said that they smelled smoke and turned to see the projection room in flames." My mouth twists as I think. "I wonder if everyone would have survived if Clyde had yelled *fire* instead of trying to put it out himself."

"That's so sad," Claire agrees. "What about the people who weren't in the stairwell?" She skims her finger down the article till she finds the spot. "Ah."

I read aloud. "'Officials believe they must have taken too long to exit and succumbed to the smoke while still in the audience.' But why would three people stay in the audience when everyone else ran out because of the smoke? It's not like they wouldn't have noticed that everyone else left."

"That *is* really strange," Claire agrees. "We should get going, though. I don't want to be late."

"That's true." I close the book and just hold it for a moment. I swear I hear the voice echo in my head from my dream. *"Mattie?"*

On impulse, I call, "Hey Gisela?" She's fiddling with the tea set nearby and looks up. "Could I buy this?" It's strange that I feel so drawn to Matilda's journal, but I do. I really want to read what she wrote now and figure out the connection with the newspaper clippings.

The lights in the shop flicker as Gisela approaches the counter. She glances up with a smile and says, "Ah, the Lanternites are saying hello."

"*Lanternites?*" I repeat.

"There was a fire in the theater nearby over a hundred years ago—"

"Yes! It's in the newspaper clipping here." I point at the diary and then realize what I did. "Sorry to interrupt you."

Gisela laughs. "It's okay. Clearly, I get excited about history, too." She gestures around the shop. "All the store owners in the area know about the Lanternites. That's what we call those who passed in the Lantern Palace Theater fire. They like to roam around and let us know that they're still here, making sure we don't forget them. Sometimes they flicker the lights. Holly, who owns the salon, says that they mess with the music there. Just little things to say hi. We don't chase them away. They're harmless. And I imagine they're restless for a reason." She shakes her head.

I look at Claire in time to see her eyes getting big. She tightens her grin and glances at the door playfully, like she's jokingly suggesting that we get out of here. I have to chuckle at her reaction.

"That is so cool," I answer. "Is it okay if I buy this from you? I'd love to dig into the history here."

Gisela pokes at her chin thoughtfully. "Ten dollars okay? I'll put it with the monthly donation to the Historical Society. They weren't interested in the journal, but I think that makes us all even."

"It's a deal." I pay and collect my treasure so we can rush off to work, but when I turn, I get a sudden bout of vertigo, and the world slants dangerously. I stop moving for a moment, and it passes.

Claire touches my arm. "You okay?"

"Yeah." I rub my birthmark for a moment as I look around. "Maybe I need more protein for breakfast." That bagel was top notch, but maybe an egg with it tomorrow?

"I've done that before," she says. But she doesn't leave my side as we exit the store.

As we're leaving, I spot Beau in the window of the building across the street. He appears to be deep in conversation with someone. I wonder what it's about. Funny how, if I had made one different choice in my own history, I would know.

———

That night after work, I swap my dress slacks for joggers and bring Matilda's diary to the dining room table to read over dinner. I take a bite of my homemade Hawaiian fried rice, place the newspaper clippings on the table, and start with the first journal entry.

I don't learn much about Matilda, just that she's starting a tailor shop with her sister Rosella Spurling, which I picked up already from the newspaper clipping. However, I do discover that journals are pretty mundane, as I suspected from my previous experience with them.

I have nothing better to do, so I continue reading Matilda's journal as the evening goes on. She shares a couple funny stories about customers, like one lady who either seemed to whisper or yell with no middle volume. She talks about knitting scarves to sell at the shop, which is a neat hobby that we share. Otherwise, I flip through several pages with nothing of note.

Partway through her archives, though, she mentions a man named Ansel and refers to him as her beau. I do a double-take, but I quickly realize that she was just using the word for boyfriend. They started seeing each other soon after she and her sister opened the shop, and according to her diary entries, he was particularly swoony.

"Well, this could turn into a decent read after all," I think. Unfortunately, the spice level is zero, as she mentions that she doesn't "kiss and tell, even with my own diary." Drat. I'm guessing that the most that happened when he was courting her was a polite kiss, if they were serious for a while. Actually, the kiss and tell comment was probably a joke. Ansel seems like a decent guy based on her commentary about him, as he brought her flowers, complimented her, and often walked her home after work. Her sister Rosella, as it turns out, was married and lived nearby with her family.

"I wonder if Mattie ended up marrying Ansel," I ponder aloud. I'm nearing the end of the diary, so I'm hoping that there will be a resolution ... until I recall that this is a diary and not a book. Real lives don't play out the same way novels do, unfortunately.

After several more entries about her work experiences and her beau—a word she uses a lot, and I imagine her blushing every time she writes it—I find myself losing interest. Even worse, I'm starting to think about Beau Blackwell and then, somehow, Aaron.

Luckily, I catch myself in the loop. Recognizing the problem is half the battle, right? And I switch gears. Focusing on Aaron is bloody stupid, and I know it.

Instead, I reach for the last of the newspaper clippings. This is another one about the fire in the theater, but it seems to be a wrap-up. And it's a front-page story. Yikes.

THEATER FIRE REVEALS WEB OF CORRUPTION

Local Mafia Boss and Mayor Convicted in Startling Scandal

A catastrophic blaze that tore through the city's popular Lantern Palace Theater has unveiled a sordid tale of greed, betrayal, and corruption, shaking the community to its core. The courtroom was packed with onlookers yesterday as the trial of notorious mafia boss Vittorio "Ashes" Calvino reached its dramatic conclusion.

Calvino, the owner of the Morgan building, which houses the now ruined theater, was convicted of orchestrating the inferno in what authorities believe was a brazen scheme to claim both fire and property insurance. The flames consumed much of the building from the second floor upward, leaving the first floor and basement remarkably unscathed—a detail investigators say points to the calculated nature of the crime.

Tragically, the fire claimed multiple lives. Their names are solemnly memorialized below this article.

The community's mourning turned to outrage just a few days after the fire when it was revealed that the city's own mayor, Edward "Eddie" Flanagan, had colluded with Calvino, offering protection to the mob in exchange for personal gain. While Flanagan now faces a lengthy prison term, Calvino has been sentenced to life without parole due to multiple charges of involuntary manslaughter. Several other members of the crime family will go to trial for their roles in this tragedy.

To compensate the grieving families of those who perished, the Morgan building will be sold. Proceeds from the sale, a bitter solace, are to be distributed to those left in mourning.

While the trial offers some resolution, residents remain haunted by the loss and betrayal that has marred the city's history.

Haunted indeed ...

"I'm glad they caught the guy," I say aloud. Then I peruse the list of victims and spot a familiar name: Matilda Conrad. "Oh." I guess her story ended not long after the last entry in the diary. How sad.

The smell of cigarette smoke washes over me for the second time today, and my shoulders collapse in frustration. It's almost like *I'm* being haunted by it at this point. Or am I?

Old books always have a musty smell. Maybe I just didn't notice it before. I lift the book to my nose and sniff. Like a literary sommelier, I pick out the notes of stale paper stench—musty old book, cigarettes, and a flowery perfume overlay. They tell a story, but I don't know what that is yet.

So Matilda died in the fire and her line ended there. Her diary ended up in a desk belonging to her sister and passed down through the family till they dropped it off at Gisela's Wunderkammer, along with some of her other belongings. I think it was a pair of boots, a tea set, and a suitcase. Is that right? Maybe there are other things.

I can't explain why I feel so fascinated by this woman who left too soon, other than it maybe being a genetic thing. My oldest sister, Rhiannon, would have geeked out with Fallon (sister number two) and me about it, the same way we did about the mystery surrounding an old mansion in the Seattle area where we grew up.

More ghosts of my past dance through the room. Rhiannon, Fallon, and I loved creepy stuff, and there was a whole lore surrounding a murder that was rumored to have happened in the 1940s at Cedarbrook House, near Seattle. It turns out that it wasn't true, but the three of us spent so much time researching and guessing and scaring the crap out of each other with the idea of something untoward happening there. It was delightfully macabre with just the right amount of accessibility, and for three brazen teens, it was catnip.

As I recall those fond memories, I also feel a sinking sensation in my chest about how Rhiannon always took over and made me feel small. Being the middle child of five, I always felt like I was desperately trying to catch up to the older ones so I wasn't considered a baby with the other two, desperately trying to be cool, be heard, be alive in a big way.

I was brilliant with the pranks, in my humble opinion, which fed our ardor for the mystery chase, but it ultimately got me nowhere with my elder sisters. Rhiannon perpetually saw me as irresponsible. As the baby. Fallon mothered everyone in the most cuddly, nurturing way possible, but with Rhi, it was almost as if a lioness had entered the room, and the rest of us just weren't worthy of leading. She loved me, and loves me still, but we butted heads.

Actually, I butted heads with a lot of people. So I shouldn't be surprised when I recall this.

Maybe I'll text Rhi and let her know what I found ...

Or maybe not. That feels like a pit, as opposed to a sweet cherry, right now. And I don't go for those.

Now that my brain is properly away from the Thoughts That I Don't Dare Think About, I open the diary again and read a little more.

Finally, in one of the last entries, I see something of interest.

Dearest Diary,

Something peculiar happened today as I walked home from work. Ansel, ever so thoughtful, joined me for the journey, and he suggested we take a turn along Carriage Row before he walked me to my apartment. The sun lingered in the sky, casting a golden glow over the evening, and I happily agreed to prolong our time together.

But that is not the peculiar part.

While passing an alleyway, I heard a commotion—a truck with several men unloading crates. At first, I thought nothing of it, but then I noticed they spoke in hushed tones. The sound of their boots against the wooden gangplank was louder than their conversation.

One man, wearing a bowler hat, stopped whispering and fixed me with a glare so sharp, it chilled me. He spoke curtly: "Move along, lady." He even shooed me as though I were no more than a stray cat.

Ansel, dear Ansel, wouldn't allow any trouble. He nodded politely and said, "Good evening, gentlemen. Don't mind us; we're merely enjoying a stroll." With that, he tipped his hat, took my arm, and led me onward.

Yet he was uneasy enough to avoid the alley on our return, taking us the long way around. I asked if he believed those men were up to something improper. Ansel only chuckled, saying such things typically happen near the warehouses at the far end of Main Street. He assured me that both my shop and apartment are in perfectly respectable areas. I'm doubly relieved as my great-aunt and -uncle own the building my apartment is in and live downstairs— that's the only respectable way I could live on my own. I would be frightened for their safety when I'm at work.

Ansel is ever so kind, and his words reassured me. Still, a small part of me cannot help but wonder— what were those men doing in the alley?

Below that line, the paper was slightly burnt, and a note had been added underneath.

Maybe this is why Rosie is always on me about my cigarettes! Will I ever learn?

It was signed *Mattie*.

This has become an interesting distraction from my own problems. And to think that I vowed to leave the past in the past. Between Beau and Mattie, I'm not sure I can keep that promise anymore.

I frown. It seems like I have more questions than answers at this point, at least as far as the diary is concerned. What was going on in that alley? Was Ansel involved? Did he really want to protect Mattie or just keep her nose out of whatever was happening?

And if Matilda went by Mattie, it's a little weird that the voice in my dream said her name. Are the souls of those who passed in the fire at the Lantern Palace Theater—the Lanternites, as Gisela referred to them—trying to get me to read this diary? Why?

As I put the diary aside for the evening—let's face it, I'm done—I knock the book off of my desk, and it lands on the floor. That's when I stumble upon something else odd. It flips open to reveal that a chunk of the diary has been torn out. The spine was crushed a bit, so I never noticed before.

Where is the rest of the story, now that it's gotten interesting?

Chapter Five

The Zangari Event Center team is supposed to meet this afternoon to discuss progress, now that Kenzi is back in town. I arrive early in the Rosewater meeting room, a mug of herbal tea in hand, mostly to keep my hands warm. The room is in the back of the building, facing the lake, and there's a huge picture window, where I'm standing, contemplating. A chill hangs like a gaggle of ghosts by the window, no matter what the firm does to fix it. I know because I've handled the budgetary details. We've tried opening the vents all the way half an hour before meetings, adding a space heater, even replacing the window itself with a new state-of-the-art energy efficient window. But the spirits remain.

As I'm pondering the window and warming my hands, I'm reminded of a similar moment of reverie, when Signore Zangari said I looked like a painting. The difference between the two lakes couldn't be starker, with the warm Italian sun beating down on the scintillating water, compared to the steel blue-gray of the Steel City sky blocking out the sun, shrouding the world in its cozy blankets of depressing clouds like the atmosphere of a Dickens novel. Sweet, tortured November, how I love you.

The thought of Aaron with his arms around me in Castel Gandolfo crosses my mind next, obviously, and I nudge it away gently. It's replaced by a vision of Beau with his arms around me as we looked out our hotel window at the pool so long ago. I was only twenty when we made the trek across the country with our meager belongings packed in his beat-up old Jeep and my trusty used Subaru, named Rue, both because it's short for Subaru and also because Rue McClanahan is my favorite Golden Girl.

Funny enough, the hotels we stayed in on our way across country to start our new life together in Pittsburgh reminded me of the Golden Girls' home, very 1980s Miami-fancy with their big palm and floral patterns on the bedspreads, pillows, and curtains, twenty years too late. Plus, a few stains on the walls and carpet that *wouldn't* have been seen in the ladies' home. We were college kids, and though our parents were kind enough to help us relocate, we still didn't have a ton of cash. Or sense. That weekend in Vegas, where we splurged on a nicer hotel with a pool, was one of my fond memories of us, though. That was during the happy times. The times when we thought it would all last forever. When what happened in Vegas turned into promises I couldn't keep for long. Especially the I do's in the all-night chapel. But just the memory of that sweet but too short time ... mmmm.

"Thinking about budgets?" Kenzi asks as she enters.

I give her a look.

"You were smiling and gazing out the window. I could only assume."

"I'm not that ridiculous." I approach the table and sit by her elbow, setting my tea down. "Actually, I was thinking about a painting." I flip through my phone to find an image of *Tea and Reverie* and then tell her the story as she looks it over.

"I remember hearing about that while I was in Castel Gandolfo," Kenzi says. "It used to hang in a restaurant in town. It's rumored that the artist got upset with the owner of the restaurant and stole it. No one has ever found it, though, and it's been over a hundred years. No one even knows where the artist lived or if he still has family in the area."

"That sounds like an Ella story." Ella is the youngest of the Zangari clan, and she loves the local folklore. She was really inspired by all the artifacts that the team was digging up when they were excavating.

"It is. She was talking about it one evening when she came over for dinner."

"I like that kid. She was very animated when she told stories. So passionate about everything she discussed."

"I love that you're calling her *kid* when she's just a few years younger than us."

"She's a kid. I remember being her age. *I* was definitely a kid." And the mistakes I made at the time have haunted me ever since. I feel my eye quirk as I recall my most important one, but I don't think Kenzi notices. "Signore Zangari said there was a rumor it was smuggled to America."

"I wonder if anyone ever tried to track it down." Kenzi sighs like she's thinking about where the painting may have ended up.

"Muffins?" Logan pokes his head into the room. He has a large plate in one hand and a small plate in the other.

"Yes, please!" Kenzi hops out of her chair and takes the smaller plate, which is labeled *gluten-free* and has three cranberry walnut muffins on it.

"Maybe those aren't for you," Logan jokes. "What if they're to share?"

Kenzi gives him a playful pat on the arm. "I might buy that if anyone else here ate gluten-free."

Logan grins and then offers me the plate with the regular muffins, and of course, I take one. Logan is our resident baker at Baker & Willow, though he's not the one the company is named for. Once he found out that Kenzi has celiac disease, he started experimenting with a variety of treats that she can enjoy too, and that made working here even sweeter. The pair of them really are adorable. Ah, *amour* ...

"I'll see you later." And Logan pops back out of the room as quickly as he came.

"While we wait," Kenzi begins, "were you able to look at that diary the other day? The one in the antique store?"

"I did. Honestly, I think I have more questions than answers now. I wanted to see what she wrote about, but then her story became really interesting." I fill Kenzi in on the newspaper articles and the last entry in the novel about Mattie and Ansel's evening walk.

"That's so incredibly sad," Kenzi says. "I don't like stories that end like that. I hope Ansel was able to find love again. He sounds so nice from what you described."

"I agree." I take a bite of one of the regular cranberry walnut muffins—wow, I need to find me a guy who can bake like this!—and chew thoughtfully. At that moment, I feel the strangest sensation wash over me, a deep sadness, almost like my heart itself is crying. *How very unlike me to feel on that level.* I must be losing it. Maybe I need to practice harder at being cold and uninterested in human emotions.

Worse yet, I feel the room lurch suddenly, and I squeeze my eyes shut to keep from feeling queasy or losing my balance. Luckily, I'm already sitting. When the world rights itself, everything looks strange. I blink. Maybe my eyes are dry from being in this room with the space heater. But there it is again. Before, the room was a blinding white with a watercolor of rosebushes and a waterfall gracing the far wall, but now it's completely paneled in mahogany with rich blue velvet curtains. Though I feel lost, I can't help admiring the opulence. The beautiful carvings on the chair rail. The vaulted ceiling. The crystal globes encasing the sconces on the walls. Whoever decorated this dream room has class.

Maybe I passed out?

"Miss, with all due respect, I can't send the police on a wild goose chase just because a pretty young lady has a hunch."

I can't see who spoke, but it's a man's voice, oily but firm. I smell smoke and turn my head slightly to see a cigar resting on an ash tray. An open box beside it is labeled *Romeo y Julieta*, with a picture of the young couple at the famed balcony printed on it. I recognize it from my antique shop hopping. It's a popular brand from the early 1900s, especially among the upper classes. A box like this likely wouldn't be cheap, being in such good condition. I wonder if the owner found it in this house. The room I'm in looks incredibly well-preserved, and I feel like I've been transported back over one hundred years.

That is, if I didn't pass out and happen to be dreaming this.

Tearing my eyes from the box, I look around the room, hoping to spot the speaker, but he's not showing himself. Suddenly, the cigar smoke grows heavy and oppressive. My lungs feel like they're constricted, almost like when I wore a corset for the renaissance faire. I sit up straighter and take a deep belly breath, only to start coughing. As I gag on the smoke, my eyes water, and I squeeze them shut and then open a couple times.

"Want some water?"

As I blink the room into focus, I see Kenzi thrust a paper cup in my direction. In her other hand, she's holding the pitcher of filtered water that sits on the sideboard. I nod and sip the water, hoping that will take care of ... whatever the heck that just was.

"Sometimes I choke a little with the gluten-free muffins, since they tend to be drier, but usually, the regular muffins are fine." Kenzi is looking at me sympathetically.

I look down and see the muffin in my hand, recalling that I had just taken a bite when things went sideways. "Ah. This is great. I think the air is just a little dry from the space heater."

"Yeah, I hope we can figure out how to warm this room properly. Maybe I'll talk to Miranda about looking at the blueprints. We might need to adjust the venting." Kenzi shrugs. Miranda Baker is one of the owners, as well as Kenzi's mentor. "Could be a down-the-road project."

"Good idea." I nod, but I'm starting to feel a little unnerved. What the heck is happening to me?

On the way home from work, my mind is putting in overtime. This is starting to get weird. How many times am I going to have bizarrely realistic daydreams? Or are they something else? I think Claire would recommend that I see a neurologist, but maybe I should see the lady at the metaphysical shop instead. I'm torn.

And I'm so not telling Claire till I get a better grip on what's actually going on.

Despite the delightfully dour mood that fall always brings as everything around us dies and the world turns wet, slick, and brown, I find that I want to create koozies with some brighter colors this evening: pinks and oranges. I park at the lot beside Spin a Yarn and dodge the drizzle on my way to the door. I'm sure they will have the right colors for what I have in mind.

Inside, I find a beautiful bubblegum and tangerine ombre yarn that will be fun to work with. Some weirdos like brightly colored coffee cup koozies, so I'm sure these will sell well. I pick up some cute patches to sew on, too: axolotls, macarons, strawberries, bows, and unicorns. I don't know if all these items are in right now, but I think they have been recently. I've been trying to keep up with my niece, Fallon's daughter Annabel, about what's trending. Half the problem is that I can't understand what's good or bad based on all the slang she uses. Kids these days.

I make my purchase and then head to the café part of the building. It feels like a soup night, and they have a fantastic clam chowder here.

I debate about eating in, since I love the atmosphere. It strikes me as an old Irish pub transported across the sea and time. The walls are white with huge dark wood beams framing the doors and window and exposed on the ceiling. The counter is the same weathered wood, and the wall behind is filled with shelves of antique bottles, similar to the checkout in the other part of the building. Finally, though, I decide on takeout, so I step up to the station to punch in my order: clam chowder and a half turkey and Swiss sandwich.

As I wait, I lounge on the bench by the takeout area and close my eyes. What a day. I open them again and look around at all the groups of people gathered for dinner—friends, families, a couple strays, like me. The plants seem to be getting out of hand. That's something charming about this place. The owner loves plants and has them everywhere, in both the shop part and the café. Here, they are behind the counter and in the window, but a few creepers droop over the windowsill and scurry over the shelves. It feels homey, earthy, and lived in, without seeming messy.

As I'm musing about the plants, I realize I'm being watched, and my gaze darts around the room to see who it is. I don't see anyone I know ... until I spot Beau. He's staring at me with those warm, soulful eyes, and he looks like he wants to say something, but obviously, we are nowhere near each other, so he doesn't, since I wouldn't be able to hear him. Then I realize that he's not here alone.

At the table are two young adults, who I'm guessing are Emmett and Vivienne, his nephew and niece. They have grown up so much: they were toddlers the last time I saw them. They both have the Blackwell eyes with the heavy, dark brows. Emmett's seem heavier, brooding, while Vivienne's are softer, with an almost doe-eyed innocence and manicured arches above. It's astonishing how much they look like adults now when I remember them as babies. Rae's babies. Now I see Emmett with his hoodie and disheveled hair, joggers and enormous tennis shoes. Vivienne with her little turned-up nose, thick hair pulled back in a long braid, and a very grown-up purse. How ... *how did I miss all this?*

I mean, I know *how* I missed it. I know *why* I missed it. I *chose* to miss it. It's just ... when you see the passage of time like this, it hits you. Hard.

My eyes flicker back to Beau, and he's still looking at me. He knows I caught him staring. I raise my eyebrows and form an O with my mouth. Unintentionally, of course. I didn't mean to draw attention to myself. Or us. Or what used to be us.

He glances at the kids, back and forth, saying something hurried, and then they turn to look in my direction as he stands. I hold my position. Emmett glowers, while Vivienne smiles politely. I wonder why they split reactions. What did he say?

When I'm certain that Beau is walking over here to see me, I stand. Awkwardly. But then, I summon my Morgan Magic and remember who I am.

"Hi?" Okay, not quite. I'm not sure what else to say. Or why that came out as a question. "Having dinner?" What else would he be doing here? This is a great start! Morgan Magic, my ass!

"Yeah," Beau begins. "I thought we'd eat out tonight." He puts his hands in the pockets of his dress slacks and shifts on his feet.

I glance across the room at the kids and catch Vivienne chattering as her gaze darts back and forth from us to her brother, who looks bored and annoyed. Maybe that's just his personality?

"That's nice," I reply. "I was on my way home from work. Thought I'd grab some yarn. Then I decided I didn't want to make dinner either." We both laugh awkwardly. Hard to believe we used to be so close.

"That's good." Beau looks around for a moment, and I have to wonder why he came over here. He doesn't seem to actually want to talk to me.

I decide to give him an out. "I'm sure you guys had a long day too. Please don't let me interrupt your dinner. It was nice seeing you." And it was. It was really nice. Like opening a favorite book to that one page, at the start of the best part, while you lounge in a huge, comfy chair.

But he doesn't leave. "Morgan, I ... it was nice talking to you the other day. But you surprised me. I didn't expect ... I never thought I'd see you again."

My eyes grow wide. "I agree. It was a happy coincidence." I give him an encouraging smile.

"You're doing okay? Since you fell?"

I can't help but laugh. "Pretty much. It's ..." Do I actually tell him what I'm thinking? "It's probably nothing. Just a couple weird little incidents. I'm good though."

He frowns. "Are you sure?"

"Positive."

"That's good." Beau scratches at his beard in a way that I'm sure is more for comfort than for addressing an itch. "Would you like to get coffee sometime? Maybe just catch up?"

I feel a bit like Anna at the end of *Frozen* where the ice recedes slowly from her heart. "Maybe catch up?" I repeat. "Are you sure?" Yes, more Morgan Magic. Maybe I need to have that defragged and rebooted.

Beau frowns like he was caught off guard and then chuckles. "I wouldn't have asked if I wasn't sure. But you don't have to say yes."

Now it's my turn to laugh. I rub my birthmark as I realize how silly that was. I guess we both have comfort ticks. "Sure. Maybe this weekend?"

"Number eleven." Someone behind the counter calls out my order and places a bag in the to-go line.

"That's mine," I say. "Can I give you my number?" Already, I'm pulling my card out to write on the back.

Then I see him nod, so I scribble my phone number on it and hand it to him.

Rather than look at the number, Beau looks at the front of the card, where my name, position, and company are listed, along with company email. "You like working here?" We're back to small talk.

"I do." I pick up my order and turn back to Beau. "Text me, and we can arrange a time to meet."

"I will." He turns to go. "Good seeing you." Then he smiles. It's tired, but it's there. And it meets his eyes.

"And you too." I pat him gently on the arm and turn to go back out in the rain.

When I get to my car and I'm certain that no one in the café can see me, I roll my shoulders, swing my hips, and do a couple dance steps before hopping in. I don't know why I felt like this was a dance-in-the-rain moment, but maybe a mix of wondering how he was, wondering if he held a grudge against me, and wondering what he would be like now all blended together into a tiny bit of a happy ending to our story.

And some wet socks, but really, who's counting?

On Saturday, Claire asks if I want to join them to bake cookies for a fundraiser Hawthorne High School is hosting next week—her sister Shannon has a kid at the high school—and I jump at the chance to do so. I was stuck trying to decide if I want to plan a trip to go scuba diving with whale sharks or kite surfing ... not with whale sharks. I've done both, but it's been a while, and I'm starting to get that itch again. I need to have some *adrenaline-soaked adventure* on the calendar so I have a Big Exciting Thing to look forward to. I gave up the idea of completing a marathon in each state a long time ago. Partially because I don't enjoy running.

We spend the better part of the day making thumbprint cookies, lady lox, pizzelles, and apricot *kolache*—an Eastern European butter cookie that looks like a blanket wrapped around sweet apricot filling—and I find that I'm strongly opposed to the lack of chocolate on our menu, but also outvoted. These are the traditional cookies of the region!

BUT CHOCOLATE!

I recall the amazing dark chocolate with sea salt, olive oil, and some other things that Aaron and I ate in Italy, and I feel like my soul is waltzing with the memory. *La mia vita da sogno*—it's my dream life!

But if we spent every day eating fantastic chocolate in Italy with gorgeous men who I shouldn't be thinking about, then how would that be special? It wouldn't. So I'm here baking cookies with my best friend and her mom. Which, incidentally, is also special. Just not in a get-your-blood-pumping kind of way.

Oh! And I didn't need to even write in my diary to come to that conclusion. Look at me figuring out my life!

As I press the pizzelle batter and pretend to sing Italian songs—"*Oh solo mio*"—which I've been asked to stop doing only once so far today, I realize that we are rapidly heading toward Thanksgiving ... and then Christmas. I had already planned to fly back to Seattle to spend Christmas with the whole Sturm clan, but I still want to decorate my apartment. It's not a problem. I could use the décor I already have. But I wanted to change it up a bit. Maybe some different colors this year.

"Where can I donate my old Christmas decorations?" I ask. I lift the top of the iron and remove the soft cookie with a fork. "I'd like to get some new stuff; just not sure if I can find a place where a family in need could have the other stuff. It's still in good shape."

Eloise looks thoughtful. "Maybe check with some of the local churches? Or the homeless shelters? They might need something to make it more festive there."

"That's a good idea." I make a mental note to reach out, and I add a dollop of batter to the iron and press again.

"That reminds me … Mom, did you ever go through the boxes in the attic? We may have some things to donate from those, too." Claire asks. "They were still here when I moved back in. The ones that were here when you bought the house."

"You know, I never did get rid of those." Eloise pulls a tray out of the oven and sets it on some potholders to cool. "Who knows what's up in that attic? I need to go up sometime and take care of that."

"Why don't Claire and I take care of it for you?" I offer. Eloise doesn't do well with stairs thanks to arthritis in her knee. "I don't mind taking the boxes with me when I donate mine, if the stuff is in good condition. And I can always find somewhere that will take it or throw out whatever is damaged or isn't needed."

"That would be nice," Eloise says. "Thank you."

"Claire, you want to look when we're done with this?"

"Sure. I don't have anything else I need to do." Claire shrugs. "Except that *Lattes and Love Notes* novel that you said I had to read to catch up with you. I think it's the third one."

"That's important, but I think it can wait." Then I pause. "Wait a sec. What attic are you talking about? I live in the attic." My apartment has high ceilings, and there's nothing above it. Maybe she meant to say the basement?

Eloise laughs. "You don't live in the attic. These old buildings usually have a small side attic where the roof meets the floor. It's a triangular-shaped area on either side of the house so the main part of the room looks square. There is a door on either end of your apartment for the side attics, but I had a built-in created there so it's not obvious that it's a door."

"I have secret passageways in my apartment?" I feel my stomach jump at the concept. This sort of thing excites me. I know I'm weird.

"Basically," Claire says. "Can you hand me the spatula?" She gestures to the drawer I'm standing in front of.

I pop it open and hand her the tool. "I'm in."

A few hours later, Claire and I are in my living room in front of the built-in bookcase.

She flips the living room rug away from the front to give us space. "Mom said there's a little latch up here." Then, she stands on tiptoe and maneuvers her fingers around at the top of the bookcase, near the wall. Soon, I hear a little pop, and she slides the case away from the wall.

"That's so cool!" The end unit is on small casters that are practically hidden, and several sliding mechanisms, like you'd find holding a drawer in a dresser, fasten the unit to the next one so it doesn't roll away when you slide it forward. Behind it is a doorway leading under the rafters in the steep part of the roof. It's almost as tall as a regular doorway, so we won't even need to duck to go in.

We knew it would be dusty back in there, so we don the paper masks that Claire insisted on, flip on the lights on our cellphones, and enter the Cave of Wonders. Ooooh!

It is incredibly cobwebby and dusty in the side attic, and there are a dozen boxes at either end, some cardboard and some wooden, all mixed together. We walk to the collection on the right, closest to us. The cardboard ones are marked: dishes, knickknacks, newspapers. I wonder what state the newspapers are in. How old would they be?

"Let's get all of these out of here," Claire says. "Mom should go through each of them to figure out what she wants to do with them."

"Agreed." I test-lift the one marked *dishes* and, discovering that it's not too heavy, I carry it back through the doorway to my living room.

Once everything is out of the attic, we only have a dozen boxes, which won't be too bad to carry downstairs. But why do it all now? Claire and I look at each other, and I know she's thinking about how much *our* knees will hurt trekking up and down the stairs with all of this.

"Are you doing stair math, too?" I finally ask. It's only one flight, but still.

"I was just thinking that I should ask Logan to help carry this stuff when he and Kenzi come over for dinner tomorrow."

"Oh, that's good! What if we make a couple trips, and then any time I come down the stairs, I bring another box? Then it won't be so overwhelming."

"I guess that's fair. It's not his project anyway, so he'll probably argue with me."

"I can't picture Logan arguing with you."

"You didn't grow up with him." Claire laughs and shrugs. I'm sure they butted heads just like any siblings do.

We end up carrying six of the boxes downstairs before we decide to take a break. "What if we take a peek in that wooden box?" I suggest. "It's not labeled, so it would be smart to check before we try to carry it downstairs."

"If we were smart, we would have left the box labeled *dishes* up here for Logan to carry."

I have to laugh at that. "Riiiight. But I'm curious. Let's just look." Who am I kidding? I'm already working the latch, trying to loosen the decades of grime from it so it will open.

"Eh, why not?" Claire squats beside me and watches as I prod the fastener. Finally, it opens, and she helps me lift the lid as its hinges creak in protest.

Inside, the box is piled high with stiff straw, powdery with age. I put my mask back on and gently shift some to see what's under it.

"I'll grab a garbage bag." Claire jogs to my kitchen cabinet and returns with the bag, which we fill with the ancient straw.

"Look at this!" I remove a small glass bird from the box. It's painted in faded browns and yellows, but it looks like a goldfinch.

"Aww!" Claire removes a pink glass elephant and holds it up for me to see. "These are lovely. Mom mentioned them a while ago, but I never opened any of the boxes before."

"I wonder who they belonged to." I shift the straw again and find an apple, its red paint chipped in places to reveal the clear glass beneath.

"No idea." Claire finds a glass star next and examines it. "The house belonged to another family before my parents bought it in the 1970s. It was a single-family home at that time, but at some point in the past, it had been two separate apartments like it is now. Mom changed it back to two apartments a couple years ago, before you moved in."

"These ornaments look like they're from the early 1900s. I wonder who lived here then. Do you know who owned the building?"

"We could probably look up the records. They might have belonged to the owners or a renter. But I imagine the family who owned it would have taken all their stuff with them. Someone would have tracked them down if they left it there."

Just then, my hand brushes something that makes a rustling sound against the straw, and my heart stops as I'm filled with visions of little mice making their home in there. *Please don't be mice. Please don't be mice.* I bite my lip and shift the straw a bit to find a few pages with writing on them.

"Oh!" Claire says. "Looks like a manuscript."

I frown and shake my head. "Not that many pages." I peer at the first page. Though the pen has faded, I can see a neat script dancing across the lines, large looping letters, almost joyous. "It's Mattie's." How strange. Why would these pages be stuffed in this box? Did I sleepwalk and somehow put them in here?

Glancing back at the cabinet and the entrance to the attic, I shake my head again. "I didn't do this."

"Of course you didn't," Claire says. "There's no way you would have known the cabinet opened without me telling you. Did you really think you put that in there?"

"I thought maybe I was sleepwalking, like the other day."

Claire screws up her mouth and shakes her head vigorously. "No way."

Then, without even speaking, the two of us lean over the first page of the diary like Nancy Drew and George. Or maybe Bess. Actually, Claire is like a blend between the two. Anyway ...

Dearest Diary,

I was doing a final fitting with a gentleman for his trousers today when I overheard the oddest conversation.

He was in front of the trifold mirror, up on a box so I could adjust the hem. You have to get the hem just right so it gives a clean, professional line. Mr. Conti is very particular when we make him suits, and I certainly don't want to disappoint him!

A rough-looking man entered the shop, but he didn't say anything. I called out that I would be with him in a moment, since Rosie was taking her lunch break. But Mr. Conti said something about the man being one of his associates. The man waited till I had finished hemming the pants. Then, when I went to the back to get the suit jacket, I heard them whispering. It sounded serious, like Mr. Conti was upset about something. He said something about "the goods" and that the shipment was late. The other man said it wasn't his fault. And then Mr. Conti said, "You may have to teach him a lesson, if you know what I mean."

I was shocked by what I heard, but I just gathered the jacket and made some noise as I was coming back into the main room so they wouldn't think I heard them. The last thing I heard was something about how "the mayor won't talk."

I always wondered what business Mr. Conti was in that allowed him to spend so freely on fancy suits. He owns a couple buildings in Hawthorne, but he had to buy them with something. I hope I just misheard.

I pretended that I didn't know anything as I slipped the jacket on him to make sure it fit properly. I even suggested a couple different colors of pocket squares that would look nice with the brown and black tattersall pattern of the suit.

I frown. I think tattersall is like a tight, narrow plaid. Very classic.

As he was leaving, Mr. Conti nudged the man and told him not to forget about meeting at The Brass Bell after the eight p.m. whistle. I think he's referring to the train that stops on the south end of Main Street at the Hawthorne Station. That whistle is always at eight p.m., when the last crowds of the day get off. The Brass Bell Saloon is across the street.

Maybe Ansel was right about mysterious happenings around the warehouses on that end of town. Not that he said he thought that. But he did say that that is the only place where those things happen. I just hope I'm wrong about Mr. Conti being involved. At least he only buys a new suit every few months, so he won't be buying another for a while! I don't want my hands dirty!

Yours,
Mattie

Never mind the hopes I had for a steamy romance in this diary! This is a strange little mystery now! "This is wild. I wonder what else happened."

"Yeah—"

"Hey, Claire!" Eloise's voice pierces the air around us. My apartment door is ajar for exactly this reason.

"Mom?" Claire calls back.

"Is there a website we can look these plates up on? They have a stamp with a deer on it."

"That's Hartwell & Co.," I call out. "Sorry," I mouth to Claire. "I got excited."

Claire gives me a sideways smile. "She's right," she yells. "Hartwell & Co. is early 1900s, if you want to look it up. I'll come help."

"If she's opening boxes, I want to see this china." I set the handful of papers on my desk and follow Claire downstairs.

When I see the pile of dishes in perfect condition on their dining room table, I approach. "These are lovely." I pick one up and admire the ring of flowers and stags encircling the plate. It's one of their staple patterns from that era, in blues, greens, and reddish-brown. I set it back on the pile and wait while Eloise is searching online to estimate the value of the collection.

A dusty plum-colored hatbox is nearby, and I lift the lid. Inside are several chic velvet hats that were popular in the early 1900s in a variety of colors and styles—a couple fascinators, a toque, a straw hat with striped ribbon, and a huge picture hat with silk flowers, wilted and pale with age—and underneath the last hat is a faded brown leather ring box.

"Today keeps getting more and more interesting ..." Claire mutters. She lifts the box and opens it to reveal a gold filigree ring with a diamond in the center. She plucks it delicately from the box and holds it up to the light. "Engagement ring?"

"Maybe ..." I say. "Diamonds weren't exclusively for engagement rings then." I wonder ... I pop the soft ring-holder part out, and beneath, I find a folded bill of sale, the paper yellowed with age. Gently, I unfold it and tip it so we both can see it. The name on the paper is Ansel Vale.

Chapter Six

Vandermere House is a gorgeous, stately three-story Victorian home on the north end of Main Street, as I can see from the picture that greets me on the homepage of its website. I'm so excited to go there this evening. In fact, it feels like it's almost calling me. I look at the lovely building for a moment and am surprised to find an ache in my heart that I can't explain. Stranger things have happened lately, so I ignore it and I scroll down to read about the structure that houses our evening's activities.

When it was first built, it served as the living quarters for important politicians but has played many other roles in the community over the years.

After its first life housing political figures, Vandermere House became the local post office for a year while the new building was being erected. Following this, it has been a dental office, bakery, and funeral parlor.

Now I'm not sure if I want to crawl around in the basement of a former funeral parlor. I might be changing my mind about tonight ...

Today, Vandermere House proudly provides space for the Hawthorne Historical Society and

Hawthorne Makers Market where talented local artists, crafters, and authors sell their wares on the first floor, the law offices of Brighton and Grimm on the second floor, and four apartments on the third floor. The basement has become the home of The Blind Tiger Escape and Speakeasy, which maintains the period charm of the building, allowing visitors to step into a bygone era.

While the idea of escaping a blind tiger tonight sounds straight up my alley, I was assured that it's sadly not what it sounds like. When Claire invited me to join them at the escape room this evening, she obviously predicted that I would be excited and told me that it's actually an old slang term for a speakeasy.

I was disappointed, but still intrigued. I do like a good puzzle.

God, I sound like my grandmother. Again.

I finish drying my hair and let it fall in its natural waves around my shoulders. With my coat on my arm, I jog down the stairs to meet with Claire so we can carpool.

When we arrive, I peer up at the building. In the daylight, the red-orange brick with the brown, cream, and navy wood accents appears more regal, but in the light of the spotlights striking the façade, it's rather imposing. Then I see Kenzi with her friends Lauren and Macy walking up to the door and pull my attention back to this evening's festivities. It's bound to be a fun night!

Once inside, we head down the stairs to The Blind Tiger, where we plan to grab a drink while we wait for our turn to go into the maze of rooms. I slide my hand down the walnut banister, slick from decades of men and women doing the same. As we near the bottom and pause, likely waiting for someone to move so we can enter the room—I can't see around the corner—my hand slides over grooves in the railing, and I peer at it in the dim lighting to see what it is.

Old houses like this always have carvings and markings that I find intriguing. When my sisters and I were tiny dancers back in Seattle, the Rose Garden Theater where our recitals were held was full of markings from those who had been there before us. There were several little rooms under the stage where we would change for our numbers, and all over the walls and ceilings, students for decades had carved and written their names and messages.

Everyone loves to leave their mark.

This one practically makes my heart stop, though. I rub my fingers over the zigzags that almost look like someone's name. Up and down like mountains, forming what looks like M-A and then some other lines. The Cassandra part of my brain—clad in all her ancient Greek glory—screams "Mattie," while the sensible part says, "Shut your mouth! It could say anything. Maybe it's some random marks."

Before I can debate myself any further, though, the room opens up, and I jog down the last couple stairs to join my friends. They are checking in with the hostess, and we are apparently registered as the Highball Honeys. They must give every group a cute 1920s-themed name, which is fun.

The entire room is done in vanilla with huge walnut built-ins for the shelves of booze, the bar itself, and the tables and chairs. All the cushions and the voluptuous couches are upholstered in tufted crimson velvet, and they are calling me to come lounge. I've always been baffled and impressed by the feminine urge to sit down on touchable couches like this in a sexy pose and take pictures.

Claire feels it too, and she raises an eyebrow at me like she read my mind. I grab her hand and drag her over to a fashionable couch with a painting of three gentlemen shooting billiards above it. When we arrive, wordlessly, she holds out her hand for my phone. I drape myself luxuriously across the seat and rest an arm on the back.

"You're too much," Claire says.

After a couple smiles and then pouty faces, I finally get up. "You get to be too much next!" God, I love this.

We all five end up taking turns posing and then convince one of the servers to take a group picture before we wander to a table and place an order. I get a Perfect Manhattan, which is made with bourbon, vermouth, bitters, and cherry juice. I know this is a sweet cherries kind of evening, especially since I get to spend it solving puzzles with friends.

Someday I'll be Miss Popular in the nursing home. Can't wait.

Claire gets an Old Fashioned, but the others order a Sidecar and Bee's Knees, which are both apparently drinks from the era, according to our menu. We go with a Chinese-food-themed platter for snacks with egg rolls, shrimp toast, crab Rangoon, and more. My mouth is watering just thinking about the egg rolls.

But somewhere between the server leaving and me mopping up my drool, Kenzi decides to start playing with her necklace with her left hand ... using over-exaggerated motions.

"Hey, what is that?" Lauren grabs Kenzi's hand and holds it out for all of us to see. "When did this happen?" Then she rolls her into a hug so fast that I actually didn't get to see what we were looking at. I'm guessing it's an engagement ring.

When I make eye contact with Claire, I know she was in on it. She's wearing a huge grin. Finally, Lauren lets go of Kenzi, and it's Claire's turn. She jogs around the table and squeezes her. "I get another sister!" Kenzi tears up, and then Claire tears up, and I'm certain I need to say something ridiculous or I'll tear up too. The Morgan handbook clearly states *no crying*.

"Who's the lucky guy?" That works. Some of my Morgan Magic, right? Incidentally, that's a great thing to yell when someone announces a pregnancy too. I might be saying that from experience.

Our crew all bursts into laughter while Kenzi and Claire dab at their eyes so their mascara doesn't run, and the next thing I know, we are swarmed by servers delivering drinks and food. *Hello, egg roll, my old friend ...*

Kenzi fills us in on the proposal as we gab and snack. "We were walking through the Hall of Architecture at the Carnegie Museum, and we stopped at the Florence Baptistery doors. They're called the Gates of Paradise, and I was reading the placard there when I felt this weird stillness. When I turned, Logan got down on one knee and said, 'Love, like art, takes patience. It's shaped by time, care, and devotion. I thought that being here with these masterpieces from across time and all around the world would be the best place to ask you to spend the rest of your life with me. Would you do me the honor?'"

"My brother said that?" Claire cries out. Then she snorts. "I thought he was just wooing you with gluten-free pastries. That's pretty deep!"

I gently smack her arm. "You give him a lot of shit, but he's a pretty good guy."

"He really is," Lauren says. Macy nods. And Kenzi beams. Then Claire concedes with a grin and a shrug.

"Can I see the ring?" I ask. Kenzi presents a beautiful trio of pear-shaped diamonds flanked with small round diamonds on either end. The whole ring resembles a tiara. "Aww, that's beautiful!"

As the group starts chattering about wedding ideas, my mind drifts a bit to the ring box Claire and I opened just this afternoon. I wonder what Ansel's proposal was like. Probably nothing as elaborate as some of the proposals I hear about today. Of course, a friend from back home said that she and her boyfriend were changing the cat litter when he suddenly said, "Oh, yeah. Here's this," and handed her a ring. I hope Mattie's proposal was more romantic than that.

I take a swig of my Manhattan, finishing it off just as the host approaches us to say that the Highball Honeys are up next to enter the escape rooms. My stomach tingles from the liquor and the excitement of our pending win, because I know we're going to kick ass at these puzzles.

Maybe I overestimated my level of awesomeness. These rooms aren't as easy to bust out of as I thought.

In the first room, we're in a parlor where a minibar is set up across the room from the entrance. There's a record player by a settee and a selection of probably twenty records. The wallpaper is covered in a brightly colored garden with dozens of little yellow sparrows peeking through the foliage. Nothing else really stands out as spots to search for clues. Macy puts a record on at random while we're searching through the rest of the records for something obvious, till Claire suggests that one of the records might tie to the liquor. We search till we find a song about a cocktail and follow the instructions in the song to mix the drink. We pour it into a glass that then turns red and discover some colored buttons by the door. Pressing the red one pops it open.

It sounds faster than it really was.

In the next room, we encounter a printing press with piles of newspapers, flyers, and menus. Beside the exit door is something like a set of three open wooden lockers, where I'm guessing the employees would hang their coats. The clock-in box is just beyond that. It's strange, though: If you pull the lever, a drawer slides down to reveal something like a combination lock. Kenzi points out that some of the cocktails are animal names—The Cat's Pajamas, Fox Trot, Bear Growl, Gilded Sparrow, and Bee's Knees—like the names above each of the hooks: Kitty Patterson, Beatrice Anderson, and Leticia Barratt. *Cat* and *Bea* are obvious, but the third one is harder till we start saying the names out loud—*Bear* from Barratt. Once we use the pricing from The Cat's Pajamas, Bee's Knees, and Bear Growl in that order on the lock, the door pops and leads us to the next room.

The third room, which ends up being the hardest, looks like a lounge or living room. Several chairs and a couch are huddled around a fireplace. Newspapers, magazines, and books are scattered on the coffee table and end tables. The mantle holds a porcelain sparrow on a mound, which might be a music box. An old portrait of a family of six all in formal attire rests above it, their eyes indicating that they were clearly bored by the time the photo was taken. A quick glance at the rest of the room doesn't reveal much we can examine for clues except maybe the hat tree near the exit door, where several coats and hats rest, and the sideboard against the wall there.

I wander over to the picture, and spotting a sign below it, I read about its history.

Armand and Rosella Spurling and their children, 1919. Hawthorne, Pennsylvania. Donated by their great-grandchildren Amanda Riley and Daniel Shields.

"Oh ..." I take a closer look at the picture. This was Matilda's sister's family. Rosella owned the tailor shop with her.

Kenzi's musings interrupt my reverie. "No wallpaper, no floor tiles, no ceiling medallion ..." She seems to be taking stock of the architecture till I realize she's hunting for things to count or untangle.

I nod at her. Returning to the game, I glance at the sparrow, which could be interesting, aside from the fact that now there is another sparrow in the space associated with Mattie and her family.

When I pick it up, I discover that it is actually a music box, so I wind the key. A haunting tune pours from the bird, and my friends pause their perusal to listen. I recognize it, but I can't think of what it is. Probably something from the prohibition era ... I hum along, hoping my brain will start filling in the gaps.

Claire lights up finally and starts scat singing to it, and that's when we all collectively say, "Oh!" While the music box plays the song with a tinkly, sort of classical tone, Claire is swinging the notes so it has more of a jazz feel.

"'Mack the Knife?'" Lauren asks.

From there, things start to fall into place. Because the song is about a murder, I wander to the bookshelf and hunt for books that feature a murder. Eventually, we gather *Hamlet* and *A Murder on the Orient Express*.

A few minutes later, I am examining the sideboard when I spot a tiny carving near the wall on top of the flat surface. It looks like a crude bird cut in with a pen knife, but it's barely noticeable since someone filled in the carving with paint the same color as the desk. "What about this?" I say. "A little sparrow, just like the music box." I point at the carving, and everyone gathers around to see for themselves.

Lauren runs her fingers over the carving. "But what do we do with this?"

"Morgan, didn't you say that you like to poke furniture?" Claire laughs.

I explain to the group about the rolltop desk in Gisela's. Obviously, next, I press down on *this* bird. Nothing happens, so I prod, tap, and nudge, but again, nothing.

"What if we're supposed to look where the bird is looking?" Macy says. "When you create an ad, you're supposed to have the person in the image look where you want the viewer to look, like at a button to click or at the product if it's in a magazine." Macy does a lot of modeling, so she must have inadvertently learned some of the tricks of advertising over the years. She places her finger on the sparrow's beak and gently follows it toward the left edge of the sideboard. Once there, she wraps her hand under the lip of the wooden top. We hear a pop, and a drawer is released from under the piece.

As if choreographed, we all squat to see what's in the drawer: six liquor bottles, all the same size, but the amount of liquor in each bottle is different. After a significant amount of rearranging the liquor bottles by rainbow order, size, and then weight, we manage to get them in the right order. There are six keypads, too, so we punch in copyright dates, page numbers, and volume numbers from the books, newspapers, and magazines where we found clues. But we only have five items with numbers, so there is still one spot left.

That's when I realize that the biggest clue in the room might just be the answer. "What about the portrait? There are six people there." Six Spurlings ... and I think their last name actually means *sparrow*. So fitting that the room is decorated with them. I feel warm with excitement as we get closer to winning.

"Sure, let's go with six." Claire punches that number in, and we hear a clang like a heavy metal bolt dropping. The door pops open. We did it!

I thought this would be the last room because it was so complicated, but there's another room beyond with a basement feel to it. It's actually chilly, less inviting than the other rooms.

The walls are all brick, and the lighting is dim. There are stacks of ledgers on a big table in the middle of the room and crates stacked along the walls. A safe is partially hidden behind the crates. Oddly enough, there isn't an actual exit door anywhere, but I'm guessing that the bricked-up archway somehow opens to let us out. It looks like it was bricked hastily, with slops of mortar running down and crooked bricks. I wonder if it's supposed to look like the next room is hiding something.

Shockingly, we manage to piece together evidence from some wanted posters Claire found and the ledgers from the table to unlock the safe. There's a sheet of escape instructions inside that tells us exactly what bricks to push to open the bricked-up doorway. From this room, we enter a tunnel that appears to lead back to the bar.

Once in the tunnel, victory music blares, and rainbow lights flash and play on the walls, bouncing off of a series of disco balls (isn't that anachronistic?!) that lead back to the main room.

A plaque hangs in the hallway directly across from the opening that we just walked through, so I pause to read it before following the party lights. It says, *During Prohibition, bootleggers used a system of hidden passages under the homes and businesses of Hawthorne to smuggle booze. When authorities discovered the operations, many of the entrances between the buildings were bricked up. This was common in many towns at that time.*

Some glops of mortar attract my eye, and I step closer. They must have repaired some of the brickwork here, maybe closing off the main part of the basement after prohibition.

Kenzi points at the sign and says, "Probably some mafia stuff, too, since we're so close to Route 19." She leads us back to the bar, and upon exiting the tunnel, we are accosted by staff who pose us with accoutrement from the era and take pictures on all of our phones. We have the pleasure of holding the sign that says "The Highball Honeys Tamed the Blind Tiger Escape Room!" I imagine there is a *womp womp* sign for those who can't get out and need the staff to unlock it for them.

"Back to the mafia bit ..." I begin as we head to the coat room. "Is this common knowledge?" Seems like everyone is in on this except me.

"A lot of it is just rumors, but I guarantee there is some truth to it if you dig around online," Kenzi answers. "Having secret passageways under the city is pretty cool, though. I bet a lot of the old buildings here have them."

I can't help but think about that on the way home and even when I'm back in my apartment. What would the men that Mattie was trailing bring into town, and would they be using the tunnels to hide things?

I open my phone to double-check the time that I'm meeting Beau tomorrow morning for coffee and pause to admire my new phone background. It's *Tea and Reverie*, or at least, it's a copy based on the artist's drawings. I smile for a moment, until the smell of smoke washes over me again, pulling me from the reverie to the present. And I thought I was having such a good day! Maybe a window is cracked or something? Ugh. I check to make sure everything is shut and locked, but they already are.

I'm not going to let it bother me, though. There has to be a logical explanation.

Casually, I shove it out of my mind. I need to get some sleep or I'll need coffee to make it to meet Beau for coffee. And then I'll be wound up like a crazy person all day.

Actually, just thinking about Beau calms me, and I mentally meander through sweet memories of us. One of my favorites was when we decided that I would be joining him to go to Pittsburgh. The calm, the storm ... it was all there at once.

It was the spring of my second year at Stonegate, the first college I attended, near Seattle, and he was about to graduate. That huge day had been looming on the horizon for the entire year, and I always wanted to slam on the brakes. It felt so final. We both knew he was going back to Pittsburgh, saying goodbye to Seattle and everything there.

Somewhere inside, I wanted to just yell, "Take me with you." But the thing is, Beau doesn't do rash. He takes his time and makes sure that the decision is the best. He likes to weigh his choices carefully, deliberately, especially big ones. He had been debating master's programs the year before, and I watched him make lists of pros and cons. For each school, I was on the cons list and felt like it was a bit of a joke. The first time he wrote my name there, he gave me such a meaningful look afterward that I couldn't take it seriously.

"So you think you'll miss me? Is that what you're saying?" I immediately climbed into his lap and kissed him like he was trying to walk out the door that minute and taking his breath away would stop him.

"I'm not going anywhere for a while," he responded, the soft hum of his deep voice buzzing my bottom lip.

But as the months went by, that *for a while* became *soon*, and I started putting up supports to keep my heart from collapsing when he left.

That spring though, with only a couple months before his graduation, we decided to brave the chill of the midmorning Seattle air and headed out to Snoqualmie for a hike. Some of the plants were starting to show their tightly wound buds, giving promise of a glorious burst of color in the coming days. We had a lot of rain the previous week, and the melt from the mountains combined to create a serious rush as the river raced to the ocean. Closer to the river, it was pretty loud, but that in itself, with Beau's hand in mine, created a peace that I'd never felt before. Like life goes on no matter what, and what's important will stay with you.

If it's meant to.

That's where we had our first serious conversation about what happens next.

"I've been thinking about this for a while," he started. "Would you consider transferring to a school out east ... and coming with me?"

I looked at him for a moment before answering, because my throat was strangling my scream of joy to turn it into a calmer response. It didn't work. I shrieked anyway and threw my arms around him. "Yes! I thought you'd never ask me to come!"

Laughing, he responded, "I didn't want to ask because I wasn't sure you would. I know you love it here. Your whole family is here. But you know, I think you'll like where I'm from too."

I felt the same: afraid to ask because I didn't want to hear the answer if it was a no.

I hadn't noticed while we were hiking, but clouds had paraded in, and just then, a roll of thunder echoed through the valley. "Is it supposed to rain?" I hadn't seen anything about it before we left to hike, but I might have looked at the wrong time.

"I didn't think it would. They were calling for a ten percent chance."

"I guess there's always a chance." I know he knew what I meant. And I wrapped my arms around his chest and squeezed, snuggling my face into him and closing my eyes. I never wanted to let go.

Kissing me on the forehead, Beau pulled me from my daydream. "We ought to head back to the car so we don't get wet." A flash in the sky triggered urgency in his voice. "Or get struck by lightning."

"Fair point."

Together, we jogged back over the trail and made it to the parking lot right before the sky opened up and drenched us. I started laughing and pulled Beau toward me, intending to enjoy the silliness of kissing in the rain. He was stiff for a moment and then caved, and I felt all the love he had for me in that one instant. I couldn't believe that I got to go with him so this would never have to end. Grabbing his hand again, I had started dancing toward the car when a crack echoed through our daydream and brought a huge tree branch crashing down into our reality on the other end of the parking lot.

"Car!" Beau called. He took off and nearly ended up dragging me forward because I was so surprised. We both jumped in. I was laughing, but Beau looked a little too serious.

"Hey." I massaged his soaking wet arm. "That was fun. And we're about to start on a new adventure." I leaned across the gear shift and planted a wet kiss, from the rain, on his mouth.

"I know." Beau touched my cheek, his dark brown eyes darting back and forth as they searched my hazel ones. "I was just thinking how close that was and what it would be like to lose you."

Chapter Seven

I'm meeting Beau for coffee shortly, so I dress in jeans and an oversized navy V-neck sweater. Then I debate whether I look too casual. Am I swimming in this sweater? Should I run down and see what Claire thinks? Nah. She won't be alert enough to say anything other than, "You're fine. Go away till I've had *my* coffee." I twist around and try to catch my butt in the mirror. *Looking good, girl!* The jeans are at least on point. The angle and position of the pockets give me a nice shape. I'd smack my own ass if it wouldn't mean a trip to the chiropractor afterward.

Drawing a deep breath, I crush the butterflies in my stomach. I'm just meeting him for coffee. Why am I overthinking this? I sigh and decide that the outfit is fine. The man has held my hair back while I puked up Boone's Farm, so I'm sure he has managed his expectations.

I add my favorite necklace, a gold chain with a heart charm, five birthstones adorning the side, one for each sister. Fallon got us these for Christmas a couple years ago so we all match, even Mom. My daring pink spinel for August is nestled in the middle. I'm glad she chose that over peridot, since the jeweler used such a bright, bold version of the stone. It's like a shot of espresso.

Roar.

I still have half an hour before I need to leave, so I return to the chunk of Matilda's journal that we started reading yesterday afternoon. I actually forgot about it by the time we finished sorting through the boxes that Claire and I carried down yesterday and digging around online for information about the treasures. Why was I so interested in all the stuff we found in the attic? No idea. It just felt ... important to me. Like if someone took the time to care for it so long ago, then surely we should give some of our time to learn about it. I feel like I know the person who used those plates, who wore those hats, who hung those ornaments on their tree, just because I got to be with their things and understand why they were special.

The Hartwell & Co. plates were actually worth more than we expected. Whenever we get curious, we end up down the strangest rabbit holes. Finding out the value is easy, though. The bigger problem is that we have no way of knowing exactly who all this stuff belongs to. Eloise can easily check who owned her home before, since she has the deed, but it's unlikely that they're still around to claim the boxes or tell us who to give them to. She said they were downsizing when they sold it, so she would probably have to track down their heirs. And it's unlikely the heirs would know anything about the boxes. If they belonged to someone before that, who knows if we would be able to trace ownership, since the house is so old.

I play with my necklace as I think about it. Then I get an idea. Maybe Matilda's sister would know, or her family. Since we know the diary was hers, maybe her family lived here at some point. Or maybe Ansel did. I wonder if Gisela would connect us with them. It could all be Mattie's stuff in the boxes, and the family was just keeping it in the attic and forgot about it.

I flop on the chaise part of my couch, place a burgundy throw pillow on my lap and the missing pages on that. Then I flip them open to the second entry.

Dearest Diary,

I've done something so horrible! I broke Rosie's trust, but I dare not tell her. Today, one of our clients, Mr. Turner, asked for some repairs on a suit. He's short for a gentleman, with a slight build, and I got an idea when he dropped the suit off: I was going to look around near The Brass Bell and see if there was any suspicious activity. I didn't know what I was looking for, but I felt in my heart that I would know it if I saw it. And I did.

After work, I brought the suit home in a bag, along with a dress shirt I was making custom for the teenage son of another client, Mrs. Green. I made her dress for her daughter's wedding last year. It was a beautiful blue, the same color as her eyes, but I digress. Her son is going to work for the family business this summer, so he needs a smart dress shirt to look professional. He's not a full-grown man, yet, so his chest measurement is a little closer to mine. Tonight, when it was dark out, I put on the shirt and suit, with a few tucks and safety pins here and there. I slipped on an old pair of boots that had been sitting in the entry of the house for a few months. I believe they belong to Mr. Anderson, who cares for the yard for my great-aunt and -uncle. Bless them for renting this apartment to me so I can have some independence! But Mr. Anderson hasn't worn them in a long time. They are always there!

I pulled my hair up in a knot on top of my head and hid it in a newsboy hat that I promised Ansel I would repair for him. Because it's dark out, I don't think anyone would think I wasn't a young man, maybe a teenage boy, especially because I paid careful attention to how I walked.

I lit a cigarette and adopted a leisurely pace as I strolled down Main Street toward the train station. It's several blocks away, and I found it difficult to walk in the pilfered boots. I should have thought to wear extra socks so they didn't slide on my feet. Goodness, though, they were certainly more comfortable than what I normally wear! Men are lucky in that regard!

When I approached the train station, I looked around, but I don't know what I was looking for. I don't know what day Mr. Conti and his friends are supposed to meet! When I approached The Brass Bell Saloon, I paused outside to light another cigarette. I felt a little bit of triumph for that, as it would be hard to find another excuse to stop outside, unless I was tying my shoe or hunting for something, but nothing else would allow me the freedom of looking around me, of observing.

A gentleman stepped through the door just then and asked me for a light. I handed him my matchbook and waited. He took a deep drag on the cigarette and handed it back. Then, he nodded and walked over to join a couple other men. I didn't want them to think I was spying, so I looked at my hand as if I were checking a pocket watch and then crossed my arms and peered through the saloon window, like I was waiting for someone. When I looked from the corner of my eye, I saw them go down the little alley between The Brass Bell and the building next door. Edging my way along the building so as not to raise suspicion, I finally peered down the alley and saw a door into the next building slightly ajar.

I took a major risk and also ducked down the alley, pressing myself to the brick of the building beside The Brass Bell. My plan was to pretend I needed to relieve myself, as men do, if I got caught. I could play at being a drunk, I supposed. Luckily, I didn't need to. When finally I was beside the door, I could hear a conversation within, though even blessed with hearing like that of a bat, I had to strain.

They mentioned something about a shipment from Clarksburg, which I believe is south of here. Something was said about "the goods" again, and then about some "valuable pieces."

They mentioned something about "that Valenti painting," and I nearly gasped aloud. I remember a headline in the paper a couple months ago about a painting by Angelo Valenti, an Italian artist who had moved to America, being stolen from the Novak Arts

& Music Museum in D.C., where it was on exhibit. Surely that's the painting they were talking about!

I crept back to Main Street, but as I rounded the corner, I saw Mr. Conti leave the saloon. I rushed to adjust my hat and lean against The Brass Bell casually, as if I had been standing there before, causing me to burn my wrist badly with my cigarette. I couldn't let him see me. I had to stay quiet, but that burn really hurt! I couldn't move, but then I caught them glancing over at me. I finally looked at my "pocket watch" again, sighed, and moved along down the street toward home. I was hoping he would think I was meeting someone and they never showed up. I pulled out my "pocket watch" after a few steps and twisted my neck enough to see down the street. Mr. Conti was rounding the corner into the same alley, so I sped my steps away. I paused near one of the shop windows a couple blocks away to make sure I wasn't followed, and it seemed safe. Then, I walked up Oak quite a distance before cutting across to Maple and backtracking to Barrington.

I pause in my reading and do a double-take. I draw the map in the air to help me visualize what she said. If she went up Oak, took a side street, and then came down Maple and ended up on Barrington, which is parallel to Main, then it's likely that she lived on my block. Maybe even in my house. I wonder ...

When I finally got home, I took some ice from the ice box for my burn. It's red now, but I'm hoping it won't scar. I'll never hear the end of it from Rosie. I hung up the clothes I borrowed to air them out, but tomorrow, I'll dry clean them before my sister gets to work, just in case they smell like cigarettes or perfume. I wouldn't want my customers to suspect that I was wearing their clothes. That would be quite the scandal!

I'm not sure what to do about the painting that I suspect Mr. Conti is involved in stealing. But I do know that these rends won't mend themselves. I'll spend the rest of the evening sewing in the safety of my home, thank you very much!

Yours,
Mattie

Well, that was unexpected! I place the pages on the end table and rub my birthmark thoughtfully with my thumb. Then I apply my lipstick and head out the door with my coat and purse in hand. I'll have to save more Mattie for later or I'll be late for coffee. Her story is getting more and more interesting, but I have my own story to create right now.

As I walk from Barrington to Maple to Main, tracing Mattie's path, my thoughts shift to Beau. All these years, I've carried one damning idea with me: Beau hates me. It's woven itself through every activity that I've done. I've recalled it in every relationship I've been in. It has pounded like a drum as the bass beat for my story for the past thirteen years.

Beau hates me.

And it's my fault. For all my confidence and my ability to crush down Bradley—I mean, hello, it's easy—that tiny voice speaks the truth like a Cassandra whispering constantly in my ear. And I believe her. I made the best man I've ever known hate me.

So to find out that he actually wants to hang out with me ... it just doesn't compute. When we ran into each other in WellSpring, a little part of me, that Cassandra part, was holding my breath. I knew he wouldn't yell or express his anger. Even Beau has a limit to what he will put up with, but it's been so many years that I couldn't imagine him raising his voice, even over that. His steadiness was expected. But asking me to join him for java ... that's a clear *I don't hate you* from him. That implies warmth.

I mean, how often do you ask someone you hate to meet up with you for a cup o' joe? That is, if you're not a politician doing it for a media opp.

Warmth, I can do.

But I'm curious why he wants to meet. To catch up, right?

Moments later, a tiny ray of sun peeks through the heavy, almost charcoal clouds, and I take it as a good sign. I enter Lyon's Den Coffee and appreciate the heat of the room for a moment as I unbutton my wool coat and look around for Beau. I'm early, and he's not here yet, so I get in line for my usual flat white. I take off my beret and flex it in my fingers, but not nervously. Soon, though, I hear a voice behind me.

"Morgan?"

I turn around to see those same warm eyes smiling at mine. Older, wiser, but the same as the ones I fell in love with in that heady rush of young hormone-induced passion blended with a deep knowing that he was my person.

Can a person have more than one person?

The stark contrast between Beau and Aaron washes over me like a tsunami. Beau's quiet gravitational pull, where you want to curl against him and purr. Aaron's atomic magnetism that you know will end in combustion, a volcanic eruption of two strong personalities so certain of their own paths being the right one that they collide.

The calm and the rush, both equally attractive ... how do I always get caught in the undertow?

I smile gently. "Yeah" is all I say because I don't want to scare him with the way our entire past just came back in a heartbeat. Besides, I still feel immense guilt for leaving. Yeah, me. The one who never feels embarrassment or blame or any of the negative energies aimed at myself. Guilt, the one thing that I'll likely never get over, sent me on a trajectory through the stars, searching for ways to feel like I was in control while *losing* control. My stomach flattens as the feeling wells up. "How's your day going?" And I'll never let him know. I can't go back to that day. I'll leave the past in the past.

"It's good." His eyes search mine, as if they know something is hidden there. We step up to the counter, and he glances at me again. "Flat white?"

"You remembered."

He orders mine, along with an Americano. Then he gives me a sly, sideways glance. "You want a doughnut?"

I have to laugh. "Sure, why not. Chocolate cake with glaze. Thank you." I get out my wallet, but he waves it away and pays for our order. I give him a genuine smile.

When our order is in, we approach the end of the counter to wait. He tips an eyebrow toward the window. "It's Morgan Weather out." His voice is warm but rugged. Then he smiles like a cozy fall day.

I actually close my eyes for a moment as the memory comes back. He used to refer to the days where the clouds hung like thick wool socks as Morgan Weather. His favorite kind of days. The clouds were pregnant with rain or snow and cuddly possibilities of us curled up on his couch, each studying for our respective programs.

And being in his orbit meant that I absolutely needed, in my heart of hearts, from the depths of my soul, to go with him.

I look up through my lashes at him and give him a soft smile. "Are we here to talk about the weather?" I joke.

"Vivi wants to be a meteorologist, so we talk about the weather a lot." He shrugs and hands me my drink when it's plunked onto the counter. I wrap my hands around it, feeling the heat spread through my fingers. When our doughnuts arrive, we head to a table.

"I'm not exactly *surprised* by how big the kids are, but honestly, I'm amazed that it's been so long since I've seen her and Emmett." I hang my coat on the chair and sit.

Beau does the same. "Thirteen years is a long time." His expression is hard to read, but I take it as a neutral comment, even though the tinge of guilt crinkles my stomach.

"Yeah." How else can I respond? "So you said you wanted to catch up? What have you been up to all these years? I know part of it, obviously." I open my hands and then wrap them around my coffee again.

Beau leans forward and sighs. Then he takes a bite of his bourbon caramel apple doughnut—which looks both bougie and bucolic, somehow, almost hipster—and chews thoughtfully for a moment.

I had to train myself to be patient when we were dating, to give Beau the space to examine things, turn them over in his mind, before responding. Beau is thoughtful and quiet, so he will sometimes ponder carefully before answering something. A couple times early on, I thought he zoned out, but he assured me that he just wanted to take the right tact with something. I learned to appreciate the extra care. I'm glad to see that this has stayed the same.

"So, a couple years after you left, when the kids were still really little, Aurelia, er, Rae—" He looks at me for confirmation, and I nod.

"I know, your sister." I give a wan smile.

"I know, well, Rae was on a couple medications for anxiety and to help ween her off of the painkillers. She had lost her job at the pharmacy before that ..."

I put my hand on his arm, intending the motion to be soothing. "I remember that part." That had been my final straw.

"Right." He pauses and takes a sip. "We were trying to help her get back on her feet. But the medications weren't working. Her doctor kept tweaking them. And then there was a bad interaction a few months after you left." His hand moves to his beard, scratching at his jaw gently. As Beau stares into the distant past, over my shoulder and somewhere beyond the wall of the café, the whole story clicks into place for me.

"So that's when she passed." I prop my elbows on the table and rest my chin on my hands. "I'm sorry."

I didn't get to know the luminous Rae that Beau had described before we moved here. The one who used to help him find all the treasures on scavenger hunts their parents created and would sneak him cookies when their mom was baking and picked him up from a party where the kids were drinking in high school because he was too afraid to tell his parents. (Spoiler alert: They would have been thrilled that he decided to leave instead of drinking with them.) Rae was his rock, a hell of a stable, sturdy big sister. I actually was excited to meet her, but she broke her leg skiing and then couldn't get off the pain meds and then stole from the pharmacy ... being a pharmacist was a huge goal for her, and she ruined it with her addiction. She went downhill fast—maybe that's a bad way to describe it, what with the skiing accident—but during Beau's senior year at Stonegate, she completely changed. He didn't really realize how bad it was until we were in Pittsburgh later that summer, ready for a new school year with him starting his master's and me starting my junior year at a local college I transferred to, ready to start our new life together.

When we arrived, Rae oscillated between anxiety and depression. A few times, Beau suggested that we let the kids stay over at our house to give her a break to work on her healing. They were toddlers, and I was barely old enough to drink. We were newlyweds, and we were changing diapers and hiding anything breakable. Soon, it was almost every weekend. Then, Rae went into rehab, and the kids were at our house or Beau's parents' constantly.

I actually started to hate going home after class. We both had to study, and there were these adorable munchkins running around who needed so much more than we could give. At least, more than I could.

Our relationship changed. I felt like he was no longer the Beau I fell in love with, the sweet and serious quiet man who was perfectly content wrapping an arm around me as we both worked on our classwork. Now, he was quick to anger. Not that I wasn't. We both just needed ... space, time, help?

It was so much more responsibility than either of us could take. Anyone would have cracked. And we shattered.

And under the crush of overwhelm, I decided to tap out.

A person can only be so strong. And it wasn't my family mess. I was new. I felt like an outsider. I felt like so much was demanded of me, a virtual stranger. So I asked for a divorce.

As I mentally wander through the catacombs of our past, I shudder. In the present, my gaze refocuses on his eyes, and I feel my own well up. There's just so much!

Before he can see it, I blink and take a sip of my coffee. I'm too late though.

"You don't have to cry on my account," Beau says gently. He takes another bite of his doughnut and then swallows. He looks thoughtfully at the pastry before looking back at me. "Do you want to try this? It has so many layers of flavor: sweet, rich, smoky, salty." He reaches across the table with the doughnut, a peace offering.

Sharing food? I guess he really doesn't hate me.

When I hesitate, he looks at the doughnut like it offended someone. "Sorry; I don't know what I was thinking. I guess I'm just used to eating with the kids."

"Hey, I'm game." I don't want him to feel embarrassed. Also, I had already decided to buy one on my way home to try tomorrow. Or tonight. I lean forward and take a nibble of the proffered pastry. I don't regret it. "This might be the best doughnut ever," I murmur around the deliciousness in my mouth. And to think that I, Morgan, actually played it safe with my favorite chocolate cake doughnut. *Girl, live a little!*

"I know, right?" Beau sips his Americano and grins. He's always had a crooked smile, where one side could light up the sky and the other looks like he has a secret. I used to live for that smile.

"So back to your story ... you adopted the kids and raised them on your own?" I glance at his hand to determine if there might be a Mrs. Blackwell, but he probably wouldn't be sharing his doughnut with me if there was.

"On my own." He says it with air quotes. "Mom and Dad were there for me, of course. And Aurelia's life insurance helped with sitters and nannies and summer camps for a while. We made it work."

I decide to lighten the mood a bit and ask what the kids are doing, besides soccer and driving, which is a little scary considering the last time I saw them, I was giving them baths and counting piggy toes. We talk about prom and SATs and all the other things that high school kids worry about before Beau turns the conversation back to me.

"Well, I'm definitely *not* journaling," I begin. This prompts a wrinkled eyebrow from my companion and then a confused sip of coffee. "Anyway, I thought about it." I brief him on some of my recent adventures, leading up to the diary found in the local antique store. As I finish and go for a sip of my coffee, the acrid smell of cigarette smoke assaults my nostrils momentarily, and I frown hard, as if that will chase the scent away.

"You okay?" Beau asks.

"Yeah." I breathe out forcefully through my nose and then make myself smell the coffee. Just. Coffee. No. Smoke. Mind over matter, right? "It's nothing." But I can't exactly lie to Beau. He has this angelic quality about him that makes you want to confess all your sins and let him tell you that he believes in you. "Actually, I sometimes think I smell cigarette smoke, and it's slowly driving me mad."

The lightning strike appears between Beau's eyebrows again. "Morgan, that's not good. How long? Did you— Have you seen a doctor?"

The rush of Beau's concern for me makes my face burn with embarrassment. Yes, another emotion I never have. Getting the whole rainbow today. I'm guessing this moment is red by how hot my face is. "It's a new thing. Since I fell." I clear my throat and my emotions at the same time. "But I was cleared by the doctor; no concussion. I'm guessing this is just a residual ... hiccup."

Beau looks questioningly at his doughnut before returning his gaze to me. "I know it's not my business, but I'd get that checked out." Then, ever the curious mind, he asks, "Have you thought about what the trigger might be?"

Why didn't I think of that? "I haven't yet, but I definitely will now. I've been inside each time it happened, so it's not the cold. I'll make a note next time. Thank you." I take another sip of my flat white. "You know, you sound a little like Ansel in Mattie's diary." I give him a wan smile. "Thanks for that."

Beau also doesn't mince words. "I want you to take care of yourself." At least he's gentle about it. "I know you like to put on a brave front, but ... you're important. Maybe see someone about this."

"I'll keep it in mind."

He pops the last bite of doughnut in his mouth and chews for a moment. "Are you sure Mattie lived in your house?"

I dab a little icing off my lip and squint as I think. "Yeah. Based on the directions she listed in her diary, it's pretty likely. It would be an odd coincidence that she lived in another house on the block, since her stuff was in my attic. Why?"

"I was just wondering why the ring would be in the box with the receipt if that's her stuff. Maybe it was where Ansel lived." He shrugs. "But if it's Mattie's apartment ... If Ansel *didn't give* it to her, it wouldn't be with her stuff. If Ansel *gave* it to her, then she would probably be wearing it when she died. I can't imagine any woman *not* wearing her engagement ring, but if she wasn't wearing it, then it would probably be in her jewelry box. So why was the ring in the ring box with the receipt, with her stuff?"

Again, cigarette smoke wafts across my awareness, and I vanquish it mentally. "You're right. That doesn't make sense at all." The heavy blanket of coffee scent slams back into place, as it should be before I continue. "Maybe he never got a chance to give it to her. Could they have been living together?"

"Living in sin?" Beau touches his heart like he's clutching a pearl necklace, so I have to laugh. "At that time, I doubt it."

I finish my coffee and set the cup on the table, rotating the bottom in a circle as I determine a good response. "I think I just wanted a little bit of a happy ending for them. Like it was all wrapped up nicely, even though she left too soon." The air leaves my lungs when I see Beau's face.

"I know what you mean."

I feel as if his eyes could see into my innermost thoughts, knowing that I wanted a happy ending for us too. My eyes grow wet again, completely of their own accord. "We should probably go." I give him a tight smile as we both stand. "It was good seeing you."

"It was good seeing you too." He slips his jacket on and gathers our trash. Then, when we reach the door, he says, "We should do this again. Maybe you can try the spiced cherry and black sesame doughnut next time. Live a little."

Those sweet cherries ... I snap my head back to look at him. "Come again?" I give him a hard blink as I think about what he just said.

Beau laughs, and I practically feel the air vibrate with his warmth. "The part where I asked you to do this again? Or the part about the doughnut?"

"Yes to doing this again." I can't help the sweet smile I give him here. "But, what was that doughnut?"

"Spiced cherry and black sesame. It has cinnamon and some other fall spices. Just a little sweetness. When you live with teens, you get to hear about all the best treats all over town, so I have a bit of an in."

I laugh. "Yeah, let's do that. Let me know when you're free." I touch his arm and look into his eyes when I say, "See you later."

When I arrive home, Eloise is hanging a fall wreath on the door to her apartment. It's covered in leaves, pinecones, and berries in cozy browns and soft yellows with a hint of orange.

"New wreath this year?" I pull off my beret and fluff my hair. Not that I'm going anywhere, but you know.

Eloise steps back to admire her door. The wreath looks lovely against the sage paint. "Yes. I thought it was about time I made a new one. It's been years."

"I love this one. And I love that you decorate the interior door just for me." I laugh and give her a hug.

She gives me a joking look. "It's for all of us, but yes, especially you."

It dawns on me that Eloise might be the right person to ask about something from the diary. "Hey, you've lived in this area a long time. Do you happen to know anything about mafia operations locally?"

Eloise looks thoughtful for a moment. "Well, when I was younger, there was a pizza shop nearby that was a front for their activity. You didn't see many people going in, and they hardly seemed to sell any pizzas." She pauses, and then she adds, "I knew that from when I worked for Hawthorne Township as the secretary for the office manager. We handled permits and gathered information for the businesses. It was always ... *fishy*." She pauses so it's clear what she means. I nod. "A few years later, when I was the office manager, they were no longer in business, and the owner had been arrested for *money laundering*." I love how she stretches out that phrase like it's so scandalous that she has to enunciate it.

I raise my eyebrows. "Wow, now that's a story! Claire made it sound like nothing interesting ever happened in Hawthorne." I sit down on the hallway bench and pat the seat beside me for her to join me.

She sits and then clasps her hands on her lap. "I don't know that she knew about that. It was before she was old enough to pay attention."

"Good point." I chew my lip for a moment. "What about earlier activity? Like ... over a hundred years ago."

Eloise laughs. "I don't know that far back. I'm not that old." I give her an *I know that* look and encourage her with a wave. "Route 19 and other roads that connected Pittsburgh with cities farther south have always been a corridor to get goods from the South and DC to Pittsburgh for the mafia to sell to collectors.

Mostly antiques and paintings. I think they passed some through Pittsburgh and up to New York City, but I can't be certain. There is a large Italian population a little south of here in Clarksburg, West Virginia, and I know that some of them were connected with the mob, maybe even that far back."

Clarksburg? "Mattie mentioned Clarksburg in her diary." I feel like dancing. Things are starting to connect!

"Oh?"

"I read some of the new section this morning, and she mentioned that she overheard some men talking about a shipment from Clarksburg."

"Ah, well it could be anything really. I wouldn't jump to conclusions too fast." Eloise pats my hand and makes a move to stand up.

"The language sounded like it was illegal." I suppose I'll have to let the conversation go if she needs to leave, but I really want to press for more info. I have a gut feeling ...

"Hmmm, well, maybe it was mafia activity." Eloise straightens the wreath on the door and smiles at it before turning back to me. "I don't know how you would find out now, unless something specific was mentioned. Then you could search online to see if it comes up in any articles or anything."

Realization crackles through my skull. "Mattie said something about a painter. I should look him up and see where his work might be. That could shed some light on it. Thank you!" I pop off of the bench, excited for something to research.

I jog up the stairs to my apartment and race to my laptop at my desk by the window. It's going to be a fun afternoon!

I spend a good chunk of time digging around online for mentions of Angelo Valenti—the painter that Mattie overheard the men discussing—and manage to track down some of his work. He was an acrylics artist in the late nineteenth and early twentieth century who lived in Italy and then moved to the United States. Several sites claim that he lived near Philadelphia, while others claimed Pittsburgh, Boston, or Chicago. I'm guessing that there is more than one Angelo Valenti and the records aren't clear.

What *is* clear is that a painting of his had been stolen from the Novak Arts & Music Museum in D.C. in 1910. Bingo. I think I found the connection! Unfortunately, there is no information about the painting, not even its name. I finally give up when Fallon calls and spend almost an hour talking to her and the kids.

After a quick dinner of homemade chickpea stew, I end up meal prepping for this coming week, reading a bit, and deciding to go to bed early. I shoot a quick text to Claire to let her know that I will fill her in on the research and coffee with Beau tomorrow and climb into my bed. I know she will be excited to hear about all of it!

The diary is still spinning through my mind as I sleep, though, so I have bizarre dreams. The oddest by far is that I'm walking past a bar, following two men down an alley and straining to hear a conversation between them when they duck through a doorway.

When I return to the main street, another man walks by, and I pretend to pull a pocket watch out to look at the time. I appear to be struggling to make sure he doesn't see my face, and I end up burning my arm on the cigarette that I'm smoking as I hastily cross my arms. I feel like I'm gagging on the smoke, and my arm is throbbing from the burn. I can only assume that I'm lying on my arm funny, causing the pain, which wakes me up enough to adjust my position and go back to sleep.

When my alarm hums through the room, I drag myself from sleep and tap the button. I feel groggy, heavy. And then, as if I needed this, a smoky scent creeps into my awareness. My first thought is that something is burning, maybe an electrical fire—this *is* an old building. Then, when I'm fully awake, I see the pieces slot into place like a Tetris board.

I turn on the bedside lamp, willing myself to think sane thoughts in the semidarkness because the conclusion I just came to is totally nuts. A tingle on my right arm makes me reassess, though. I push up my sleeve and give my birthmark a hard look. It's round, almost too perfectly round for a birthmark, and light brown. It's also in the exact spot where Mattie burned herself with her cigarette in her diary entry, as well as the same spot that was scorching in my dream.

Chapter Eight

I'm starting to think that I'm falling apart. Or maybe just going insane.

"Just" going insane.

Clearly, something happened to me when I banged my head. It seems that it either a) messed up something in my head that now makes me smell cigarettes at random times or b) set off a series of wacky coincidences that are leading me on this journey, possibly led by a ghost, to figure out ... what, exactly?

Wait. Why *am* I so interested in the diary and Mattie's story?

Sure, I'm curious about what the men in the tailor shop were talking about, just like she was, but is that it? If I really am being led by a ghost, then wouldn't I be on a bigger mission? Surely she's not like some crazed dead author, going, "Pick up a copy of my book to find out more about this wild tale!" I could grab a book at the library if I wanted that level of excitement.

These thoughts swirling through my head like leaves in a dust devil are distracting me from the numbers I'm supposed to be focusing on, like all day. Worse yet, I have a weird little hunch about why Mattie and I have the same mark on our arms, but I find it pretty disturbing to go down *that* road. So I don't. I keep shoving that memory away and tucking it safely out of sight when it pops up.

This whole thing is messing with my ideas about who I am, why I'm here, and the fact that I believe I get to check out of this lifetime when I'm all done and have dotted all the Ts and crossed all the Is ... shoot. I think my brain is scrambled. You're not supposed to cross your eyes.

The point is that my purpose in life is to be an absolutely solid rock star in my little spot in the financial world, where I guide the companies I work with, currently Baker & Willow, to major successes and possibly world domination. I know why I'm here. I don't play games, and it seems that I'm locked in the middle of one.

Can a spirit screw with you? Like, for fun?

And are they even real?

I spent a good chunk of my childhood messing with my own sisters by making up ghost stories, reciting them with a creepy voice, and banging around, pretending to be otherworldly. When my youngest sister, Lacey, was little, I made noises in the basement as one of our other sisters walked her past the stairs so she thought there were ghosts down there. She ran past the stairs for years after that, and we would all laugh, so maybe this is payback.

Wow, and you think you know Karma, that you and she are cut from the same cloth—brazen, fashionably late, but always welcome—but then you find out she's after you, too. Huh. Some friend!

I rub my temples as I stare at the screen, debating whether I could be having a brain bleed or a psychic attack (which I think is total bullshit, by the way, but I'm not ruling anything out). I just don't know what's going on, and because my head doesn't hurt, I feel like asking questions is crazy. And I'm not crazy. My therapist assured me of this years ago!

I desperately need to talk to someone about this before my brain explodes, though, and this isn't something I want to share with Kenzi, even though she's in the same building as me. I resist the urge to clock out early because Claire is probably busy with patients.

Finally, at the end of my workday, I pop over to the Hawthorne Youth and Teen Health and Wellness Center. Yes, I told Claire they should shorten their name, but she's "not in charge" and "didn't want to bring it up." *I* would have brought it up.

Anyway ... I walk in close to time for Claire to clock out and smile at Leslie and Bree, who are behind the desk. Bree immediately says, "I'll let her know you're here," and steps into the other room, her box braids flying because of how fast she bounced out of her chair. I guess I pop in often enough that I get the royal treatment.

After I've been in the waiting room a few minutes, Claire steps out of the back with her fuchsia puffer coat on over her royal blue scrubs. "What's up? Let's go." She nods at the door.

"You're done?" I look at my watch. "I thought I'd have to find a game to download to my phone. Don't you have another half hour?"

"I was just doing some paperwork. I can finish tomorrow." Claire shifts her bag to her shoulder as we exit.

"Thanks for leaving early. I felt so weird today. I really needed to talk to you."

Claire pauses at the door. "Want me to check you out? Do you need your head examined?" she jokes.

"Probably." I give her a look. "Is there a good place to talk?"

"Let's just pop into the library." Together, we walk down the street a couple buildings and enter through the heavy double doors framed by a set of sturdy columns. The building is a little imposing, having been here well over one hundred fifty years, and you can tell that the people of old-timey Hawthorne adored their bastion of knowledge by the extra intricacy in the design of the building. A row of large arched windows punctuates the front, framed by carved stone lintels and decorative brickwork, creating inviting spaces where readers who gather to discuss literature or lose themselves in a book can also enjoy the ambiance created by Main Street.

These little reading nooks would have been the best thing ever as a kid. It's pretty great as an adult, too, but I don't have nearly the reading time I had as a kid—or a desire to leave the house—so I've only read in the nooks a couple times.

I slide into a cushiony bench area across from her and peel off my wool coat, showcasing my cardigan and hot pink Roma t-shirt combo, which I was proud to pull off as office casual today with a pair of cute dress pants. I immediately spill the weird dream from last night.

"I thought you wanted to talk about Beau." She gives me an exasperated look. "We can get to that later though. So why is the dream bothering you?"

I get ready to voice the weird idea that's been dancing in my head like a drunk cat all day. Once I've spilled, I sum it up with the words I hadn't actually spoken aloud: "I think I was Mattie in a past life, and my mole is where she burned herself with a cigarette in the dream."

"Ohhhh." Claire frowns, and I'm not sure how to take it. Is she thinking? Confused? She reaches across the little table, pushes my sleeve up, and examines the mole. "It looks like a normal mole. A little big, but normal. I'd keep an eye on it as you get older, though. Definitely have a dermatologist check it—"

"God, Claire." I sigh. "I really just wanted to talk about this weird thing. I don't need medical advice."

"I thought you said you might need your head examined." A smile quirks her lips. "I was excited."

"I mean, probably." I huff out and deflate against the back of the bench. This is starting to wear on me. "Claire, what's wrong with us?"

"Why are you roping me into this? You're the one who thinks the ghost of your past life is prodding you to read her diary." Claire lets her hair out of the claw and starts massaging her scalp like she's coaxing away a headache.

"Every time I try to have a conversation with you, though, and I say this because I love you, but you just want to give medical advice."

"That's what people come to me for." Claire's brows lower as she gives me a tired but clearly upset look.

"I don't know that this is a medical thing, though. I don't know that it can be solved with rational thinking or making sense of anything." I shrug. "I keep smelling cigarette smoke, and my mole looks like a cigarette burn that Mattie had."

"I think it can be solved with rational thinking, though." Claire punctuates the air with her pointer finger. "You have been so obsessed with this diary since you got back from Italy. Maybe it's just a nifty story. A good distraction from Aaron. Maybe it's just a coincidence that you found the second half in your apartment." She takes a long breath. "Maybe the world isn't laid out all neat and tidy like a fairytale." She ends with a sympathetic look.

I can hear the clipped tone that Claire is taking on, though, and I get it. "I didn't say it was a fairytale. I just think that some things are worth exploring. Maybe there are weird and wild things out there for us to discover." I raise my eyebrows and give her an exaggerated look. "Maybe there are adventures to be had ..."

Claire sighs. "Hard pass. I had enough adventures today. My last patient has had stomach issues for a couple months now, and her labs aren't showing anything. I'll be researching next steps to help her feel better, since I'm out of ideas."

"I'm sorry to hear that. I'm sure that's hard for her and her family."

"Yeah. It's frustrating digging into this stuff and not always having an answer. I want to help them all. I want all my kids to be healthy and happy."

I give her a wry smile. "I understand."

Claire looks out the window for a moment. "Sorry if I always lean back into medicine. It's just, that's what I do all day. I solve problems. I'm used to having an answer. It's upsetting not to, even if it's something that isn't a medical issue."

"Yeah, I'm sure it is." I join her and watch a stream of cars heading for the middle of town. "Maybe we should get out of here. It looks like it's going to rain again. Want to stop for some soup at Hazel's?"

"They have a great loaded baked potato soup. I'm in." She grabs her bag, and we both drive over to the restaurant.

I find a spot on the street, and as I shift the car into park, I suddenly get hit with the smell of cigarette smoke again, sneaking up on me like leg day—I always forget that one is coming till it's here. I told Beau I would make note of whenever that scent creeps in, so I take stock of anything that could affect the air or what's triggering me to smell it. That's when I hear the guttural buzz of a diesel engine. Just ahead, a beat-up pickup is pulling out of the alley and onto Carriage Row, leaving a cloud the color of charcoal behind it.

As the smoke clears, the smell of cigarettes does too. I guess that was the source this time. When the truck disappears down the road, I realize I'm right across from WellSpring Robotics. I wonder if Beau would like some soup, too ... Maybe I'll text him when we're leaving and offer to—

Just then, my phone buzzes, and I glance down. It's Aaron. It just says, "I miss you."

I feel like I pressed pause on the world.

I realize that the cardinal rule of breaking up with someone is that you block their number so this sort of thing *doesn't* keep happening, so you can manage to dodge their gravitational pull at least temporarily till you can regain your common sense and just ignore them, at which point, you've already blocked their number and don't need to. However, I forgot.

I know that's lame. My finger hovers over the button to open the text as I think about how gorgeous he is. And ... maybe I'm just shallow, okay?

Why am I arguing in my head for this? Argh.

No. I'm not shallow, and there is a lot to my former relationship with Aaron. Morgan energy in, pushover energy out.

I throw my phone in my purse, eye up the heavy, dark clouds pressing down on us, grab an umbrella to ensure that it doesn't rain, and duck into Hazel's to grab a bowl of soup at the bar with Claire. Geez. I don't need more trouble today.

―

Beau turns me down for the soup. He's picking up pizzas for the Hawthorne High theater department's final rehearsal before the first performance of *The Mystery of Edwin Drood* this weekend. I make a note in my phone to check on tickets because I love this play. And, of course, I'd love to support the school and see Vivi in action as Princess Puffer. Beau said that Emmett is running audio for the play, and that has been a main interest of his for a couple years, so he's a part of it too.

That was a whole lot of information for a couple texts! And Claire watches me out of the corner of her eye the entire time, judging but not saying a word. I'm not in the mood to ask.

A bit later, Claire and I leave Hazel's with happy bellies full of loaded baked potato soup and salad. We're in our thirties, so we always eat our vegetables. I realize that doesn't sound very Seize the Day Morgan, but most people in our age bracket need veggies or we cramp up or our eyesight worsens or ... something. I'm not Claire. I'm sure she knows.

Across the street, an older woman is walking into Gisela's, and she looks vaguely familiar. Seeing her reminds me, though ...

"Do you think Gisela would be willing to give my contact info to Mattie's family?" My heart picks up pace as I get excited about connecting some of the dots. "Her diary was in that desk, so I bet the desk was hers, if not her sister's. Maybe they would want the boxes from our attic."

"I don't think it would hurt to ask her about it." Claire taps the button to cross at the light, and we enter Gisela's a moment later.

"Any news about the lake painting?" The woman we saw entering the shop is at the checkout desk, addressing Gisela. Claire and I browse around nearby while we wait, and it's hard not to hear their conversation.

"I'm sorry, but I haven't heard anything." Gisela gives her a sympathetic smile and pats her hand. "I hope it turns up for you. It sounds lovely."

The woman sighs and shifts her handbag from one forearm to the other. "It would be nice to finally see it in person. It would bring me some peace knowing that it's been found."

Gisela places a hand on the woman's hand. "I understand, Angela. I'll let you know if anything comes in that looks like what you described. I have your number."

Sighing again, the woman fiddles with some of the tchotchkes on the desk. "I know you will. I just feel like we're so close to finding it. It's making me more anxious." She laughs. "And thank you for letting your friends at the other stores know. It makes me feel better knowing that everyone is watching for it."

"You know I'm happy to help." Gisela smiles and picks up a small box that appears to be filled with trinkets. "Anything else you needed today?"

"Oh, no. I'll just look around for a minute. Thank you, though."

"You're welcome."

As the woman steps away from the counter, Claire and I approach.

I smile and greet Gisela. "I know this is sort of weird, but I found a bunch of stuff in my attic that I think belongs to the family that owns the desk we found the diary in."

Gisela's eyes grow wide, and she sets the box of trinkets down. "Really? Why do you think it's theirs?"

"The other part of the diary was in one of the boxes, along with a ring box that had a bill of sale for Matilda Conrad's boyfriend. She mentions him in the diary."

"That's absolutely amazing!" Gisela places both hands on her heart. "What sort of things did you find there?"

I brief her on the items and realize that the air is awash with cigarette smoke and an overlay of flowers. The scent has been growing for the past couple minutes, but it wasn't strong enough that I registered it. I squeeze my eyes shut for a moment as if that would pinch off the scent without anyone noticing I'm bothered.

"You smell it too?" Gisela whispers.

Now my eyes are wide open, and I'm staring at her like she's the crazy one. But Gisela looks at ease, hands resting on the counter, head tipped to the side, a gentle smile on her face. I finally say, "How did you ...?"

"I have clairalience." Gisela scrunches her lips tight, a sympathetic smile.

"Claire-did-what?" I mutter. When I look at Claire, she shrugs.

Gisela laughs. "It means that I can smell things that are"—she looks up like the answer is on the ceiling somewhere—"not really there."

"God, that sounds awful," I say. "Like when you watch *Encanto*, and you realize that all their gifts are really horrible, but the worst one is Dolores's because she can hear things miles away. I always wonder if she can hear people in the bathroom or hear them saying mean things about her."

"I wonder that too." Claire shakes her head as she joins the conversation. She turns to Gisela. "So, do you smell dirt and decay all the time? That could be a sinus infection or something worse. You may want to see an ENT."

I actually start laughing. "I'm sorry. She's just like that." I place my hand on Claire's arm and give her a serious look. "This isn't medical. It's like seeing ghosts, but she smells whatever they smell like."

Claire gives me a look. "Like dirt and decay."

Thankfully Gisela steps in. "It's more like they are sending a signal. In this case, I'm guessing you, Claire, *couldn't* smell cigarettes and maybe perfume or flowers a moment ago."

Claire shakes her head and glances at the door like she wants to leave.

"It's just someone giving you a message." Gisela turns back to me. "Actually, I'm not sure who it's for. And I don't know what the message is. I could ... look into it. If you want."

"Like a palm reading or a séance or something?" I ask. When I look at Claire, she has *hell no* written all over her face.

Gisela nods. "Mediumship. No charge. I'm pretty curious now that we've talked about this."

Little tingles of excitement in my stomach give me the signal to go ahead. This sounds like it could be fun! "I'm in. Claire, let's do this."

Claire pulls her work-bag-slash-purse protectively in front of her body and locks her jaw. "Fine." Her tone is neutral, but her body language is pretty clear that this is *no bueno*.

As we're walking to the back, it strikes me that Rhiannon would be so into this. She always loved the woo woo stuff when we were growing up, and I know she sees someone to pull Tarot cards for her every once in a while. I take out my phone, thinking I might text her, thinking that maybe I need to get over this feeling that she disapproves of me. When I open the texting app, though, I immediately get distracted because hello ADHD.

I have texts from both Aaron and Beau. Well, isn't this so very grab-those-sweet-cherries. When have I ever in my life had two men texting me at once when one wasn't related to me?

Discretely, I open Aaron's text, against my better judgement because I figure I will leave him on read like a good girl and just satisfy my need to be rid of the red notification dot. After his initial *I miss you* is another text with a picture of him holding up a cup of coffee, like we're going to clink mugs and say *cheers*. He's outside at a café, and there's a book on the table, one of the mysteries he likes by Owen Graves.

Beau, on the other hand, has sent me a selfie of him holding a huge stack of pizza boxes with Vivi beside him. She's holding the phone, and they're both grinning like they're about to get the party started, and my goodness, it's about the cutest thing I've ever seen. The text accompanying it just says, "Theater crew hero!"

I smile, and I can feel it not only on my face but in my heart. Funny how he's worming his way back in there without seeming to be trying.

When we enter the back room, I slip my phone back into my bag without responding to either of them—I'll get to that later—and glance at Claire, who's eyeing me up like she knows I just read a text from a boy. I swear, nothing slips past her, like she has clair-something herself. All these clairs!

But no eclairs? *Sacre bleu.*

Gisela motions for us to sit down, and I finally exit my head and look around the room. It's small but cozy, furnished with four evergreen wingback chairs and an antique coffee table with an inlay of fabric covered in needlepoint wildflowers, protected by a pane of glass. A deck of cards rests on the table. The matching end tables each have a standard-looking lamp on them, covered with a scarf in rainbow colors. The room appears to have a blush thanks to the subdued lighting.

I lean back in the chair and cross my legs, excited to see what will happen next, but my companion looks like I asked her to chill with me in a morgue. This isn't her scene, and I can tell by her darting eyes and the way she sits stiffly in the chair. "What now?" I ask.

Gisela must pick up on the vibe. "I'll make this quick. Don't worry." She smiles, lights an incense burner on the end table, and closes her eyes. After taking three long, deep breaths, she clasps her hands on her lap.

"There's a woman here," Gisela begins. "She has a long dress on, and her hair is pulled back. She's wearing a hat. Her outfit looks like maybe Edwardian era, something over a hundred years ago. Is this Mattie? She's dancing, so glad to be recognized."

I nod, unsure of how else to respond.

"Now I'm seeing a flame," Gisela continues. "It's small, but it's growing. Now it's covering everything." She wrinkles her brow, maybe like she's concentrating. "We know about the fire, Mattie. I'm sorry."

I frown in sympathy. Then I clasp my hands around my knee and wait to see what else she sees.

Gisela takes a long breath in and out. "And now I see a hand. Maybe she's showing me her wrist. Okay. Now she's tapping on her wrist where there is a scar."

I bite my lip and rub at my wrist. This is getting eerie. "The scar is a cigarette burn, according to one of her entries," I explain. "She bumped her wrist, and I have a matching birthmark."

Gisela nods. "Okay, now she's showing me a box. Morgan, is there a box that's important. Maybe one from the attic?"

"Not sure. There were a couple dozen in there." I definitely have some boxes in my life right now.

"Ah. Right, I forgot." Gisela rocks back and forth in the seat for a moment. "Yes, now we're going back to the scar. I see two right arms with scars or marks on them." She opens her eyes and reaches across the coffee table. "May I see?"

I pull my sleeve up and offer my arm to her. "Is this what you saw?"

She hums in response. "Yes, and Mattie is dancing again. Now, I'm seeing ... the emoji with the two women dressed as bunnies." She chuckles. "I'm not sure what that means, but it's something with your relationship with Mattie. Was she a great-aunt or something?"

My mouth feels incredibly dry right now, and my stomach is tight, but I somehow manage to squeak out, "Could she be a past life?"

"Ah." Gisela closes her eyes again, and her lips turn up in a smile. "She's dancing. I think that's a yes. That's why the scars match. She was showing me that she's you. You carry that scar from your previous lifetime as a reminder of who you were."

Funny that I had no idea who I was, but I've been rubbing this thing my whole life.

Despite the warmth of the room, a chill works its way down my body. "Interesting." I feel seen in a way I've never been seen before. It's like having a piece of me pulled out and put on display. *She's me.* "What do I do with that information?"

"I'm seeing a book. Maybe her diary? And the pages are flipping, but I can't read them. It looks like there's something important there, but it's not for me to see. It's for you."

"Got it. I'm assuming Mattie wants me to keep reading her diary." I imagine very few people have the pleasure of reading a diary that they wrote in a past life, so I'm curious if I have a mission now.

Do I *want* a mission?

I guess that's everything now. All the mysteries are solved. "Oh, while you're doing this, anything important I need to know? I don't want to bust my head again. Should I stay home from work tomorrow?"

Gisela chuckles softly. "She's just dancing. I think that's up for you to decide."

Claire and I leave the shop a few minutes later, and neither of us seems to know what to say.

"That was weird." Claire has her arms crossed over her chest, bag held tightly to her body. I glance at her, and she looks worn out and bewildered.

"Agreed." I keep pace with her as we return to our cars. "I guess I was expecting that, after the odd dream, but it still feels bizarre to be confronted with all of that."

When we reach the cars, I wave and hop in. We zip over to our spots by the house and head inside together, where I give her a quick hug. "Thanks for doing that with me."

"You're welcome." Claire squeezes me a moment longer. "I'm glad I could be there for the strangeness. Don't ever make me do that again, though."

We both laugh, and I respond, "Of course!" before jogging up the stairs to my place.

Once inside, I surprise myself by opening Beau's text first and responding to the picture with a heart and then, "I'm sure you're their favorite adult now!"

When I open Aaron's text, I hesitate long enough that a reply from Beau comes through. "Always!" with the smiley emoji that has a monocle. I find myself grinning and feeling warm all over. He's always been a sweetie.

I type several responses to Aaron—cheeky, average, clever—deleting each before I realize that I don't really want to say anything back. My heart isn't fluttering. My stomach isn't quivering. My skin isn't chilled from missing his touch. There's just ... fond memories. And no desire.

Huh. Well, that's something.

I finally settle on, "Looks like a nice afternoon there! Whatcha reading?" which ignores the *miss you* part of the text and also shifts to a friendship mode I didn't ever expect. I don't want to hurt his feelings, but we really, truly, aren't going to get anywhere by keeping up the flirting and the longing.

Next, I fish some containers out of my fridge and end up with butternut squash risotto and a grilled chicken breast, all with sage and parmesan. As I heat them up in the microwave, I wander to my desk and pick up the diary. If Mattie wants me to keep reading, I have plenty of time this evening.

Once I settle at my table for dinner, I open the diary to the next entry and immediately catch the fragrance of cigarette smoke mingling with flowers. I sniff the book, just to be sure, but it's definitely in the air.

"Hello, Mattie," I say with a slight quiver in my voice. Does this count as talking to myself?

As quickly as the fragrance came on, it dissipates, leaving me to smell my dinner alone. I bolster myself with a little belief that she's not here to harm me, and hey, I'm the one in human form. I'm in charge, right? Morgan Magic, sweet cherries, supreme confidence. Anchor in, girl! Whew!

The first entry I read dives right into the action after Mattie's stroll down Main Street, mentioning her fears that something is going on and also that she doesn't know what to do about it. She thinks that her client, Mr. Conti, is involved with some shady business, probably smuggling paintings and antiques, but she obviously doesn't want to confront him and doesn't feel comfortable sneaking around again. Plus, the repairs on Mr. Turner's suit are done, so she would have to find something else to wear.

I feel her worry. Aside from concern for herself, she's also concerned about her sister and their shop. If she upsets the wrong people, she has a lot to lose.

The next diary entry is from a couple weeks later, so I'm curious what has passed in between. Maybe nothing worth writing about.

This one is interesting for a couple reasons, though.

Dear Diary,

My world keeps getting stranger and stranger, and I find that I need to do something about it. I'm not the type of person to sit idly by and allow odd things to happen. I've always been a bit of a snoop, despite the feeling I often get in the pit of my stomach to stop. It's strange how this happens. It's like there is some strange force urging me on!

"I feel you, sister," I say aloud. My arm suddenly feels warm, almost like someone is touching it, and though I know no one is there, I turn to look before I can even think about it. Now I'm spooking myself!

Today, I decided to do the right thing and approach the mayor about the goings-on in town. Normally, I would think that going to the police would be the right step, but Ansel knows Clarence Vandermere, who runs the Vandermere Foundation. He met the Vandermeres at a charity for the town library last winter, and they are close with the mayor, since they donate to a lot to community investment projects like the library's new roof. I stopped by Mr. Vandermere's office, and he agreed to ask the mayor to meet with me. I was ever so grateful. I never thought that being courted by an English teacher would turn out to be such a blessing! Aside from our long discussions of literature, of course! I have always been a fan of Austen, but Ansel introduced me to Wilkie Collins' beautiful works that feature incredible women. I could go on and on about the heroine in No Name, *but that should be a separate diary entry! I hope he continues reading when he finishes his law degree and begins his career as an attorney, so these lovely discussions don't go away.*

My breath catches when I recall the newspaper article that I read at the beginning of this adventure. I flip to the front and pull it out again. My memory was correct: the mayor *was* involved in setting the fire at the theater. My heart aches for Mattie as I realize how this is going to go. Maybe, though, it was a different mayor. Maybe?

My meeting with the mayor didn't go as well as I had planned, though. He didn't seem to take me seriously at all when I told him about the conversation I overheard with Mr. Conti in the shop or when I mentioned what I overheard outside The Brass Bell. He even had the audacity to say, "Miss, with all due respect, I can't send the police on a wild goose chase just because a pretty young lady has a hunch." He completely discounted what I heard! "All due respect," my foot! It's obvious that something is going on, but because I'm a woman, I am disregarded.

I'm so angry just writing these words that I could spit.

I smoked two cigarettes after our meeting just to calm down enough to go back to the shop, and then Rosie was upset because she could smell the smoke on me and was afraid it would soak into the dress she was working on. It's for a wedding for one of the Vandermeres, no less.

There's something familiar here. I reread the last couple paragraphs of the diary entry before it hits me: I've heard that phrase before. I heard what the mayor said! Maybe it was in a movie. Maybe I can convince myself that ...

No! It wasn't. I was there, and a chill ripples down my body as it floods back to me now. The blue velvet curtains. The box of *Romeo y Julieta* cigars. The oily voice. Somehow her memory crossed over into my reality. And *I* remember. I read on a little now, but with a heightened sense of trepidation.

He treated me like a silly woman and then ushered me out! I had a sick feeling the whole time we were in our meeting, and now I have to tell Ansel what happened. I hope that doesn't change his relationship with Mr. Vandermere. It seemed that they were going to do wonderful things for the school library once the community library projects wrapped up.

I hope Ansel won't be upset with me.

I feel a pang of sorrow for Mattie. Maybe this is why the ring box was in the attic. Did he break off their engagement because she was doing dangerous things? Or because she ruined his chance to get funding from the Vandermeres? That doesn't make sense either, though. Why would she have the ring box if he broke off the engagement? Would she have kept the ring?

There's nothing else of interest in this entry, and I'm getting tired, so I opt to soak in the tub and read Margot Ashford's latest, *Espresso & Entanglements*, and enjoy the drama of yet another person's life. While in the tub, I discover that I now have a new book boyfriend, Lance. He sets an astonishing standard that I'm not sure can be attained by mere mortals, with his attention to Sienna and her needs (eyebrow waggle here), his charm and intellectual witty banter (swoon here), and Ashford's description of his smell. For someone who's been suffering under a frequent cloud of hundred-year-old cigarette smoke, six pack abs and the scent of dawn breaking over breakfast on a cabin porch in the Hamptons is otherworldly.

I wonder if I can buy that in a candle.

I don my favorite pink satin pajamas and climb into bed to read a little longer—it's been a day!—and then my phone buzzes. I tip it and see that it's Beau, and I actually bookmark my book for him. That's a step forward, but I don't know what direction it's in, since I don't know what the heck we're doing.

> Pizza was a hit! How was your day?

Now here's where it gets tricky. I haven't really gotten to know late-thirties Beau. I knew early-twenties Beau, who was everything to everyone and determined to be a success with everything. A perfectionist times ten, but with a creamy caramel center. I have no idea what his stance on the afterlife is now, but he was staunchly in the *that's laughable* camp when we last connected.

> Odd. To say the least. I read more of Mattie's diary. Found out some peculiar things. Still have some questions.

When I don't see a *read* notification right away, I return to my book, but only a minute later, I get another text.

> I'd love to hear more. Coffee?

> It's kinda late for that.

> Saturday? Vivi got a job at Lyon's, and I'd love to surprise her at work.

> That's adorable.

Maybe I shouldn't have typed that. Eh.
Beau responds with a cheesy grin smiley.

> I'm purely in it for the leftover pastries she will be bringing home at the end of her shift.

> You've got it all planned out.

> Life is exciting. Next up, I'm going to get a field guide and start identifying birds by their songs.

> Try not to sneeze while you're enjoying the great outdoors. You'll knock a rib out of alignment.

I guess this counts as sexting when you're in your thirties. And I remember when I was all excited to grow up ...

Beau laughs at my comment, and the three dots appear.

> So is that a yes for Saturday? 9 am?

> That's a yes. Sounds good!

> Okay if I pick you up? Or would you rather meet there?

> Is this a date?

Blunt? Yes. Surprising, coming from me? No.

I imagine Beau sitting in his living room, feet propped up on the coffee table, scratching his beard and looking at the screen, debating how best to answer. I set the phone down and continue reading, giving him time. I know he's looking for the best way to respond, but I honestly don't know which way it should go. Do I want him to say yes? Will it be weird? Is this weird?

It's no weirder than talking to your past life while she's huffing cigarette smoke in your face, so really, Beau, just hit me with—

> Yes. If that's okay with you. I don't want to assume anything, but I did enjoy our coffee the other day. I'd like to see where this goes, especially knowing how it was before.

> Before everything.

Oh. Well then. Worst case scenario, this could land me a free pastry. Best case ... I dare not even think about it.

Chapter Nine

We end up with a strangely beautiful day halfway through the week, and Claire and I can't resist going for a walk through the neighborhood that evening after work. Dressed in leggings and sweatshirts, we clamber down the steps to the street and head south along Barrington at a decent pace, like we're being chased by the chill that's sure to return tomorrow.

The trees that line all the streets in our area are a dour brown this time of year, echoing the mood of the brooding gray skies. It smells earthy outside from the recent rains, and wispy loose hairs dance around our faces in rhythm with our walking.

After a couple minutes, Claire asks, "So how's your head?"

"Still intact, surprisingly," I sing to no tune in particular.

Claire chuckles. "I mean, since you banged it. It's been a while. You're good?"

"Yes, I actually am. Especially since I know where the smoke smell is coming from now."

"Mmm," Claire responds. "You know, I thought about what you said the other day."

I twist my mouth and look up as I try to recall what she's talking about. "I'm sure it was brilliant, but

I don't remember. Enlighten me." When I glance at her, she's giving me a look, probably about my confidence.

"About how I always respond with medical advice."

We walk in silence again for a moment before I prompt her. "And?"

"And it's safe."

"Well, yeah. It's what you know. But what you don't know can be figured out." I give her a sympathetic look. "You mentioned that you were working with a patient whose stomach problems you couldn't figure out, right?"

"Right."

"It's the same with everything else. If you don't know, you can ask, look it up, talk it through. That's why I wanted to talk to you that day. What I was thinking sounded absurd. And it was true! I just didn't know how to approach it. But it was better with the two of us, you know. Sometimes, you just listen. You don't always have to have the answer."

"I know that's true. I just *like* to have the answers. I like that people can always rely on me for that. It scares me when I don't. Like with Mom's rheumatoid arthritis. I don't have the answers. I have to ask around, and it makes me feel ..." She holds her hands out like the answer will drop from the sky.

"Vulnerable?" I offer.

"No. Stupid." Claire jams her hands in the kangaroo pocket on her hoodie, and I pat her arm in solidarity.

"Girl, you're anything but stupid." When she doesn't respond, I add, "I'm sorry you feel that way."

She gives me a sour smile. "We all have our days, I'm sure."

"Would it make you feel better if I told you I felt stupid the other day, the day we ate at Hazel's?"

"Maybe ..."

"I got texts from Aaron and Beau at the same time—"

"My goodness!" She feigns surprise. "Aren't we popular!"

"Yeah. Yeah. But I didn't answer right away. I waited till I got home. Then I went to answer Aaron, and I felt *nothing*. Just some fond memories. I realized I was pretty stupid to keep hanging onto him for so long. I knew we weren't going to work, but I kept trying to make myself think we would."

Claire hums in response.

"I kept perpetuating a bad idea." I frown. It was fun. And he was great. But I always knew it was a bad idea. "Maybe I got excited about trying to make it into something that did work. Maybe I'm addicted to that feeling. Like figuring out a puzzle."

Claire takes a deep breath and lets it out. I know something important is coming, if she feels like telling me. "In the spirit of opening up and talking things out ... Do you ever think that maybe you've continued to pursue a relationship with Aaron for so long because you don't believe that you deserve happiness after what happened with Beau?"

I actually stop walking. "Oh." Was I really doing that? Can someone do that to themselves? "Do you think so? Maybe ... maybe I didn't feel like I deserved to be happy. I mean, I was happy with Aaron, but there was always an edge. Like I thought that I was going to lose him at any moment, any time we were together, whether he said it or I said it. Like you're driving with a nail in your tire, and it's bound to deflate or pop, but you keep driving and hoping you can get to the next gas station before disaster strikes."

"Yeah. Like that." Claire is looking at me with concern, her eyes darting back and forth between mine. "I didn't mean to crack you open with that, but it's an epiphany, right?"

"Oh, crap. You know what?" I start walking slowly again, and she joins me. "I may need to start journaling."

With that, Claire jokingly smacks my arm. "Sure you will."

But now, she's got me going. Am I really torturing myself by bouncing back to Aaron all the time? I kept thinking that he felt safe, so he was calling to me, but really the safe feeling was that I was growing used to the uncertainty. I was craving imbalance. God, what's wrong with me?

It's not like there's anything in my life that made me feel like I *should* be unsafe or unstable or anything. Just that blip with my marriage to Beau. And that was, honestly, nobody's fault. And it seems like Beau has forgiven me ... "Oh, there ya go." I'm a little embarrassed that I said that out loud, and I know I'll have to answer for that.

"Go on ..." Claire prods me.

"Beau forgave me—" Then I begin again. "Not verbally, but he seems to have. I think he has. I always thought he hated me, like he somehow held onto anger for why I left all those years ago, but I don't think that's true. I think I'm forgiven."

"Should you have a conversation about it? Or does it seem like he's healed from that time?"

"I think it would be weird right now to ask him his thoughts on that topic."

"Yeah ... what else were you going to say?"

I need a deep breath for this one. "I don't think I've forgiven *myself* for creating that hole. I feel like it's my fault for not stepping up and shouldering my portion of the work, for bowing out."

Claire lets out an exasperated sigh. "But you were like, twenty? Twenty-one? What woman that age is ready to take on what you were expected to take on? And I'm not blaming Beau here either because all of this just fell on you guys."

"He did sort of invite it. I don't think he wanted to burden his parents with the responsibility after Rae started down that path. They had her to worry about, so we took on the kids."

"Right. Still, you weren't at fault." She shakes her head to emphasize it. We walk on for a moment before Claire continues softly. "Forgive *yourself*."

But can I?

Saturday morning, I'm not sure I'm ready for everything I have planned for the day. First, Beau will be here any minute to pick me up for an official coffee date. And second, this afternoon, Amanda Riley will be stopping by to pick up all the boxes from the attic. Amanda's great-grandmother was Mattie's sister, Rosella. Amanda and her brother were the ones who took Mattie's things to Gisela a couple months ago.

Since Claire and I were talking about forgiveness, that's what is on my mind when I greet Beau at the door. *He's forgiven me for leaving, but I still haven't forgiven myself for giving up.* But all the thoughts in my head melt away when I see him. He looks nice, wearing a thick mocha-colored sweater and jeans, along with his navy wool coat. There is a simple Beau-ness to the outfit and the carefree and warm feeling I get from seeing him, almost like it was effortless for him to be here. Like he's not nervous at all. Like we just fell back together. My breath catches in my chest as our eyes lock.

"Fancy meeting you here." He quirks that sideways smile, knowing how corny that was. Also knowing it would make me laugh.

"Come here often?" I respond in a flirty voice. He chuckles as we slip from the porch down to his simple gray sedan. "This is your ride? You really haven't changed."

"Everyone expects the robotics guy to have some futuristic state-of-the-art car, but I find that stuff to be unnecessary." He opens my door, and I climb in, adjusting my beret to have something to do with my hands as he circles the car to join me in the driver's seat. When the engine hums to life, he looks at me for a beat. "No, I didn't build it myself. No, it doesn't turn into a rocket."

"I'm disappointed. I had expectations." I give him a sad look and jokingly put my hand on the door handle like I might get back out. Then I give him one more shot: "Is it at least a Transformer?"

He looks around as if someone might be listening and then leans toward me like he's about to tell me a big secret. Then he whispers, "No, but it has a seat heater," and presses a button on the dashboard.

I don't even notice if the seat gets warmer, but I do notice the warmth growing in my chest and the musky scent of cedar and allspice that wafts my way. For the first time in several weeks, my nose is happy. I feel like the shell around my heart has suddenly cracked open, like I can take a deep breath but don't really need to, like all is right with the world. That's the smell of peace, the smell of home.

I lift my hand, about to touch his beard, finger the strands of silver adding grace notes to the melody of his jaw, but at the same time, he sits up and puts the car in gear, and the moment is gone. Though his aroma remains a cocoon around me as warmth seeps from the car seat all the way to my bones.

We park, and keeping my hands to myself, I walk side by side with Beau from the car to Lyon's Den. Immediately, I spot Vivi in the Lyon's red polo and black visor. She's behind the counter, hair back in a braid, nodding as she intensely watches someone who is pointing at a cup. No doubt she's stressed, though the morning rush is pretty calm around here on a Saturday. I'm sure she will appreciate friendly faces.

When we're almost to the counter, she notices Beau, and her whole face lights up. She flicks her hand in a wave and mouths, "Hi, Dad!" I almost start crying when I realize what she said.

I look at Beau, and he's beaming, hands in his coat pockets, looking proud. I wrap a hand around his arm. "Well done ... *Dad*."

"I never thought the kids would call me that, but I like it."

We get our flat white and Americano, along with their special autumn spice eclairs with fig jam and buttercream, and find a table by the window.

"I don't know how you did it." I sip my coffee and just admire my company for a moment.

"What's that?" Beau tears a bite from his eclair.

"Raised them. Never mind. I was just musing. She seems sweet."

"It wasn't easy, and as I said, I had help." Beau smiles at Vivi as she's working, oblivious. "She was the easy one. Emmett has always been a bear."

"A bear?"

"Grumbly. Brooding. Crabby."

"Perfectionist? Oldest child syndrome?"

Beau nods thoughtfully. "You might say that. He has a couple memories of Rae, not much. I think he has some unreal expectations of how everyone should have done things so she would still be here. Like if he had orchestrated it, it would have played out differently."

"Man, I feel for him." I smile sympathetically. "I guess he's seeing someone about that?"

"We all are. He's just having the hardest time coping with unmet expectations and a desire for a do-over."

A weighty pause presses against us. "I can understand that." I shift the conversation and ask about the assistive devices he created to help the hearing impaired communicate, and this shifts to an idea he had about translator glasses with a speaker over the ear, which then shifts to travel. We end up talking for well over two hours, long after our drinks and treats are gone. It's honestly the most wonderful time I've had in forever.

We haven't even noticed that many of the customers have cleared out till Vivi approaches us as she's wiping off tables in the dining room. I look up to see her standing there with her big doe eyes, looking back and forth between Beau and me like she's going to explode with words.

"Hey, nugget," Beau says. "How's your first day?"

"It's good!" she says. "I know how to make some of the drinks, and I ran the cash register. Did you know that it tells you how much change to give if someone uses cash? Remember when you told us that we would have to know how to figure out change when we were learning to count money? Totally not true. You were messing with us!" Vivi barely pauses to take a breath as she's gushing at us.

"I wasn't *lying* or anything," Beau clarifies. The contrast between Vivi's verbal diarrhea and Beau's snuggled in a blanket calm is almost comical. "I worked at a golf course snack shop once where we had to count up the change for customers. I didn't know everyone would have high-tech registers now."

"Says the robotics guy," I mutter playfully.

Vivi turns to me and switches her cleaning rag to the other hand. "Hi, I'm Vivi. You must be Morgan." She thrusts out her slightly wet hand to shake mine, so I return the firm handshake. "I don't remember you, but I know I should. I was really little though."

"No worries," I answer. "It's nice to meet you again. You've grown up since I last saw you." Despite the steadiness of my voice, I feel a raw burning sensation searing through my gut like wings with dragon sauce turning my insides to molten lead. It's like a combination of guilt and a desire for her to like me. Like I'm meeting the parents of my date. I've never met someone's kids.

Before I can say anything else, she lets go of my hand and turns back to Beau. "Dad, Delaney wants to go to the mall at the end of my shift. She said she'd give me a ride, but I forgot my wallet at home." She opens her eyes just the tiniest bit wider and pokes her lip out like she's jokingly pouting. Then she holds an open hand in Beau's direction.

I'm struggling to keep from doubling over with laughter. She's clever.

Beau's eyebrows go up. "Don't you have some birthday money from your grandparents?"

"I do ... but it's in my wallet." Her argument sounds logical.

"You remembered your purse, but not your wallet?" Beau says.

"I didn't think I'd need it today. I needed my phone and my lippy." Again, she sticks out her well-lipsticked bottom lip.

"Alright, no need to resort to manipulation." Beau really is a big softy. "I'll stop at home and bring your wallet back here."

"Oh." Then her face lights up. "Yay! Thank you!" She turns and sprays a table near us, wiping crumbs onto the floor rather than catching them properly with her rag. At least the table is clean, though.

"You're welcome," he answers. Turning back to me, Beau says, "Did you want to see the apartment? We live on the top floor of the WellSpring building. I had it renovated when I bought it, and they did a nice job with it."

"Sure, I'll tag along." I pop my beret back on, and the two of us head outside. It's only about a block to walk to Beau's building, so we hoof it. To the left of the WellSpring window is an archway with a rounded black cloth awning. Beau unlocks the door there and leads me up two long flights of stairs—I'm guessing they accommodate very high ceilings—to the top floor.

When he unlocks the door on the top floor, I'm struck by how simple, clean, and lovely the space is. It's open concept with twelve-foot ceilings, so it feels breezy, especially with the pale blue-gray walls and white trim. I feel like I'm in a luxury loft in a big city instead of little Hawthorne.

"This is beautiful." I follow him in and take in the space while he approaches a door off of the living room. It must be Vivi's room because he returns with a wallet in his hand, and he's tucking a couple bills inside. So sweet.

"Found it." He grins and then watches as I explore every nook and corner.

"This really is nice. How old is the building?" I touch the charcoal granite countertop in the kitchen, admiring the gleam.

"Built in 1899." Beau leans against the counter before he continues. "It was mostly gutted in the 1950s and redone, then updated in the late 1980s to comply with code for water and electric."

A part of me wonders if Mattie ever came here when this was … whatever it was in her time. "It's nice that they updated it over the years," I respond. "I imagine it would be a pain to redo an entire building that had knob-and-tube wiring. I've heard nightmares from my coworkers."

"I wouldn't have bought something that needed that much work." He chuckles. "I only did some minor updates and renovations so we could move in. We had a small house nearby for a few years, but I always wanted to live above my shop. It took a long time before the right building was on the market, though." The silence as Beau pauses here is weighty, and he licks his lip and looks away from me before continuing. "Once this building came available, I knew immediately it was the right spot."

I nod in agreement. The apartment has a good feel, and it's a nice place with a convenient location. "I guess when you know, you know."

His eyes search mine for a moment. "You do."

When we are back on the main floor, I notice an alcove under the stairs with a door. "What's back there? Furnace?"

"Basement." Beau pats the door. "It's about the only space that hasn't been touched, aside from a rare cleaning. I avoid going down there." That makes sense. He never did like dirt or dusty, creepy spaces.

I chuckle as we exit the building. "I don't blame you. There are probably rats down there dressed like Dickens-era carolers."

Beau lets out a sudden belly laugh. "I'd love to see that! Maybe we *should* go down there."

"Are you asking me for another date?" I push open the front door and step outside, greeted by the chilly air.

"If you're into checking out hundred-some-year-old basements for a date, then I guess I am."

"You're weird." But I'm glowing as I smile at him. He's my kind of weird. "I feel like creepy basements are a fourth or fifth date thing, though."

"Good point. I don't want to rush things."

"So now that I know you have a creepy basement," I continue as we press toward the coffee shop, "are there any cool hidden passageways or anything in the building? My house has strange little side attics, you know."

"That's true ..." Beau looks thoughtful. "I think that all the fun stuff like that was cleared out during the renos in the fifties and eighties." Then his voice drops lower. "Except the basement."

"You keep enticing me." I cackle as I think about us exploring some cobweb-coated subterranean world. "What if I pick up a dozen spiced cherry and black sesame doughnuts, and we skip ahead to that fourth date to check out this space."

Beau opens the door to Lyon's Den and places a hand on the small of my back as we enter. I feel like his fingertips are scorching my spine as he does it, like I have a heightened awareness of the heat of his touch as it dredges up the ghost of our earlier relationship. "As tempting as that is, I really don't think I can eat another doughnut right now. And, I have to be honest: I don't think my basement is very exciting."

As the door closes behind us, a sudden downdraft filled with the smell of cigarettes catches me off-guard, and I wrinkle my nose. "I-uh. Yeah. I mean no." What the heck? "Sorry; smoky smell."

Beau frowns and the lightning bolt appears between his eyes. We step inside, and he looks at me with concern. "What brought that on? Stress? Being around me again isn't stressful, is it?"

I'm so surprised for a moment that I can only return his gaze. Then, I finally answer. "No. It's fine. It's nice. I think … I think the smoke is supposed to be a message. Like the strangest game of hot and cold I've ever played."

In response, Beau squints at me like he's staring at a flat-earther, and I think I ruined things again.

I hold up my hands, palms facing him. "I know it's weird. Please let me explain." I brief him on what Gisela said and how it lines up with the smell of smoke appearing. But instead of continuing to stare at me funny, he actually looks a little relieved.

"That's strange, but I've heard stranger." He glances over at the counter, where Vivi is punching something into the register, and watches her for a moment. "I never told anyone this, but sometimes, I feel like Rae is right there with me when the kids are doing something important." He tips his chin toward his niece. "Like at her dance recital in the spring. At Emmett's final high school soccer game this year. A few other times. Like she hasn't really left us at all."

This man is determined to make me cry. "I get it."

"Let me drop this off, and then I'll run you home." When I nod, Beau approaches the counter and hands Vivi her wallet. I see them exchange some words, and then she grins broadly at him.

A few minutes later, Beau is walking me up the steps to the house on Barrington, and I feel a little quiver in my stomach. It's been a long time since I've had a real date. Keys in hand, I turn and smile at my companion.

But Beau cuts off whatever pleasantry I was about to give. "You still have that phoenix tattoo?"

I chuckle. "You think I had it removed?" My right shoulder blade was graced with an intricate phoenix soon after my eighteenth birthday just because. No really. I came of age, and I knew a phoenix was perfect for me. Always fire. Always rising.

"Not really. I was just thinking about how perfect that is ... since Mattie passed in that fire."

I'm speechless. Maybe I knew. Somehow. I guess trusting my gut and just going with things works out sometimes. She is me, after all. "I don't think I ever would have put two and two together."

Beau's eyes are soft as he looks at me, and then he pulls me in for a bear hug, cupping his hand behind my head. It feels like he missed me. *I* missed this. My face rests against his chest, and I take a deep breath of him, appreciating this moment, the softness of his sweater and his heart.

"I didn't realize how much I needed this." I squeeze him back and breathe in his scent for a moment before letting go.

"I needed this, too." When he pulls away, he runs his hand down my arm and catches my fingers in his, lingering there. With a squeeze, he says, "I'll call you. Let's grab dinner soon." As he jogs back to the car, he glances back at me with that crooked smile, and I admit that I watch until he gets inside before I turn the key in the lock and open my own door.

———

That afternoon, Claire and I patiently await the arrival of Amanda Riley. She shows up with her husband, Callum, and her brother, Daniel. I remember seeing Daniel's name along with hers beside the photo in the escape room.

I had wondered if I would feel anything strange when they arrived, since both Amanda and Daniel are direct descendants of Mattie's sister, which is sort of my sister, which I know is weird. Mattie worked with her sister, so I imagine they were close, though from the way she writes about her, I think that Rosie was the one in charge, the big sister not only in birth order.

I know from experience that sisterly relationships can be challenging. Anyone with as many sisters as I have would know that. Actually, I imagine that having just one could make it challenging. Are *all* sibling relationships challenging? Like you're packed into a house together like sardines, and you think you'll all be close, but that really doesn't happen till you're not in the can anymore. You can't be as close in the heart when you're that physically close all the time. It's like cramming two people into the same sock.

Being the middle sister, I am somewhat close with everyone. Rhiannon, though ...

One time, she and I and Fallon were going to surprise Mom and Dad for their anniversary. We had it all planned out. Honestly, I walked in on Rhiannon and Fallon planning it and demanded to be part of the committee. Everyone was assigned a task. I had just gotten my license, so I got a little pissy with Rhiannon because she didn't give me anything to get at the store.

"You and Fallon get all the jobs where you run to the store," I said. "I'm stuck at home with the babies." Granted, Haley and Lacey were thirteen and ten, so they weren't exactly babies. But sixteen was so grown up in my eyes. Rhiannon and Fallon were in their early twenties, so they just didn't see it.

But what hurt was the argument. Fallon tended to go along with Rhiannon, but Rhiannon told me that day that she just didn't trust me. "You're so impulsive, Morgan. How do I know that you'll get the right cake and not just pick what you want?"

"Sometimes, Morgan, you are unpredictable," Fallon added gently. Then she turned to Rhiannon. "But maybe we can let her pick up the snacks. I think that's fair. She can have some responsibility." Fallon has always been the peacemaker.

Rhiannon had walked away from the disagreement with skepticism, but I did exactly what she thought I would: I went rogue with the snacks, picking up my favorites even though the party was about Mom and

Dad. I get it now, but it became a major fracture to our potential friendship.

"Everything is over here." Claire interrupts my thoughts and gestures to the pile in the living room. Our guests eye up the boxes.

"Great," Daniel says. "With the three of us, we should make quick work of it."

"We can help, too," I say. I'm happy to note that I haven't smelled cigarette smoke since they arrived, so maybe this will go smoother than I thought.

Together, the five of us carry all the boxes out to Daniel's truck, filling it. Claire and I make it back inside the house just as it's starting to sprinkle.

"Did you hear Amanda say that they are taking it over to Gisela for appraisal? I bet it's all in the shop next week." Claire is looking out the window, and I join her to watch the raindrops as they get heavier and faster, pelting the roof over the deck like a dozen kids dancing on bubble wrap.

"Glad they threw a tarp over everything." I frown at the sky, willing the rain to slow down a bit to protect Mattie's goods as my heart aches a little, presumably for what once belonged to me. I force out a long breath to chase the feeling away and change the subject. "Hey, are you doing anything later?" When she shakes her head, I mention that Beau's niece and nephew are performing in *The Mystery of Edwin Drood*. "Want to see if there are tickets for the showing tonight?"

Claire raises her eyebrows. "Are you sure that's a good idea? You just started seeing him. Isn't that sort of stalking?"

I frown, giving it some thought. "I don't think so. If I see them, I'll be honest. I love the show and wanted to support the school, especially after Beau mentioned that they are both in it."

Claire twists her hair around her finger as she ponders this. "I suppose that would be okay. Let's check for tickets." She strides across the room to the office nook in the kitchen and flips her laptop open. "Looks like they have a few left. Do you mind sitting toward the back? It's not a huge auditorium, so I don't think it will affect our enjoyment."

"Nope. As long as they have two seats together, let's do it."

That evening, we find our seats in the auditorium and wait for the curtains to go up on *The Mystery of Edwin Drood*. I always liked this play for several reasons. First, it's both spooky and silly. It pokes fun at itself. Next, I love that people cared enough about Dickens' story that they chose to finish his unfinished manuscript—when he died, only half of the installments had been published, and there were no notes for the remainder of the book. Finally, I love that the audience gets to decide who the villain is, and then the troupe acts out the ending based on the audience's choice.

I'm impressed by Vivi's performance as Princess Puffer. Her character runs a grimy opium den in London. She does a great job speaking in a gravelly voice without diminishing her stage presence. She's scroungy and mysterious, and she seems to know everything about everyone. I love that she breaks the fourth wall by winking at the audience and aiming clever jokes directly at us. There are a lot of layers to this character, both comedic and tragic, and Vivi plays her well!

After the show, Claire and I exit the auditorium together slowly, as the entire audience seems to be in line to greet the cast. Because it's a local production, most of the attendees stop to talk to them, and the players are beaming, as they should be, still in full stage makeup. I guide Claire around the line and pause close enough to Vivi that she sees me when the person in front of her moves.

I wave at her and say "Great show!" When she waves back and calls out, "thank you," Claire and I keep going toward the exit. By a set of double doors nearby, I see a group of teens dressed all in black and wearing headsets, likely the stage crew. Emmett is among them, and I smile politely at him when he catches me looking. He turns to his companions, says something, and makes a beeline for me.

"Hey. Hang on," Emmett says.

I touch Claire's arm so she stops moving, and I offer Emmett a smile as I wait to see what he has to say. I'm surprised he wants to talk to me, and honestly, I'm a little nervous about why. When he stops in front of me, I tip my chin up to make eye contact. I'm decently tall, but he's much taller.

"You're here." He doesn't say it with heat—it's more observational, like he's measuring me.

I bite my lip and then reply, "Yes. Beau said you guys were doing *The Mystery of Edwin Drood*, which I love. I thought I would check it out and support you and Vivi ... and the school."

He fiddles with the cord on his headset. His response carries some unexpected edge. "You know, life hasn't been easy without Mom. Beau stepped up and took on her role *and* became our dad."

"I know," I answer kindly. "Beau told me—"

Emmett suddenly turns and puts a hand over his earpiece like he's listening to something, and I smile politely, about to wave and exit so he can get back to his work. Then he drops his hand and says, "He talks about you sometimes." After a hard stare and a twitch by his mouth that I think is almost a frown, he continues. "You already walked away once. He doesn't need more heartbreak. Not from you."

I suppose this is one wound that will never heal with time, for any of us. My heart still aches for what I went through, for what the kids went through, for how Beau kept trying to pull everything together and then ultimately had to cobble together the family, adulthood, a life on his own. I never expected this though. I never thought, first of all, that I would see any of them again. But I especially never thought that Emmett would react this way if I did see him. I imagine the pain that he has held in his heart all this time, and I feel that he needed someone to blame for the hard times. And that someone is me. And I know that I deserve it and also don't at the same time. Those two feelings collide and crush me.

The two of us look at each other for a moment as tears well in my eyes. I feel like a child, looking up at him and being scolded. Claire puts her hand around my arm and pulls gently so I know it's time to exit.

"It was nice to meet you," Claire says to Emmett, even though I never introduced them.

Emmett puts his hands in the pockets of his zip-up and continues to watch us, completely emotionless.

Claire guides me through the exit into the cold night, where the tears finally spill onto my cheeks. "I know that hurt," she says, still holding onto my arm.

Once we're in the car, I grab a tissue from my purse and let the tears fall like rain. "I'm awful," I whisper.

Claire pats my arm and sits watching me. "He's not being cruel—he's being loyal. He's protecting Beau. And he's a kid. You know he doesn't understand the full story. He's never been faced with a decision like that. He couldn't possibly get it."

I'm still rattled from the experience. "I didn't mean to hurt them," I say through a sniffle. "I just knew I couldn't stay or I wouldn't be the person I wanted to be in that situation. I was near my breaking point. And I wasn't mature enough to be their mom back then."

"And Beau knows that or he wouldn't be talking to you now. Remember that Emmett doesn't understand. We don't even know what he knows about that time."

And I'm haunted by the ambiguity of his statement. Did Beau talk about me with fondness? With pain? I don't know what impression Emmett has of me based on what Beau has told him. Does Emmett remember any of the early days? Beau mentioned that Emmett has some memories of Rae. Vivi doesn't, and she said she doesn't remember me. But wouldn't he have told them the same thing? And Vivi seems okay with me.

I cry the rest of the way home and all the way up the stairs to my apartment door, but Claire makes sure I get inside okay.

"Do you need me to hang out?" Claire offers. "Want some tea?" When I frown and don't reply, she adds, "Want to do shots and play video games till we pass out?"

I snort laugh at this and feel like I'm drowning because of the tears and the volume of snot that got shuffled around from that one motion. I squeeze my eyes shut as I try to recalibrate breathing and then open them again. "I'll be fine," I manage to choke out. "I'll just head to bed and see how I feel in the morning."

I haven't felt this awful about my decision to leave Beau in a long, long time, so I suppose I had this coming. Will I ever feel okay about this? Probably not.

I walk past the desk on my way to my bedroom and notice a newspaper clipping on the floor. It's the one about when the Morgan Building caught fire during a showing of Poe's *The Cask of Amontillado*. As I'm reading over this article, I recall that Mattie died in a building that I share a name with. I shudder: another eerie coincidence. There are way too many of them. I skim the article again and decide that I'm done for the day. This has been a lot.

I place the page on my desk beside the diary and head to bed thoroughly drained.

Funny enough, my restless sleep doesn't help me feel any less awful. I awaken with the same pit in my stomach, the same feeling that I've done something really wrong, that I've hurt people. Even though so much time as has passed since our divorce, I still feel awful about the decision.

The bathroom mirror reflects the evidence of my rough night. My eyes themselves look raw. My eyelids are swollen. My sinuses feel swollen too.

On top of the general puffy feeling, Emmett's words keep echoing in my head. "You already walked away once. He doesn't need more heartbreak. Not from you."

Arguing with myself about why I left isn't going to make me feel better, so I brush my teeth and try to put yesterday's conversation aside. I can't stomach the thought of breakfast, though. I make some tea with the hope that it will shift me back to some better version of myself and recline on the couch, allowing my head to rest heavily against the back cushion. I curl my legs up and wrap both hands around the warm mug, holding it close enough to breathe in the steam full of cinnamon and cloves. It's soothing, but my mind keeps drifting back to Vivi and Emmett and all that I missed.

By leaving, I said no to wiggling their teeth and teaching them how to ride a bike. No to guiding them through arguments with friends about trading cards and fashion. No to supporting them through math problems and crushes and even more broken hearts.

And because of all the life I've lived beyond what they have, it may take a long time for them to understand why I chose me. And why it seems like I chose me *over* them rather than *in spite of* them.

I rub my eyes and sigh as I try to strangle the train of thoughts racing through my mind. I need a distraction so I don't keep obsessing over this, and I don't even feel like facing my book boyfriend right now. Maybe I should dig into the story of the fire and see what else Mattie recorded for me.

I pad across the room to my desk where the diary and the missing piece are waiting for me. There is a pull I can't explain—a tug I feel in my belly like I'm holding my breath and my lungs are longing to let it out. Mattie seems to be calling me to keep going. I notice the article beside the diary, the one I found on the floor last night, and I tuck it into the front with the others.

Returning to the couch, I snuggle into the cushions with my tea and part two of Mattie's reverie. Opening the missing piece of the diary, I find where I had stopped reading and begin sifting through her entries again.

The first few pages don't say much, just a little about the day-to-day, spending time with Ansel and her family, and some funny work stories. I find the entry where Ansel proposed to her, which was truly beautiful.

As I start reading, I sense something in the air shift, and cigarette smoke blended with a floral scent wafts through the room. "Hey, Mattie," I whisper, but before I can fully comprehend that I spoke to her again, I feel a sucking sensation all over my body, followed by a gentle breeze playing in my hair and a little flutter in my heart. It appears to be a golden autumn afternoon, and I'm on a hillside overlooking a river.

A man I've never seen is sitting on the ground across from me. He has a strong frame and a nervous smile. His tweed jacket is unbuttoned, and his matching newsboy hat rests on the blanket nearby. A small picnic basket is open at the end of the blanket, and I can see containers with cheese, bread, and grapes bursting from them.

I get the sensation that where we are has history. Like this is where Mattie and Ansel used to talk about literature and their work and their dreams.

"Mattie?"

I turn toward him and find myself smiling. He seems both tentative and certain at the same time.

"Ansel," I reply, though the voice isn't my own. After the happenings of the past few weeks, I know it's Mattie's. She has a honeyed tone, smooth and silky like she knows what she wants, but also filled with the hope and joy of youth. When he doesn't say anything else, I place my hand on his and gently stroke his fingers till he wraps them around mine. "What is it?"

With a deep breath, he reaches into a leather satchel that I hadn't noticed, almost hidden behind his leg. "I have something for you."

I think it's a blanket, which is a little odd, but I take it from him anyway. I find myself saying, "What is this?" The bulk of the blanket unfurls, billowing open to show me its secrets, and I hold it out in front of me for a moment before I realize that this is something incredibly special. "It's beautiful," I murmur, and my voice is full of love and reverence that I haven't felt in a long time in my current lifetime.

What I hold in my hands can't rightly be described as a quilt. It's truly a work of art. On a background of irregular stripes in shades of gold, russet, coffee, and olive that remind me of hills is a huge mocha and cream sparrow. I stretch the piece out on my lap and brush my hands over the bird, as if I need to touch it to truly sense the care and adoration that went into its construction by tracing the route of the maker's hands myself.

"Exquisite," is all I can say. I search Ansel's eyes and find that they have softened and that his face has taken on a look of both triumph and admiration. When he doesn't speak, I return to the quilt and find that there is more to it than I originally noticed. The first detail I spot is stitched across the top of the piece in small, determined lines—though truthfully, they are uneven, showing the skill of the tailor to be novice. Oh! "Did you make this?" When Ansel nods, I feel my heart melt. I touch the words along the top of the quilt.

You stitched my name into the collar of my coat so if I ever got lost, someone could return me to you.

"It's beautiful." I say. I run my eyes over the quilt and notice other phrases stitched around the edge by the same determined hand.

At the bottom, in the center, one of these phrases catches my eye: *Will you marry me?*

I gasp and turn to Ansel, who promptly scrambles so he's kneeling on one knee. Calmly now, he takes my hand in his.

"Matilda Florence Conrad, every stitch was for a moment that we've shared that has been truly special to me. I wanted to commemorate some of my favorite moments with you with the hopes that we will share many more in the coming years." Taking a deep breath, Ansel pulls a ring box from his pocket and opens it.

There, inside, I see the same dainty engagement ring that I found in my attic a few days ago, in my current lifetime, and my breath hitches as I think about how short their joy ends up being. My lip quivers as the thought passes through me, before I look back at his face.

"Will you marry me, Matilda?" He swallows nervously, and it's actually quite endearing.

"Yes, of course!" I find myself saying. "But I can't believe you asked me so soon!"

Ansel laughs and slips the ring onto my finger. Then he takes both my hands in his. "I've known for a while that it was you. Why wait any longer?"

The warmth of the afternoon and his smile start to fade, and I find his hands replaced with my cold mug and the chunk of diary.

"Oh, Mattie," I whisper, "you two had something so special. I'm sorry that had to end. His love for you was so big!" You would think that I didn't have any tears left, but somehow, I find that the dam bursts again, and I'm sobbing over the end of their beautiful story. "Thank you for that little glimpse into the wonderful things in your life!" I place the mug and diary on the end table and lose myself in sorrow for a few minutes, letting go of the heavy burden of Mattie's life ending right when she was in the middle of her joy. My scalp tingles, and the hairs raise on my arms. Somehow, I sense that I'm not alone.

Brushing away my tears, I head to the kitchen to warm up my tea, walking right across that creaking board to remind me that I'm here, now. Looking out the window, I note that it will be the perfect sort of day to wallow in my feelings, both those left over from yesterday and the fresh parade of sadness from Mattie's diary. The sky looks heavy with feelings as well, all shades of gray. Cars zip by on the street below, the occupants clueless about the century of time passing just a few feet above their heads in my apartment.

I return to the couch and Mattie's diary with my reheated tea and a newfound determination to discover whatever it is that I'm supposed to learn from her words. As often as I feel a pull to read her diary, I'm certain that she wants me to not just read and discover who I was in that lifetime, but also to learn about some part of her life. I'm not sure what or why, though.

When I start reading again, I find that the entry after the one about her engagement is rather interesting as well. Mattie and Ansel were walking through town together after she got off work when they noticed something strange across the street.

A wheelbarrow was parked in the alley beside the Morgan Building, and a man was mixing something in the wheelbarrow, which I thought was strange. Then, I noticed a stack of bricks slowly being transported down the stairs to the basement doorway of the building nearby. I brought it to Ansel's attention.

We watched for a moment before Ansel gripped my hand tighter and suggested we hurry along. "It's probably nothing. They must be repairing the foundation," he told me. He didn't sound convinced though, and I had a strange feeling. Maybe it was just intuition, but something wasn't right about it. I can't put my finger on why.

Frowning, I set the book down. The activities in early-twentieth-century Hawthorne are certainly odd. Wait a second …

I grab the main part of the diary from my desk and flip to the article that I found on the floor last night. Skimming, I confirm what I thought: the theater was on the second floor of the Morgan Building. The rest of the article talked about people dying in the stairwell from smoke inhalation, another one in the room with the projector, and three more at the front of the theater, nowhere near the stairs.

I read aloud. "'Officials believe they must have taken too long to exit and succumbed to the smoke while still in the audience.'" As before, I wonder why three people stayed in the audience when everyone else ran out when someone raised the alarm.

Snagging the next article, I reread it as I pace the room.

Calvino, the owner of the Morgan building, which houses the now ruined theater, was convicted of orchestrating the inferno [...]

The flames consumed much of the building from the second floor upward, leaving the first floor and basement remarkably unscathed—a detail investigators say points to the calculated nature of the crime.

[...] the city's own mayor, Edward "Eddie" Flanagan, had colluded with Calvino, offering protection to the mob in exchange for personal gain.

To compensate the grieving families of those who perished, the Morgan building will be sold.

Again, the scent of cigarettes permeates the air, and I drop into my armchair in response. "What am I supposed to do with this information? Do the bricks and the wheelbarrow have something to do with the theater burning down? With your death?"

A shiver passes through my entire body, and I have the sensation that I'm on the right track. What the connection is, though, I can't possibly imagine.

Chapter Ten

My apartment suddenly feels stifling, and I can no longer tell if it's my emotions or the cigarette smoke. I need to get out of here. I dress and throw on a coat, grab my crossbody, and head for the door. Then I jog back for my beret. I'm sure my hair is nightmarish. No need to frighten the neighbors.

When I get to the sidewalk, I finally feel like I can breathe again. The chill autumn air flits through the ends of my tresses and flips the bottom of my jacket as I stride down the street. There has to be a reason Mattie is leading me on this quest, but what is it?

I take a bite of my protein bar—thank God for chocolate—and chew thoughtfully. Mattie died in the fire in the theater. Does it have something to do with what was going on in that alley? Were they doing something in the basement of the Morgan Building and she went to the theater that day to find out ... what?

And decided to also take in a movie?

That makes total sense.

I get to Main Street and start walking the route south, toward where the train station and The Brass Bell used to be, the route Mattie took when she was sneaking through town dressed as a man. Taking another bite, I look around me, hoping to get inspiration from the town, hoping Mattie will send me a message aside from just smoke.

"Morgan!"

A woman's voice calls out my name somewhere behind me, and I turn around. I suppose the red beret is easy to spot. Standing in the doorway of the Wunderkammer is Gisela. She's breathing hard and has a paper in her hand.

Jogging back down the street, I nod to her. "What's up?"

"Come in. It's too cold for me out here." She laughs and grabs my arm, pulling me into the store. "I found something." Gisela holds up the paper for me to see. "It looks like a diary page. I found it in the box of china you and Claire found in the attic."

I do a double-take. "It's definitely Mattie's handwriting. Why didn't we see this before? Claire and I went through the boxes before we gave them to Amanda." Now it's Gisela's turn to give me a questioning look. "We had to see what was there and figure out who it belonged to, since nothing was labeled. I'm assuming everything was Mattie's, since we found that ring, and she noted that she lived on Barrington in her diary."

"That makes sense." Then she gestures at the paper in her hand. "When I was unwrapping the newspapers around the dishes, it fell on the floor. It was rolled up with them."

"Do you mind if I read it?" I take the page from her and peruse the diary entry till I find something interesting.

Ansel told me today that his father was a famous painter before he moved to America. His name was Angelo Valenti, and he created so many beautiful paintings. They were in many buildings in Italy, some owned by private collectors. When he came to America, one of his paintings was even accepted into the Novak Arts & Music Museum in Washington, D.C. What an honor!

Unfortunately, that painting was stolen. Ansel has been hoping to hear something since the robbery, which was several months ago now, but the police don't have a clue.

I didn't know that Ansel's father was the famous painter because his last name is different. Mr. Valenti shortened his surname to "Vale" so it sounded less Italian. Unfortunately, many people do not like Italian immigrants right now, and they are facing hostility due to their Catholic faith and their poverty. Many were farmers before they came here and are struggling to find work. I imagine this is why so many are involved in mafia crimes. They don't have a choice, the poor souls, if they want to feed their families!

I have to wonder if Mr. Conti knows something about the painting, since his friends were clearly involved in some questionable business. They mentioned a Valenti painting when I heard them talking by The Brass Bell. Maybe it's the same one! I wish I could find out somehow. Maybe I could find the painting for Ansel. It would make him ever so happy for his father's painting to be restored to the museum.

I couldn't possibly ask Mr. Conti about it. That would be extremely dangerous. Maybe Ansel and I could speak with the mayor together. It will take a great deal of courage to return there, but I think that he would listen to Ansel, since he isn't a silly little girl.

It still makes my blood boil to think about how the mayor spoke to me. Maybe we should approach the police instead.

That's the bottom of the back page. I look at Gisela questioningly for a moment before I find my voice. "That's it?"

"Sadly, yes." She sighs. "I didn't see any other papers besides newspapers in those boxes. They were all from early 1912, which was a few months after the theater fire, so it makes sense that everything here was Mattie's. Whoever wrapped up her things must have waited a while before doing so."

"Maybe Rosella or Ansel." A wave of sadness washes over me. "I don't blame them for putting it off."

I thank Gisela and retreat back to my apartment with the diary page, planning to turn over this mystery in my head for a bit. I'm stopped in my tracks on the front porch, though, where I find a package with my name on it. It's a small box, and it's wrapped in brown paper with a red wax seal with an owl pressed to the top of the box, closing it like an envelope. Immediately, the little hairs on my arms stand up. I grab it and take it inside, but it's strange. I wasn't expecting a package.

When I get to my apartment, I examine it further: no name, no address, no sign of who it's from at all. Weird.

Open it? Or is it full of anthrax? Funny how we have to worry about intent these days when it comes to mysterious packages.

My hand hovers over the seal for a moment before I decide that no one is that mad at me, and I'm honestly not important enough for a murder plot. I opt to rip the paper off like I did for my birthdays as a child. I do love a good (hopefully benevolent) surprise!

Inside is a card with a single line typed on it. *You always did love a good adventure. First clue: Go where time moves backward but the clocks go forward.*

I flip the card over several times like those cards we wrote in elementary school that just said, *How do you keep an idiot busy for hours? Turn over*, on both sides.

"What is this about?" I feel a little uneasy in my stomach, but I'm also excited. Did I win a puzzle prize or something? I pick up the box and strip the paper off completely, looking for a logo or emblem of some sort. I examine the owl on the seal more closely, but no dice. Maybe it's from a puzzle company? My birthday was several months ago, so I have no idea why someone would send me this.

Then I look at the packaging. No signs of wear, no tears, no dirt. This wasn't shipped, just dropped off. It's someone who knows where I live.

Insert creepy music here.

I text Claire a picture of the box and the card. "Want to solve a puzzle with me?" Then I head to the kitchen and cut a chunk of cheddar to munch on while I wait on her response.

"Always," she responds with a party popper emoji. "I'll be up in a few. I think I have an idea."

I re-read the clue and realize this is probably something I'll have to leave the apartment for, so I do some light makeup while I wait on Claire and make sure my hair is presentable. Then I add my beret.

When Claire arrives, I tell her my thoughts. "Do you think this could be a scavenger hunt?"

"Oh! That would be so cool!" Then she tips the crumpled paper up. "Any idea who it's from or why you got it?" When I shake my head, she frowns. "Then you definitely aren't going by yourself. Could be a really elaborate kidnapping plot."

"You know, I was thinking the same thing."

The two of us stare at the card for a moment, though. All ready to leave on an adventure, but not sure where to go. "Where would a clock move backward?" I repeat the card, totally clueless.

"Maybe we start with places that have clocks," Claire suggests. "What about churches? Or schools?"

"There were definitely days when it felt like the clock moved backward at school," I comment. "But we don't have security clearances, so we can't go in a school."

Claire makes a sour face. "Good point."

"Does Hawthorne have a clock tower?" I ask.

Looking pensive, Claire taps her chin. "No ... but there is a Hawthorne Historical Society, and they may have an old clock there. That might be the answer to the riddle because time goes backward—"

"—at the Historical Society. You're right. And even so, it may not have to do with a clock at all." I feel like this is the right answer, regardless of the presence of a clock. "The clocks on our phones will continue moving forward even if we're moving back in time."

"Technically, you could move back in time at any museum. Or at the Blind Tiger."

"Do you have to ruin this?" I joke. "Maybe we can just pop over to Vandermere House. The Historical Society and the Blind Tiger are in the same building, so we can knock both of those out."

Nodding, Claire looks pensive, but ultimately, I'm right. "I still think it's about a clock. I'll drive," she says, and we both head for her car.

As we pull into the lot beside the building, I'm checking their hours, and we're in luck. They're actually open on Sundays. Walking to the building, I keep turning ideas over in my head. If it's about a clock, easy breezy. If it's not about a clock, then we have to figure out what else it could be pointing us to. Inside the Historical Society, I'm struck by an eerie sense of *déjà vu* when I realize that I've been in the main room very recently. It's paneled in mahogany with rich blue velvet curtains. The beautiful carvings on the chair rail. The vaulted ceiling. The crystal globes encasing the sconces on the walls. This was the mayor's office over a hundred years ago, and I shudder as his oily voice drips into my brain again.

I shake my head and decide not to say anything. I'm honestly still not sure where to go, so we start wandering aimlessly through the exhibits. I meander past some vintage outfits and a quilt, and my stomach churns as I recall Mattie's touching gift from Ansel.

"Have you ever been here before?" Claire asks. She pauses by a display of old woodworking tools and gives them a look that plainly says this isn't it.

"Actually, yeah," I say, brushing away the trip I took in Mattie's memory. I approach a display of vintage timepieces in the back corner. Above them in large letters on the wall is the phrase *Turn back time...* I shake my head. "Aaron and I came here a while ago, and when we left, he kept singing the Cher song with this title." I point at the sign. "He has a good voice, but it was utterly ridiculous. I was laughing so hard because he really got into it. He can be theatrical when he's trying to make me laugh." It's a good memory, but I tuck it into that shoebox in my mind full of Aaron things that I won't examine again till a few years from now. "This clock display is new, though, so I didn't know it would be here."

An employee strolling through the room approaches us just then and asks if we want to know anything about the exhibits.

"Not about the exhibits, exactly," I say. This feels so weird, but I show her the card. "I was given this, and I guess I'm on a scavenger hunt. Do you know—" I stop talking when a huge grin breaks across her face.

"I do! Follow me." Together, the three of us go to her desk, where she hands me a small box with *#2* typed on the front.

"Thanks ... who gave this to you?" I ask. Not to be blunt, but ... no actually, it is to be blunt. I'm all about seizing the sweet cherries, but I would also like to know if I have a stalker.

"Someone who said you would be in with the clue you just showed me." The woman's eyes twinkle with orneriness. "The whole thing sounds super sweet. I can't give you any more details, though."

I thank her. She didn't even say *he* or *she* so I know something about the person. Again, I have that uneasy feeling in my stomach. I tear through the paper on this box and find a clock inside shaped like a cherry. On the face of the clock is the simple phrase, *It's about time.*

"Time for what?" Claire says. I shrug. No idea. "Is there a card?"

I pull a notecard from the box with a typed message on it as well. *You saw the sky catch fire here, reds and blues and greens and silvers. You said it was the most beautiful kind of chaos. Return to that hill and look up.* I have no idea what that's supposed to mean. The Northern Lights? Fireworks, maybe? When is the last time I watched the fireworks? I thank the woman again and motion for Claire to follow me outside.

In the car, we both look at the note for a few minutes. I can't come up with anything else that makes sense, so I suggest it means fireworks. Frowning, Claire leans back in her seat. Then she says, "Maybe a baseball game? A lot of times they do fireworks at the end." She squints at me when she realizes what she said. "You've never been to a baseball game, have you?"

"Not since I watched my high school boyfriend play, and they don't usually do fireworks for high school games." When else would I have seen fireworks? "Maybe Fourth of July. I know that seems obvious, but I don't remember going anywhere for fireworks for the last few years." My mind drifts back to Beau when we first got to Pittsburgh. He was excited to take me downtown to see the fireworks over the water. I have to admit it was stunning.

We fought the crowds and got a good spot in the park. He brought a bag of some of our favorite junk foods and bottles of iced tea. I had brought glow sticks, and we broke them all and wore them. I made bracelets and crowns and we laughed in the semi-darkness with thousands of people around us, but it felt like we were the only two people there, just me and my new husband, as we looked into each other's eyes. My heart was so happy, it could have burst.

I was so wrapped up in us, in the perfection of the moment, that I jumped when the first explosion happened. The crowd had grown quiet with anticipation, and when that pop echoed through the valley, I heard kids shriek and adults *ooh* and *ahh*. Beau laughed at me and wrapped me in his arms. Then, we just held each other and watched the lights in the sky and their reflection on the three rivers. I felt like I had stepped into a glowing wonderland of color, a magical and impossible place where our new beginning here seemed to indicate that our love, our joy, was limitless. We were in our early twenties, and I felt like I was invincible as long as we were together. And this new city would be our playground.

Coming back to the current moment, I shake my head, and Claire looks at me questioningly. When I finally focus on her face, I give her a wan smile. "Good memories." She doesn't ask, so I continue. "I don't think it's anywhere that far away. Maybe ... I went to a local fireworks display a couple years ago, now that I think about it. There was this hill where the women in that knitting group I was in said they liked to go to watch, just outside of town. You could see the fireworks perfectly up there. A group of them were going with their husbands, and they invited me. I brought ... Aaron."

"Okay, did you tell someone about going there?"

"I don't know that I would have mentioned it to anyone. It was nice, but it wasn't memory-making."

Claire taps on the steering wheel for a moment. "Do you want to drive over there and see? Is it nearby?"

"Yeah." I search the GPS for that doughnut place I remember seeing at the bottom of the hill. "Here. Go here and then turn just past it. That takes you up to the overlook."

When we arrive, I don't know where we need to look for the *look up* part, till I wander over a little knoll to the lone oak stretching its branches skyward. We had all picnicked there that evening before the show. There, in the crook of its branches, is another box with a red wax seal and *#3* typed on the front.

"This is the place?" I pull the box out and tear into it with vigor. I'm getting excited about where we're going next. Also, I like presents, and I am curious what's inside. "I guess I need these if I'm going to look up during the day." Strangely enough, the sun came out in time for us to tromp around up here, so I don the gift. It's a pair of aviator sunglasses with a tag that reads: *For the girl who always wanted to fly.* I hum for a moment and think about all I've done to feel like a bird. "I do like jumping out of perfectly good planes," I finally say.

"Is there a clue with this one?" Claire sticks her hand in the box and pulls out another typed card. She reads it aloud to me. *Wool and words twist together here. You once said it smells like paper and old dreams. Go where the pages never leave.*

"This one is tricky ..." My gaze gets fuzzy as I think about all the places I like to go where they have wool and words. "Like sweaters and books?"

"Oh! What about Spin a Yarn?" Claire suggests. "Wool and words."

"That's good! What about the pages that never leave?"

"We can figure that out when we get there. Come on!"

We return to downtown Hawthorne and park close to Spin a Yarn, and Claire and I hop out of the car and practically race inside. I don't think I've ever been so excited to enter a books and yarn store, and I get pretty excited about those two hobbies.

Inside though, I have no idea where to look. Where do the pages never leave? Maybe a display with classic books? A set of encyclopedias? No one uses those anymore. We end up wandering around for a while before I decide to ask the cashier if he knows anything.

"Hi, sorry to bother you, but I got this card and ... it's part of a scavenger hunt. I need to find pages that never leave. Are there any books on display that aren't for sale?"

The cashier gives me a hard look over his glasses and then takes the card from my hand. "We sell all the books we have here, bro." He returns the card to me. "Maybe check in the restaurant. The servers have been here longer than I have, so maybe they know something."

I'm very tempted to *dude* him as I thank him for the suggestion, but instead, I walk into the other half of the shop with Claire and approach the hostess stand.

Pages that don't leave? That would be menus. In the restaurant. But why would I think of that? Luckily, the server knew what we were looking for and helped us out with the clue. Then she presented us with box #4.

This box is heavy, like the second box, and I carefully open it.

"It's a book. Who is surprised?" Claire smirks and elbows me.

I return her grin with a more serious one. "I've been looking for this one for a while. I started a series a couple years ago, the Seasons of Isla Rica by Juliette Amberly, and I wasn't able to find a copy of the last book because they're out of print. This is the final book, number four, *Autumn of Us*."

Whoever did this scavenger hunt must know me really well. Or they've seen my wish list on the Odio shopping app. Maybe one of my sisters? Then a quiver tingles through my stomach. *Or Beau?* Did I mention to him that I was looking for this? It would have happened a long time after we broke up. Maybe I mentioned it when we met for coffee. I mean, I must have. Surely these are gifts from Beau. At least, I'm hoping they are.

"It's sweet that someone got this for you," Claire says. "And that someone clearly knows that you would enjoy the game aspect of it." She picks up the book to look underneath it. There's the card. She pulls it out while I hold the box in my hand, somehow unable to move as I'm wondering what this is all leading to.

I finally shake my head to clear out the cloudy thoughts. "What does the card say?"

Claire clears her throat. "*I'm waiting at our final stop. A place for warmth, caffeine, and maybe one more chapter.*"

"Well, that's obviously coffee," I say. "Lyon's?" This one was almost too easy. Claire nods, and the two of us walk down the street to the coffee shop.

When I enter, I don't see anyone I know other than Vivi at the counter. It's early afternoon on a Sunday, so it's not crowded. In fact, there's no one in line at the counter, so we walk right up.

"Hi, Vivi. Weird question for you ..." I show her the card that I'm holding. "I'm doing a scavenger hunt, and I thought I was supposed to meet someone here, based on this clue."

Her smile changes to a frown, and I watch the famous Blackwell eyebrows dip together, clouding her perfect expression. "I don't know anything about this. Who are you supposed to meet?"

"We don't actually know." Claire shrugs and then flicks her fingers in a wave. "I'm Claire, by the way. I'm friends with Morgan."

After Vivi acknowledges her with a gleaming grin and a "nice to meet you," I enlighten her about the mysterious box on my porch and the scavenger hunt.

"That sounds so fun! Let me see if anyone here knows about a clue for you." She turns and motions excitedly for her other two coworkers and then recounts the story. I can tell by the blank faces and the shaking heads, though, that we're probably in the wrong spot before she tells us.

"Maybe another coffee shop?" Vivi gives us a sorry look and asks if we want anything. Since we haven't had lunch, I get a couple ham, brie, and cranberry croissant sandwiches to go, and Claire and I return to the car to eat and think.

There are lots of chain coffee shops nearby, a couple that are Pittsburgh chains, but I don't have any fond memories of any. Most have been just run-in-and-grab sort of places. Initially I thought Lyon's because of the convenience, but maybe I hung out at one before. I seriously can't think of anything though. What coffee shop could have been a final stop? Or another chapter?

"Oh ..." Maybe the start of a new chapter. Surely not, though.

Claire is taking a huge bite of her sandwich so she leans toward me and raises her eyebrows for encouragement.

"Between the Beans," I say with a twinge of guilt. Not that I don't like the shop. It's just that the last conversation I had there was with Aaron a couple weeks before he left. It's about fifteen minutes from here. We met up there a couple times when we were busy but still wanted to hang out because it was a good halfway point between our homes. Plus, the other memory from there ... How did I not think of that before?

"I don't think I've been there," Claire says around a mouthful of sandwich.

"It's a coffee shop and used bookstore." I twist my mouth into several different expressions before I force myself to continue. "Aaron and I met there for one last coffee before he packed up and left. He talked about wanting me to go with him. I talked about wanting him to stay here. It was a really pointless conversation. And depressing."

"Aaron?" Claire lets out an exasperated sigh. "I was hoping this was from Beau."

I bite my lip and look at her. "Honestly, I was too. It makes more sense for it to be Aaron, though. We went to the Historical Society together. We saw fireworks together at the overlook. We ran into each other at Spin a Yarn and ended up back together ..."

"And he wants to see about one more chapter at the coffee shop where you had your goodbye." Claire sounds touched when she says it, but I know her thoughts on Aaron. It's broken. We both take a deep breath and let it out before she continues. "How do you feel about this? Do you want to go? It's your choice if you want to go there and actually talk to him. Assuming it's him."

I raise my eyebrows at Claire, a little overwhelmed. "It's really thoughtful that he did this. I feel like I have to go. He texted me the other day and said he missed me, but I sidestepped the comment. I hope he didn't come back to Pittsburgh just for this."

"I'll help you with whatever you decide to do." Claire pats my hand. "Maybe finish your sandwich while I drive, and you can decide when we get there?"

"That sounds like a good idea. I do think I'll have to go in and talk to him, though. It would be wrong to let him sit there all day, wondering if I'll show up."

Claire puts her SUV in drive and pulls onto the main road. "I agree. It was really brave for him to put himself out there the way he did. And this was a kind gesture. He clearly knows what you like."

I hum in response and lean back in the seat. This weekend keeps getting weirder.

When we pull up outside of Between the Beans, I stare up at their cheerful sign with the lineup of books flanked by two jaunty coffee bean bookends for a moment before I muster the courage to go in. I look at Claire for a moment without a word, and she pats my arm.

"I'll wait in the car if you want. Or I can drive around. Or I can go look at books. Your choice."

A couple beats pass while my stomach churns before I decide to answer. "Can you just pull over and wait? I think I'll go in and talk to him for a couple minutes, let him know how I feel." I rub the birthmark on my wrist for a moment, and then she finally nods. I take a deep breath and open the car door.

The thing is, even if it is Aaron, I'm realizing more and more that my heart belongs to someone else.

When I enter Between the Beans, I feel in my bones that I'm in the right spot, but since there are several bookshelves between me and the coffee shop at the back, I can't see if Aaron is sitting there. I approach the checkout area near the door where a friendly young cashier with long blonde hair is adding stickers to a stack of books.

"Hi, this might sound odd, but I'm on a scavenger hunt, and I have this clue that I think was directing me to come here." I hold out the card for her to read, and when she sees it, she emits a little *eee* of excitement. Must be the place.

She points at me with both index fingers like she's granting a wish and says, "Yes." Then, she reaches under the counter and pulls out a box covered in brown paper with the same red wax seal as the others. It's not terribly big, and when I take it from her, I note that the contents shift but aren't heavy.

"Thank you." I don't want to open it. But I also do. I mean, this is an adventure, and every part of me wants to see the end of this game, but I also believe that this game is going to end badly for the other party. I don't want to hurt anyone. Again. At this point, I feel like I'm just tromping around like a giant fire-breathing dragon singeing whoever gets in my way. Thatched roofs are also in trouble.

"Can I watch you open it?" the woman says. She's peering at me with big eyes while she leans on the desk like it's all that's keeping her from ripping into the box herself.

"Um. Sure?" I don't want to be rude, but it is my disaster, right? I can't imagine there's anything in here she shouldn't see, though. And the show must go on. With apprehension, I slip my thumb under the seal and tear away the paper, revealing the box. Then I pause. I really, really don't want to open this. What if it's a ring? But why would it be a ring? You don't ask someone to marry you unless you know the answer. And he would be here *with* the ring. And this is complicated. Okay, so it's not a ring. How did I go from a proposal in another lifetime full of so much sweetness to standing here hoping there isn't a ring—

"What do you think it is?" The cashier is verbally nudging me, and I know she's excited, but she can't possibly imagine what is going through my head.

I let out a huge breath in preparation. "No idea." Biting my lip, I set the box on the counter and lift the lid.

The first item I see is a map. Am I supposed to go somewhere else? I felt like this was the last one since the note says someone is waiting here for me. Opening it, I search for the name of the city. Charlotte. My heart falls. I only know one person in Charlotte. I smooth out the map and see that there are pinpoints drawn on in marker with little notes—"You'd love this rooftop bar," "This bookstore makes skydiving seem boring," and "Best Indian food this side of the Atlantic." And more. He took the time to map out where I would like to go in his new city.

And my heart breaks a little as I fold the map, almost like doing so is saying no to him.

When I set the map down, I notice that a key is taped to the lid of the box. Attached to the key is a fob that says, *Aaron Gilbert, Apt. 3B*. He wants me to move in with him. Another part of my heart cracks.

The final item in the box is a short handwritten letter, and it's definitely Aaron's boxy handwriting. I stare blindly at the words for a moment before I actually start to read and process them.

Morgan,

I haven't stopped thinking about you since the move, and after seeing you in Italy, something stirred that I couldn't ignore. It felt like a moment we weren't supposed to miss, like life nudging me to say something. So here it is: I'd love to try again, if you're open to it.

Life in Charlotte is good in many ways, but the truth is, it's been missing you. The brightest part of my days was always you. I couldn't let this chapter close without opening the door one more time—because my heart still knows where it belongs.

I think you'd really love it here. I've found cozy corners, great food, places that already feel like favorites—but they'd mean more if you were discovering them with me.

So, I'm writing this with nothing but hope and honesty: I want you in my life. And if there's any part of you that wonders "what if," I hope you'll follow that feeling.

No pressure, just possibility.
With all my heart,
Aaron

My own heart drops to the floor right there and shatters like a crystal vase. Tears cloud my vision as I feel the thorough dread of having to break his heart. That's when I realize that my heart was never truly up for grabs to begin with. Even when I was with Aaron, it had already found its place.

Which makes me wonder, now, what actually fell on the floor because it sounded expensive.

When you know something was wonderful, but ultimately not meant to be ... how do you move through it? How do you say no to this? This sweet and wonderful man? True, we were often like Mentos and Coke together, but there is beauty in the drama. And it was good, if not totally stable.

And I suppose he's waiting in the coffee shop for me to answer him.

I suddenly realize that I'm being stared down by ... what does her name tag say? Tiffany. I sniff and then present a decently polite smile. "Hey, Tiffany, thank you for delivering this to me. Do you happen to know if the gentleman who gave you this is still here?" I'm crossing my fingers that this can be an email. That would be so wrong, but maybe?

"Oh, sure. He said he would just read and have some coffee while he waited. Seems like such a nice guy! And this is really romantic." Her hair swings as she points toward the coffee shop at the back, and I follow the path she indicates like I'm about to tell my little sister that I forgot to feed her goldfish while she was at Grandma's and it has left this realm.

When I step from between the rows of books, I see Aaron sitting completely alone in the coffee shop part of the store. Thankfully, there are no other customers this afternoon. He's seated there with a coffee and an open book and this big, nervous hope in his eyes.

That's when I let the rest of our story pour back in. This isn't just the place where we left our bookmark. This is also the first page. I happened to be here one day years ago, browsing the stacks for some fresh new romance titles—new to the store, since it's all used books—and he was meeting someone here for a coffee date. I bumped into his table since it was close to the stacks. I apologized. He smiled, and then I smiled. That's when he looked at his watch and asked me how long I thought he should wait for his date before he assumed she stood him up.

I couldn't help but chuckle sympathetically. "Fifteen minutes if she hasn't said anything. Did you text her?"

He had, and she didn't respond. He said it had been twenty.

"Man, I'm sorry to hear that. Maybe she's caught in traffic or got lost and doesn't feel comfortable trying to text at the same time."

"Maybe so," he said. Then he grinned at me and shrugged. "Want to have some coffee?" He gestured at the empty chair.

I was a little surprised, but I couldn't say no. He was cute, and he had a novel with him. I sat down, and we spent the next two hours getting to know each other. He never did hear back from his date.

Now, I find myself standing where I had before, at the beginning of our story, about to close the book altogether.

"You came." He stands and pulls out my chair. "Can I get you a coffee?"

I open my mouth, but all that comes out is a long breath. I feel like a deflating pool floaty with my heart being tugged in two different directions. I bite my lip, and his arms drop to his sides. I get the sense that he's deflating too. "Aaron, I— I got your boxes and your gifts and your letter." I hold up the last box and work at my lip a moment before I can say anything else. "I'm so sorry, but I have to say no. Not because it wasn't beautiful—our time together truly was—but I'm a different person now. And I still can't see myself leaving here. I love it here."

"I understand. You want to be here more than you want to be with me"—Aaron holds up a hand—"and I can respect that. I'm not trying to guilt you. It's a truth, and I'm okay with that. I want you to be happy." He puts his hands in his pockets and looks like his mind is somewhere else for a moment. "After Italy ... I kept replaying those moments. It was like we slotted back together so perfectly."

"I know."

"You're the only person I would want to get chased by the cops and enjoy Italian chocolate with afterward."

I grin at the memory. That was pretty exhilarating.

"When I had to come back here for a training, I thought it was a perfect opportunity to show you just how much you mean to me, to invite you to join me with something I built for you."

Warmth rises through my body and heats my cheeks as I realize just how touching that was. That he was wooing me in a way that showed he truly knew my heart. "That was a beautiful scavenger hunt. It was really meaningful."

"I'm glad you enjoyed it." Aaron takes a step forward and then back to where he was, like he wanted to approach but decided it was better not to. "I was walking around the South Hills the last couple days, retracing our steps like I could rewind time. I thought that, no matter the results, it would be nice for you to take a trip down memory lane, too." He pauses, studying my face, but I'm not sure how to respond. "It wasn't about changing your mind. Just reminding you who we were... and showing you who we still could be."

I realize that he's giving me another chance to change my mind, and I have to say that I'm tempted. For a long moment, I turn that little folded map over in my hands, feeling the weight of everything Aaron just offered. I almost regret that it feels heavy. When my eyes meet his again, I smile—softly, but sadly.

"This is... so me. It's perfect." My voice catches from gratitude for what he put into this. "If this had happened three months ago, I might've said yes without even thinking." I look at him for a long moment. That chiseled jaw I know so well, the sharp wit, the way he always rose to the occasion—or rose to meet my stubbornness with his own. He never backed down, never blinked when I baited him.

If the true measure of a man is how he shows his care, then Aaron is a giant.

I sigh, bracing myself for the part I don't want to say. "I've been finding new pieces of myself here—pieces that don't quite fit in Charlotte. And maybe... maybe they don't fit with you anymore either." I scrunch my face sympathetically. I really don't want to have to say any of this.

I close the distance between us and set the box on the table. Then I touch his hand gently. "You gave me something beautiful today. But the best adventures—the ones that matter—they don't pull you backward. They pull you forward. And right now, I think my forward is here."

Chapter Eleven

Returning to the car in silence, I wipe the back of my hand across my face, dragging my tears with it, and climb in. Claire raises her eyebrows at me but doesn't say anything for a moment.

"Ready to go?"

"Yeah," I mutter. Suddenly, everything feels stifling, and I peel off my gloves and scarf, unbutton my coat. Then the crushing sensation is gone. I can breathe, but it's not a relief like I hoped it would be.

The ride back to the house is fairly quiet. I feel so many things swirling through me as Claire drives.

I never imagined that Aaron would go for a grand gesture. We were so clearly over. But then, of course, there was Italy. I guess I had some hope too. Part of me wishes he had done this before ... well, before Beau.

But would I have followed him? Would I actually have moved for him, given that second chance a little sooner?

I must have sighed out loud because Claire finally turns to me when she pulls up to the stoplight.

"You okay?"

"Didn't we just do this last night?" A weak laugh escapes my throat. "I don't know how much more of this my heart can take." Right now, that pitiful organ feels like a tiny hard metal ball deep in my chest.

"It's not your fault, though. Any of it." The light turns green and she continues guiding the car through the small towns near Hawthorne.

"He wanted me to go with him," I say. "He asked again."

Her mouth forms *oh* without any sound. "Did you talk to him or just tell him you can't go?"

I sigh again. "I talked to him. It was so touching. And I owed him a conversation." I finally brief her on what happened. On the map. The key. The letter. The place. "I know he put so much thought into this, and I feel awful, but I had to say no."

When I look at Claire, she's biting her lip, eyes glistening. Finally she speaks. "You know, you needed to do what was best for you. You don't owe him anything. If you moved and it wasn't the right decision, you would both be miserable."

"I know that," I whisper, fiddling with my scarf in my lap. It's one that I made a couple years ago to coordinate with my beret and gloves: a mottled red and cream with strands of shimmery gold through it. The sun peeks through for a moment and glints off the gold before vanishing again behind an angry cloud. "It doesn't make me feel any better that I broke his heart again."

"Oh, sweetie." Claire pats my hand. "Aaron will be fine. And he had to know that there was a heavy possibility that you would say no again."

I stretch the scarf out in my hands and run my fingers over the fabric, appreciating the way the nubbiness of the thick yarn creates little speed bumps that my fingers slip over. "I know. It doesn't make it any easier though."

Claire grimaces and then turns onto Main Street. "I know it's especially hard after what happened yesterday. I was hoping for a happy ending when you found that first box."

"Yeah." I chuckle softly. "Me too." And I think the happy ending I was hoping for, more and more, is from the story I started long ago: Beau.

"Want to stop anywhere? Or just go home?"

Looking around me, I feel the strangest thing. It's like I've become part of this community, its history. Like this place is home, family, and love all in one package. It's a depth of feeling I'm not accustomed to, having been a transplant in the area for so long, but I guess that not only can a place grow on you, it can become part of you.

Not to mention, I've lived here in Hawthorne longer than I initially expected. I suppose my roots run deep now.

"Home," I say with an edge of finality that steals my breath. I belong.

We pass Carriage Lane, and I feel my gaze tugged that way, my eye catching on the sturdy crimson brick that belongs to Beau. An ache in my heart pulls me from the feeling of depth just a little, like my roots wiggled out of the dirt and reached for him.

My phone vibrates in my purse, and I steel myself, fully expecting to field a text from Aaron with a sad goodbye. I don't want to prolong it, and honestly, I want Claire by my side for this, so I immediately pull the phone out, ready to reply, my stomach tight with apprehension.

But it's Beau.

> Hey! How's your day going? Vivi said you went to the show last night. It was a nice surprise for her. She was happy to see you there.

I feel Claire's gaze on me when I'm quiet for too long. "It better not be Aaron."

I shake my head and feel a little quiver in my chest. "It's Beau."

"Ah." Claire puts the car in park and turns to face me. Her expression is unreadable, but I know she's bursting to ask what the text says. I'm not feeling playful, so I give her the scoop. "I see." Again, unreadable. Then, she makes a scrunch face. "He didn't say anything about Emmett, so I guess he doesn't know."

I ponder this as we approach our door. "Is that good or bad?" I'm starting to feel worn out from this weekend. Maybe I should call off work tomorrow and just sleep.

"I don't know." Claire turns the key in the door to her apartment. "But if he doesn't bring it up, I think you should."

I let out another sigh. I'm sighing a lot today. "I know you're right. I would slowly die from the pain of wondering what he told Emmett and if Emmett talked to him about running into me."

"You know he would bring it up if Emmett told him. There's no way he would let that go without addressing what he said."

"Good point." I gnaw on my lip for a moment. "I still don't want to bring it up."

Claire gives me a look. "You know I'm right down the stairs if you need to talk about it. I'm not telling you what to say, though."

I finally crack a little smile. "I always hate it when they do that in movies. Especially when it's people our age. We definitely know better."

Claire flares her nostrils and gives a wry smile, no doubt from experience. "Don't ever operate under the assumption that everyone grows up."

"Good point." I start up the stairs to my apartment and then pause. "I'll say something."

"You better. I'll be checking your phone later." She jokingly shakes her finger at me.

"'Kay, Mom."

A bit later, I'm back on my couch with my phone in hand, just staring at the blank screen. This is a good start. Maybe by next month I'll open it and find the texting app.

Any number of things could happen that would prevent me from calling Beau to let him know what Emmett said and apologize, again, for any turmoil I caused. Lightning could hit me.

Ahem. Lightning? Hello?

With no such luck, I finally open the phone and stare long enough that it shuts down again. I'm clearly not going to get anywhere, so I set it on the coffee table. It buzzes, mocking me.

I pick it back up and see that Rhiannon has texted me. We don't talk often. Having a conversation with her always feels like putting on a tight jacket.

> I was eating cherry cobbler at lunch and thinking of you. New place down the street has the best. How have you been?

It's accompanied by a picture of her with my nephew Silas, each holding up their cobbler and grinning. The kid is fourteen, and he still lets his mom be seen in public with him. I love that kid.

A tiny plume of cigarette-scented air plunges past my nose, and I draw back for a moment. I feel an ache in my chest that I'm not sure is mine. *Is this a sign of a stroke?* No ... I think ... I think Mattie is heartbroken. I feel longing and the crushing desire to wrap my arms around someone who isn't there.

I bite my lip nervously. I don't care for these strange feelings that wash over me that aren't mine. I like having dominion over my body. I don't plan on sharing it with anyone else ... well, unless I decide to have a baby someday.

The word drops into my mind like I thought of it myself: *sisters*.

My fingers flutter across the keys—controlled by me—as I dump my thoughts into a text.

> That looks delicious! Hi, Silas! I miss you guys!

I start typing another text. "I—"

Words, words, words. Actions carry more meaning, but what can I do from here? After a moment, I finally center myself and begin again. I need to say this.

> I've been thinking about sisters a lot lately. Because of a book I've been reading. And it got me thinking about you and how we are. Maybe we haven't been super close because of our age gap and our stubborn personalities and the fact that I moved east when I was twenty and don't see you guys very often. But the truth is that I always felt like maybe you saw me as a kid that you needed to take care of, and because I didn't really need or want to be taken care of, maybe we didn't understand how to be with each other. Obviously, we're adults now, but all I really wanted was to be seen and heard. Anyway, I love you.

The thing about sisters ... you know that you should be able to be honest with them, and they will hear you and love you even if it's something hard. I don't think that was a super hard truth, and since we live in the modern world and Rhiannon and I are old enough at this point, maybe we don't have to keep dancing carefully around each other. Mattie mentioned so many times in her diary that Rosella would be upset with her about her smoking, even though Rosella wasn't her mother and Mattie wasn't a child. They obviously never cleared that old crap out and stepped into a peer dynamic. Seeing that, I know that's what Rhiannon and I need to do.

And the ache in my heart is starting to subside. Maybe I was right.

I see Read appear below my text, and I set the phone on the table. I said what I needed to. Now it's time to watch an episode of *Braving Borders*, crochet a koozy, and just clear my head.

When Rhiannon calls a few minutes later, I'm surprised, but I feel ready to talk, calm and steady. And it's a good conversation. She brings up some of the times when she felt like she was being a disapproving father—she always had more of a dad feel while Fallon had a mom feel. I talk about how I felt like I had to be a bratty teen around her, even though I was a perfect angel with our parents. I was. I swear.

"I want you to know," Rhiannon begins, "that I do see and hear you. I always did. I just sometimes didn't like what I saw and heard." She laughs. "You were something else. I felt like sometimes we both just tried to do and say things that would irk the other one."

I laugh too. "I think you're right." Then I take on a more serious tone. "You know, I'm not as reckless as I was back then."

"I would hope not." Rhiannon sighs. "It bugged me that you didn't need to be taken care of. I don't know why. We had legit babies in the house. Why did I need to baby you?"

"No idea," I say. "Maybe we made a pact in another lifetime." A chill creeps up my spine.

"Eh, maybe."

When I eventually get off the phone with her, I'm smiling. I promise that she and Silas can come stay with me over spring break—they aren't sold on going somewhere cold, but I'll soften them up. And I know that we are better off for having that bit of honesty about our past.

I finish the episode of *Braving Borders* and daydream about the beautiful market in Morocco that the hostess was wandering through. Clearly, I'm getting no closer to contacting Beau than I was earlier, but maybe I need to give it some more time so I know what to say. Emmett's words still sting, though I know I don't really have a fault in them. But was it just him taking out his frustrations? Or did Beau actually hate me, as I fully suspected he did?

To further procrastinate, I cobble together a dinner of cod with malt vinegar, sweet potato fries, and some vegetables and heat it in the microwave. There is a rule about microwaved fish at work, but in my sweet sanctuary, I can microwave any animal I like. And eat it.

No, I'm not pleased with myself. I spent four more days with my stomach in knots thinking about how I should be avoiding Beau so I don't break his heart. He has texted me a couple times, and I've responded, but every time, I've felt like I was betraying him or me or the kids or … I don't even know. That constant feeling that I've done something wrong has firmly wrapped around me like a straitjacket, and I'm not sure I'll ever be able to Houdini my way out of it. And the chains. And then swim back to the surface. And then get rescued by a helicopter.

Where was I going with this?

So I'm taken by surprise when my phone vibrates in my purse around four on Thursday as I'm walking through the parking lot at Baker & Willow, my coat pulled tightly around me, and my beret and gloves protecting my extremities from the wet chill of November. It's so cold after the inviting warmth of my office that I feel like I stepped right into a snow drift.

Flicking open my door, I duck in and rummage in my purse till I pull the phone out. It's Beau.

My stomach flutters and sinks at the same time, if that's even possible. But as his warm voice pours through the earpiece, I feel like he's wrapping his arms around me again.

"Hey, how was your day?"

"Good. It was good." I have somehow lost my social skills. They must have turned into popsicles before I got in the car. "How was yours?"

"Not too bad. Busy with a new client, and I like talking to him. So that was nice."

"Glad to hear that!" I'm happy to hear him happy.

"I was wondering if you have plans for this evening. I wanted to make chili for dinner—"

"That sounds perfect today!"

Beau laughs. "I didn't get to finish. Vivi called and said she was going to a friend's house to rehearse for an upcoming show this evening, and then Emmett got a call from work and went in to pick up an extra shift."

"Aw, you don't want to be stuck eating chili by yourself! I'd be happy to join you for that."

"I was hoping you'd say that," Beau finished. "I'm wrapping up at the shop, and then I have the commute to contend with, but you're welcome to come whenever you like."

"I've heard that rush hour can get pretty bad in that part of the building." I laugh aloud and feel a little better. "Be safe going home. I'll bring something to go with the chili."

"That sounds perfect. By the way, if you go down the alley to the left of my building, there is a lot back there. You can park in any of the spots numbered four through eight. One through four are for the second-floor tenants."

I hadn't realized before that the alley was wide enough for a car and actually went somewhere, but of course it does. I go straight from work to the parking lot behind Beau's building and park in seven. Then, I walk back to Carriage Lane, up to Main, and down the road a bit to Lyon's Den because I have plans.

When I was in elementary school, we never had desserts with our school lunches like kids do today. My niece and nephews talk about having ice cream and cookies and all sorts of other junk food, but none of it stacks up to the face-sized cinnamon rolls that our school served on chili day. It was the only day that a treat was ever served, and I swear the whole school ate hot lunch that day. The chili tasted like vomit, but the cinnamon rolls tasted like the tooth fairy and

Cinderella's fairy godmother and probably some other magical creatures had arrived to bless us all with the most delicious confection known to Tudor Elementary School.

I know that all the memories we have of childhood food are skewed. I tried bologna in college one time, and it tasted like the inside of an old gym shoe, but I hold onto the belief that those cinnamon rolls are like ambrosia and nectar.

I aim to duplicate this elementary school tradition tonight with Beau, so I step up to the counter and, as luck would have it because I have Morgan Magic, I purchase their last two cinnamon rolls. Not face-sized, but they will do.

Distracting myself with the cinnamon rolls worked for a while to quell the rolling waves in my gut, but now that I'm heading to Beau's apartment, I feel them tossing again. He buzzes me through the main door, and my heart bangs like thunder in my ribcage when I knock on his apartment door.

He opens it with his huge crooked smile that crinkles the corners of his eyes.

"Come on in! Did you come straight from work?" Then he spies the bag in my hand with the red Lyon's Coffee logo. "You took a detour first. I approve."

"You don't know what's in the bag."

"I don't think you would recycle a pastry bag from Lyon's."

"Maybe I'm weird. Maybe it's broccoli."

"If it is, it probably has icing on it that was stuck to the bag, so I might try it."

I make an *ew* face and set the bag on the counter. Beau sneaks a peek, and his eyes open wide.

"Cinnamon rolls? Does that go with chili?"

Then I have to explain why of course it does.

"Huh. Then this might be the start of a new tradition." Beau throws a dish towel over his broad shoulder, just like he always did when he was cooking. I never figured out why. I guess it's so he can wipe his hands on it if he needs to, but why wouldn't he just walk to the sink and wash them off?

The gnawing feeling returns to my stomach when our conversation dies down, so I offer to help open cans and stir. Together, we make dinner, and we don't say much. Beau seems really at ease with me already, again.

Throughout dinner, I keep looking for places to gently insert Emmett's comments and find out if Beau has any insight. I glance over at the two closed doors off of the living room. I know which one is Vivi's, so the other is likely Emmett's. I know I have to bring it up, but ... dinner is kinda perfect. And just a few weeks ago, I never thought I'd be right here with him again.

Unwinding another strip from my cinnamon roll, I pinch it off and take a bite. Awkward conversation loading in 3 ... 2 ... 1 ... But as I swallow, I'm cut off at just the right time.

Beau's face lights up with a look I know as 'bout-to-make-mischief. "You had mentioned interest in seeing the basement and maybe finding out how the rats down there dress."

I chuckle at the memory of what I said about the rats. Damn, I'm funny.

When I nod, he continues. "Want to check it out after dinner?"

"Sure. I'm still curious." I take the last bite of chili. "I wonder what was in this building before. Was there a business on the main floor before you bought it?"

Beau finishes chewing a bite of his cinnamon roll. "It was a hardware store before I moved in. They relocated to a plaza on the other end of Main Street. Bigger building."

"Right; I think I saw that one. Marek's?"

"That's it. I didn't have to do too much to renovate the shop. Mostly cleaning, painting, and adding the partitions and furniture."

"That makes it nice. What about the top floors?"

Beau leans back in his chair. "The second floor was already split into three one-bedroom apartments, so not much work there. The top floor was too, though. I updated the second floor and did a full remodel up here."

"Nice."

Together we clean up the dishes and store the rest of the chili, working around each other in the kitchen the same way we used to. It always feels like dancing when you're in tight quarters with another person like this, especially when everything flows smoothly, when your steps move past the other person in synchronicity, almost like it's been choreographed. I'm feeling a little buzzed from our interaction and how well everything is going, till my eye catches on Emmett's door again, reminding me that I need to bring up our conversation.

I take a deep breath, and Beau happens to catch my eye. He saunters over and cages me in with his hands on either side of me on the counter. I smile up at him and relax. I can always bring it up later.

"It's been wonderful having you here this evening. Maybe we can make a habit of this, if you're okay with that."

"I do like eating." I challenge him with a smile. I think I know what he's thinking, but I tend to make him spell it out.

He kisses me on the forehead. "As do I, but I meant that I would like to hang out more. Not just eat together."

I wrap my arms around his waist and nuzzle into his chest, a glow of delight emanating from the spot his lips touched. "Mmm. I'd like that too."

Beau wraps his arms around me as if I'm a treasure he's spent a lifetime searching for. The edge disappears from my breathing, and I completely surrender to the moment. I could get used to this. His right hand runs gently from my shoulder blade to my waist and then retreats to my shoulder blade again, almost like he's stroking a cat, and I know from experience that this is one of Beau's grounding moves, like he's nestling into a feeling for the long term.

Again, I know that I need to say something about Emmett, but the perfection of the moment, holding onto Beau and being enveloped in the smells of him—his woodsy citrus soap, his musky cologne, and a hint of laundry detergent—and the spices from the chili, the coziness of the room, and the gentle sound of a rainstorm starting up outside makes me never want to move. I can't interrupt this.

Pulling back a little, he looks down at me and smiles, a dimple sinking into his cheek on the higher side of the ornery grin. "Did you want to check out the basement now? Or do you need to head out?"

As time starts moving again, I catch myself glancing at his lips. The little hairs from his mustache are starting to curl over the top. All I can think is how much I want him to kiss me right now, to feel the roughness of his mustache and beard against my smooth skin.

"Hey?"

I raise my eyebrows and release myself from my daydream. For some reason, I can't stop smiling, though. "Sure. Let's check it out."

As we walk to the door, Beau slips his hand around mine. When I meet his eyes, he pulls my hand to his mouth, kisses my knuckles, and then opens the door.

My hand is tingling where his facial hair scratched it, and the little burns race all the way through my body. I almost forgot how sweet he is.

Together, the two of us walk down the stairs to the main floor, where he pulls a key from his pocket and slips it into the lock on the basement door. "I don't want the rats wandering around up here. Gotta keep them locked in."

"Fair point," I reply.

Just inside the passage, he flips a switch, turning on a bare incandescent bulb above the stairs. The area beyond the bottom, though, remains dark. A chill crawls up from my toes to the roots of my hair as we creep down the creaky stairs. Holding onto the railing, I inch my hand along and realize that the wall stops halfway down, so the stairs are open to the room I can't see ... and whatever might be down here watching us. I didn't think I would be able to creep myself out so easily, but here I am, heart pounding, wondering if there is another light switch at the bottom. Wondering if there is a furnace and a meat grinder down here. And maybe a barber shop nearby. I really shouldn't be thinking about *Sweeney Todd* right now.

I don't think we're intentionally going snail-speed slow, but it seems to take an eternity to reach the bottom. When we do, though, Beau stretches overhead and pulls on a chain that turns on another dim bulb. He leaves me at the bottom of the stairs while he walks around and turns on three more.

"I should probably get better lighting down here, but like I said, I don't ever come down, and I never bring guests."

"I'm honored," I manage to say. As my eyes adjust to the sudden brightness, I'm struck with the eerie feeling that I've been here before, and my instinct is to think rationally to get out of it. *No way have I been here before. Maybe Mattie was here once. Or maybe this is like another basement I've been in. Maybe a friend's house when I was little. Or ...*

Oh. It reminds me of the escape room. Strange, but less creepy. My heart rate slows to normal.

"What are you thinking?" Beau asks. He wraps his hand around mine and tugs me a little toward the center of the room.

I squeak out a discordant melody from *Sweeney Todd* in an effort to change the subject back to the creepiness of the basement. My throat is a little tight.

Beau guffaws. "That's ... yeah, I can see that. No demon barbers here though." He gestures to the back of the room, far from the stairs. "There is a wine cellar back there. In horrible condition." Then he points at a small set of doors near street level. "Coal shoot. Lock intact." He turns toward the far wall. "Some rats ..."

I'm jarred to attention when he says that, and I swivel my head to look where he's pointing. There, on a TV tray, is a framed portrait of ... rats? I step closer and realize that someone has photoshopped the rats from the Muppet movies into a family portrait where they are all wearing Victorian costume.

I'm moved that Beau would do something like that for my enjoyment, and I also find it hysterical. Bursting out laughing, I scoop up the picture. "Playing with editing software again?"

Beau's laughing too. "I missed hearing you laugh."

"I love this." I shake my head, still overwhelmed with mirth. Finally, I take a deep breath. "Okay, let's continue the tour."

He gestures to a stack of crates in various states of breakdown, piled in a corner. "Here are my old crates hiding a wall safe—"

"Whoa. A wall safe? You didn't start with that?" I shove away the *déjà vu* again because I'm certain I'm recalling the safe from the escape room. Pretty certain.

Beau grimaces. "I don't know what business would have needed that in the basement, but I had someone check it out. Nothing in it. Original to the building.

Still works. I have the code written down, but I have no reason to use it, so I just keep it shut."

"That's so interesting," I take a few steps and peer at it. "Maybe we could stop by the Historical Society and see if they know anything about the building's origins."

"I'd like to do that. Maybe that can be our next date." Beau brushes something from my hair, and I shudder, certain it's spiders or cockroaches or vampires or ...

Finally, I can't contain myself any longer and give a full body shimmy to get whatever it is off of me.

Beau laughs and crosses his arms. "Why, Morgan Lilith, ye who are named *Sea of Darkness*, are you getting freaked out by the basement? I didn't think anything scared you."

I draw myself up to my full height and muster all my witch-goddess powers to maintain my cool. "I don't like bugs," I say calmly. "Especially in *the hair*." I give a playful toss-toss of my locks to assure him that it really is just the thought of bugs.

"I see." He shrugs. "I can't help the bugs down here. *And* it was your idea."

"Mmm." My gaze brushes over the brick walls, and I mentally trace the arch design in the brick, so much like the escape room exit. Something feels like I need to be down here. Almost like I was drawn here, and little twitters of excitement curl in my belly. The air around me feels a little colder, suddenly, and I shiver.

"Let's head back up. I don't want you to be cold." Beau wraps his hand around mine, and I start to follow him, but suddenly, I feel compelled to pull away. Something about the crates.

"Hang on." As I walk across the room, I pick up on the smell of tobacco, and it gets stronger when I get to the wall. Normally, I would head in the *opposite* direction of cigarette smoke, but anymore, I know it means Mattie. "Something ..." Then I spot the yellowing corner of a sheet of paper sticking out from one of the crates. "Okay if I pull this out?"

Beau joins me and shifts the lid. We're greeted with a plume of dust, but the rest of the sheet is revealed. I gingerly pull it from the crate, aware that the oils from my fingers could disintegrate it in my hands. When I unroll the whole thing, it's roughly eighteen by twenty-four inches, and it appears to be a movie poster for *The Cask of Amontillado*.

Part of me is really giddy because I love Edgar Allen Poe, but this, even without that context, is incredibly cool. "I don't recognize the actors." I point at the names on the poster: Iris Stafford and Bernard Romilly. In the story, Lady Fortunato is mentioned but doesn't actually appear, so I assume that this is loosely based on Poe's story and, much like *Titanic*, is a disaster that Hollywood turned into a romance. Which, in turn, may have been a disaster at the box office since I didn't know about this adaptation.

When I look at Beau, he has a half smile on his face as his eyes flicker over the poster. "Emmett will get a kick out of this."

"Emmett?" I mutter. My stomach squeezes as I recall that we still haven't talked about him. *And I thought Mattie was my friend!*

"Yeah," Beau continues. "He's into old movies. He talks all the time about the differences in how they used to do sound and lighting and everything, compared with today. The history is pretty cool, and he knows a lot about it, considering he's still in high school."

"That's really interesting. You'll have to take it upstairs with you."

Beau agrees and takes the poster from me, grinning. "I can't wait to show him."

I really can't put this off any longer, so I suck in a huge breath and begin. "I actually meant to talk to you about Emmett tonight. On Saturday, Claire and I went to the high school to watch *Edwin Drood*."

Beau nods, frowning, so I quickly fill in the details. I really want to reassure him that Emmett didn't do anything wrong because I can only imagine what's racing through his head, but I think it's best to get straight to the point. When I'm done repeating the story—how Emmett said that Beau doesn't need more hurt in his life—I search his eyes for a moment before I continue.

"His words wrecked me, Beau. Completely and utterly wrecked me. I never forgave myself for leaving you and the kids. You gave up your whole way of life to take care of them, and I couldn't do the same. I just knew that I couldn't be the best person for them, the person I wanted to be at that time. I didn't really know who I *was* at that time. Heck, my brain wasn't even totally formed." I shake my head and refocus. "Bottom line, I don't think there was any right decision to make in that moment, but I made the one that I thought we all needed for survival. I'm sorry for any turmoil that caused. I'm sorry if that means the kids have been in therapy because they believe moms always abandon them. I'm sorry for anything that I can't even think of to be sorry for because I haven't overthought in that direction yet. I know that I was self-aware enough to know what I was and wasn't capable of handling, and that love sometimes means you have to let someone go, but there is so much after. So much that I wish none of us had to deal with."

Beau is looking at me so tenderly the whole time I'm saying this that I am forcing myself not to cry. It's hopeless though. The tears parade down my face anyway, and Beau reaches over to wipe them away with his thumb.

"You know," I whisper, "I never stopped wondering what might have happened if I stayed. I think ... I think I never stopped loving you. But I've been scared, you know. Scared of loving you completely again, failing everyone, being the wrong person for you. You needed me, and I left. I can never change that. But I can change where I love you from, and I think the best place to do it is right here, beside you."

Beau cups my chin, and I tip my face up toward his. "Morgan, you've always been the right person, and all our moments are the right moments. I'm so glad I found you again—"

A loud buzzing strikes my eardrums, followed immediately by all the lights in the basement turning off.

Matilda Conrad, if that was you, I'm not so sure I want to continue on this wild goose chase you're leading me on. You're a terrible wing woman!

I hear a soft click as Beau flips on the light on his phone. Thank goodness he had it in his pocket.

"Let's head back upstairs." He grabs my hand, and together, we proceed slowly up the steps. When we reach the main floor, the light there is on. "Huh, must be something with the basement breaker. I'll have to check that in the morning."

"Ah, okay. Well, I should probably head home anyway." I start up the next flight of stairs toward his apartment so I can get my purse and coat.

Beau follows, and we continue in silence up the stairs. "I'll walk you to your car," he says as we both slip our coats on. When we're back on the main floor, Beau takes my shoulders in his hands. "Hey, promise me that you're okay. I'll talk to Emmett. I appreciate him sticking up for me, but he didn't need to say that. I'm sure he didn't even know what he was saying."

"I am okay. And I agree. He didn't have any idea."

"I never said anything negative about you to the kids. Really. I was mad at first. Anyone would be. But, I know you had to leave. It wasn't your fight, and like you said, there really wasn't a good answer. Stay and be miserable and overwhelmed? Or go and feel guilty?"

I give him a wan smile. "It was a hard choice. I didn't belong there, trying to raise those kids. But, if you guys will have me now, I'd love to see where I fit in."

Beau squeezes my hands and smiles at me, pushing open the door onto Carriage Lane. "You're a lot to lose, Morgan. I'm glad you're back." The storm has calmed to a drizzle, which is good, since I left my umbrella in the car. It's still chilly, but it seems a little warmer than earlier, probably due in part to the heat growing in my heart. Raindrops streak the glow of the streetlights, casting halos around Beau's silhouette. Like he needs to look more angelic.

"You know, our story doesn't have to be about the past repeating itself," he says. "We get to build on the best parts of what we were while exploring how we are now."

Okay, I've had enough. I come to a standstill there in front of the building and force him to stop, too. "Beau, I swear, if you don't kiss me right now ..."

"What? You have a threat? What are you going to do?" Beau winds his arms around my waist. "You're not walking away. What if I just stand here like this, inches from your face?"

"I'll have to do it myself then." I lean forward, assuming that he'll meet me halfway because, hello, he'd have to be nuts not to, when I'm cut off again.

"Hang on."

"Hang on?" I feel like Tinkerbell with the red face, making jingle bell sounds while I'm about to boil over.

He points toward the top of the building. "You never looked up," he says gently.

I follow his finger, and there—engraved in a concrete block near the top of the building—is my name. *Morgan*. It's unmistakable in the gentle glow of the streetlight. Tugging my coat tighter, I feel the dampness settling into my sleeves, but it doesn't matter. Glancing back at Beau, I see the broad grin on his face, quirked on one side like it always is when the joy envelops him completely.

My breath catches. All this time, I've been so focused on the story that was playing out at ground level that I never noticed this. He's right. I never looked up.

He's watching me, eyes darting back and forth between mine. Then he speaks the truth that will overwrite the bass beat of my life-after-Beau with certainty. "It was always you."

I don't know who moves first, but I do know that we collide right there, on the sidewalk in the rain, in front of *my* building, and for the first time in well over a decade, my lips find his.

Nothing has felt so right as Beau does right now. His soft kisses, his warm arms wrapped around me, and the rain washing away my doubts. It feels like not even a moment has passed between the last time we touched all those years ago and now. Like a bridge found its way across that gap.

When we finally need to breathe again, a laugh escapes me. My hair is drenched, and my clothes are sticking to me, but I've never been so happy. Beau laughs too. Then he takes my hand and spins me gently. Another laugh escapes me, tear-laced and glowing. I knew this man was determined to make me cry. Then, for a few brief minutes, we waltz, right there in the wet hush of the evening. This may be my new favorite place, and it's always been mine.

Chapter Twelve

As I come up from yet another breathless kiss with Beau in the rain, I squeeze his hand, about to reluctantly suggest that I head home, when a finger of cigarette smoke prods its way into my nose.

Mattie wants me to focus at a time like this?

I take a deep breath and suddenly snap to attention with this realization: Beau owns the Morgan building.

That means that *this* is where the theater fire was.

This is where Mattie died.

I glance at the second floor, where the Lantern Palace Theater once was. Then my gaze sweeps to the alley. A cloudy memory drifts into my mind. That's where the wheelbarrow was in one of her diary entries.

Wide-eyed, I look back at Beau.

"What's up?" He places a hand on my arm. "Was this okay?"

"Um, yeah, yes. Definitely. It's okay. But ..." My thoughts are moving faster than my words can assemble. Then my brain fixates on the image in my head of a wheelbarrow beside the building, where the door leads to the basement. "There is something else in the basement that I want to see."

Jaw hanging open, Beau quirks an eyebrow. "The basement? What made you think of the basement just now?"

"Cigarette smoke."

"Oh." He says that like this is a normal conversation.

He lets us back inside, and we track wet footprints across the entry to the stairs. With both our phones lit, we trek down into the basement. A chill hangs in the air and hits our damp clothes, making me shiver. *Now what?*

I straighten my shoulders and shine the light in an arc across the room, taking in the walls, the crates, the wine cellar. I notice the door that leads to the outside. Curious, I wander over to the door and shine a light on it, then the floor. I spot clumps of dried mortar in a few places, like it was being brought in from that direction and across the floor. But where were they taking it? It doesn't form a perfect path that I can follow.

I shine my flashlight toward Beau, but low so I don't blind him, and I see that he's watching me with his arms crossed, head cocked with curiosity. I give him a confused smile and a shrug, feeling a little self-conscious after destroying our perfectly romantic moment. But this is important! Surely instinct or Mattie will take over. *What am I missing?*

Scanning the room again, I notice the crates and feel called to walk in that direction. After all, that's where we found the movie poster.

Oh. The movie poster.

Then it becomes clear to me.

I tip my phone up again and look at the walls. They all seem pretty normal. Maybe there's a brick that was pulled out of place that they needed to tap back in and cement with mortar. Maybe a lot of bricks, since they were using a wheelbarrow to mix the mortar.

I trace the archway with my light as I approach it as part of my inspection of the room. "Have you noticed any repairs to the brickwork down here?"

"Actually ... it looks like there was some work done under that archway." Beau steps beside me and gestures. "It's sloppy, and the color of the mortar doesn't match the rest of the wall. I never noticed it before. It's not very obvious."

He's right. It looks a lot like the exit area for the escape room. I wonder ...

Then the movie poster flashes through my mind, and I almost gag. "Do you know the story of *The Cask of Amontillado*?"

"That's the one where a guy traps another guy in a room in the basement and bricks up the entrance, right?"

When I look at Beau, he looks a little queasy too. I take a deep breath. "You don't think ..."

"I thought you said Mattie died in the theater." Beau places a hand on my shoulder and strokes my arm. I love that touch is so important to him because right now, I need a little help anchoring myself.

"She did. I was just thinking that maybe they bricked someone else in back there. Maybe that's why they burned the theater down." I shudder as I think about it.

"The basement didn't have any damage though. Just the second and third floors." Beau tips his phone light onto the wall and scans the area. "It was in the disclosure when I bought the building."

I can see damaged bricks just under the arch, and now that I'm paying attention, I see where Beau said the mortar is sloppy, like the brickwork clear down to the floor was hastily done. "Maybe the fire was put out too fast. Maybe it didn't do it's job."

"I suppose it's hard to be precise with a fire."

I bite my lip as I wonder what to do. "I really want to tear the bricks down. There is definitely something back there."

"You said some*one* a minute ago. What else do you think it could be?"

When I smell cigarettes again, I know it's important, but I still don't know why. "Not sure." I press my fingers on the top brick, and it rocks a little. So I press some more. After a minute, I'm not getting anywhere. I could be here all night and maybe only press one or two bricks out of place.

"Why don't I make some calls tomorrow and find out what we should do?" Beau squeezes my hand. "If someone died back there, even if it was a hundred years ago, their loved ones deserve to know ... if any are still around."

I take another long breath. "Actually, I have an idea." I take a few pictures of the wall, close-ups and full shots, and then I text them to Kenzi. "I'll see if Kenzi knows anything about the wall, just to make sure we're right and it's not load-bearing or anything."

"Let's do that. I'd rather my building not fall down."

"Ahem, *my* building." I give him a sparkling smile as I send the pictures and an explanation to Kenzi. "Maybe she can stop by with a structural engineer tomorrow."

"Tomorrow? This must be pretty important to you."

I feel a shiver work its way across my body. "I think it's been important to me for a long time."

How lucky is it that I work at an architectural firm? Late the next afternoon, Kenzi and Joel, one of our structural engineers, stop by the Morgan Building to assess the situation in the basement. Of course, I'm at work and don't really have a reason to tag along other than massive curiosity, but I feel silly taking time off for being what Pittsburghers like to call *nebby*. Can you call in nebby to work? I thought about it. But I didn't want to explain it to Logan—not that he would have a problem with it—so I figured I would drop by on Friday evening.

Kenzi doesn't return before the end of the day, so I rush to Beau's after work to see what he knows. I could text Kenzi, but I might as well see what's up in person.

I arrive in time for what appears to be a demolition party. Several teenage boys wearing safety goggles are entering the front door carrying sledgehammers, and I unintentionally lock eyes with Emmett as he's going in. He quickly shifts his gaze to the ground for a moment and then back at me. His lips tighten into something between a grimace and a smile.

"Hi, Morgan."

I smile gently back. "Hi, Emmett. What are you guys up to?"

He glances around in what seems to be an attempt at avoidance and then looks back at me. "Knocking down a wall in the basement." Then he rushes and says, "Dad says it's okay."

Chuckling, I reply, "I would hope so."

An uncomfortable silence fills the space between us, but he's still hesitating outside the door, weighing the sledgehammer in his hands. Finally, he looks back at me and swallows. "I'm sorry."

"Oh?" I say. I don't want to jump to conclusions.

"I'm sorry for what I said to you the other night." He scratches the back of his head nervously. "I was trying to protect Dad, but now, I don't think he really needed protecting." Looking away, he seems to be waiting for me to say something, but I just motion for him to continue. He meets my eyes and says, "We talked."

I nod. "It's okay. I know you were worried. I accept your apology."

"Cool." Then he turns and pulls the door back, gesturing for me to enter ahead of him. I nod my thanks.

Kenzi and Joel are just inside talking to Beau, and when I pause to talk to them, Emmett follows the other boys down into the basement.

"Wait till I get down there," Beau says to Emmett. He's holding a pair of safety goggles, too, and wearing an old tee and sweatpants.

Kenzi smiles at me when she catches my eye. "Good news! The bricked-up part under the arch isn't supportive. It can go. There is an open space behind it that's under part of the building. It's like they walled off a closet or another room."

Joel chimes in. "The brickwork is actually pretty shoddy, and the mortar is weak, like it was whipped up hastily. I gave them the go-ahead to knock it down. Should be an easy job and probably best to get that area out before it falls anyway."

Like it was whipped up hastily? Hmmm.

"We rented some sledgehammers from Marek's Hardware." Beau grins. "Joel said it should be easy for Emmett and a couple friends to knock the wall down."

I make a face because I'm not sure this is a good idea.

"Some of it was actually wobbly, so it won't be a problem at all." Joel crosses his arms and eyes me up. "They will be safe. All the boys had sturdy boots to wear, and I gave them a safety briefing. What are you worried about? There's no budget here, boss."

Ignoring the rub, I bite my lip and then decide I should let them know. "I trust you." I had to start with that. Joel is one of the best in the business. "It's just that I don't know what could be *behind* that wall. And I'm familiar with Poe's *The Cask of Amontillado* ..." I glance at Beau, and he grimaces.

Joel chuckles. "I know that one too. What are the chances, though? It's probably a heap of junk that someone wanted to disappear."

"Maybe some bootleg liquor?" Kenzi suggests. "The building is from the right time period."

Beau points at Kenzi and nods hard. "You mentioned that earlier. I bet that's what it is. Maybe machinery like a still. Anyway, we're about to find out." He places a hand on my arm and grins. "I'll report back in a bit."

"Can't I come with you?" I say. Ugh. I want to know!

"We only had six pairs of goggles in the truck," Joel says. "Sorry, but Emmett and his friends were pretty excited and got here fast." We all laugh, and Joel hands Beau a box of masks. "Good luck, man."

When Beau disappears down the stairs, I eye up the closed basement door for a minute, till I can hear a cacophony of hammers hitting bricks. I imagine the dust is pretty thick down there. I look back at Kenzi and give her a sour face. I'm not known for my patience.

"Let's go grab a coffee," Kenzi says. "It's a short walk. Beau can text when they're through."

Back in the cold autumn air, I pull my coat tighter around me and adjust my beret. Then the three of us walk to Lyon's Den and order our drinks. While we're waiting, I decide to text Claire to catch her up, since I hadn't had a chance to share yet. She responds immediately.

> What?! I'll meet you at Lyon's Den. Don't leave without me!

> We'll wait on you.

> I MUST KNOW WHAT'S BEHIND THAT WALL! Bets on there being a body?

> You watch too many murder mysteries! I thought the same thing, but Kenzi thinks it's a still.

> That would be cool.

Claire arrives at Lyon's Den while we are chatting casually, and I introduce her as Logan's sister and my landlord, which makes her laugh.

We make small talk for a bit, and I tap my phone to check the time every few minutes. Why hasn't he texted? Are they okay? Is it gross back there?

Obviously, it's gross back there, even if it's not *remains* sort of gross. Between the dust and brick chunks that are likely raining down in the cubby, it's at least dirty.

Finally, my phone vibrates, and I grab it. Conversation stops, and the group all seems to hold their breath as I read what Beau sent.

> You won't believe what we found! No

> So no missing persons?

An agonizing minute later, the response rolls in.

> No. You will never be able to guess, so don't even try!

> Okay, we're coming over!

I stand and put my coat on, and everyone else at my table leaps up, ready for action. Then another text rolls in.

> Actually, there is too much dust for you guys to be down there without goggles and masks. I'm heading up for a shower, and the boys are cleaning up. I promised them pizza.

> Nice of you!

> Thanks! We rented a couple shop vacs to handle that, and they are setting up fans blowing out the basement door and the coal hatch to suck the dust out. They get another pizza party tomorrow if they come back and take all the bricks out to the alley.

At this point, I realize that everyone is watching me, likely waiting for instruction, so I motion for all of us to sit again. Once the cacophony of chairs scooting dies down, I glance at my phone one more time, but I can feel everyone's eyes boring into me.

> That's fun! Cheap labor, lol!

> Give me ten. I'll let you know when it's okay to go down.

I turn to meet the curious looks of my fellow partiers and fill them in on our instructions.

"So *not* a still and *not* a missing person?" Claire crosses her arms and leans back in her chair. "I can't even imagine what would be back there. Why would they want to wall off anything else?"

"I bet it's something boring like old building materials," I begin, "and Beau is just messing with me." I rotate my coffee cup on the table while I'm thinking.

"Could be." Claire takes a sip of her latte, and we all continue with small talk a while longer.

"This is taking forever." I tap my phone again and will a text to pop up. *And it works!* "Oh!" Beau says that the dust has finally cleared and we can safely enter the basement, so I share the news. We scramble to clean up and get out the door.

I'm excited enough that the cold doesn't feel so bitter when we exit the shop and head back to the Morgan Building. When we get to Carriage Row, though, I see Gisela coming out of the Wunderkammer and pause to say hi.

"I thought you might be interested in what we're doing." I introduce her to our group and brief her on the basement find.

She perks up. "I wonder if it could be like a time capsule," she suggests. "What if that hole is full of boxes of things from soon after the building was constructed? Time capsules became popular in the nineteen thirties and forties, after they buried one at the New York World's Fair. That one got people to think about the long-term preservation of things they care about, to share with future generations."

"I can see why that would be appealing!" I wonder if that's what they found. It would certainly be interesting to see. "Do you want to come with us? You would probably know better than any of us what we're looking at."

"I have time," she answers. "If you guys don't mind, I'd love to join you."

"Always good to have an expert on the team," Kenzi says.

"Please come with us," I answer.

When we enter the Morgan Building, I spot Beau sitting on the bottom step from the upstairs, now dressed in jeans and a vintage Counting Crows tee. He stands when we enter and entwines his fingers with mine. I feel warmth bubble up from my solar plexus all the way to the tip of my nose. I think he likes me.

Then he nods at Gisela. "Glad you're here, too. We could really use your expertise." He motions for us to follow him, and we all trek to the basement.

He must have rented some standing lights, too, because the area is bathed in sterile blue-white lighting from several freestanding poles with bare fluorescent bulbs. I can still see fine particles in the air from the destruction, but it's not bad at all with the fans sucking most of the dirt out.

The archway is now open, and the aperture behind it is probably ten feet by ten feet, dank and dirty. As I approach, I see a pile of items by the back wall draped with an old sheet. When I look back at Beau, his crooked smile has stretched across his face, making his eyes crinkle. I assume he moved the sheet and put it back based on that grin.

I sigh and step toward the cloth. "May I?" When Beau nods, I reach for one end of it, and Claire jogs forward to grab the other end. We lower it to the floor and step back to witness the discovery from an appropriate angle.

I skim the collection for a moment before I piece together the story of what is going on here. There are dozens of paintings, all canvases without frames.

I bet they're stolen paintings. That's why they were hidden here.

My eye catches on a familiar image, and my heart skips a beat. "Actually," I begin, a little breathless, "I know that one." I point at an image of a woman gazing out at a body of water. I glance at Claire and smile, remembering that I told her the story. "It's *Tea and Reverie*, and that's Lago Albano in Castel Gandolfo, Italy." I pop my phone out of my purse and show them the lock screen, where the image that someone else painted based on the artist's sketch is displayed.

"Oh, the painting that Signore Zangari was talking about when you were in Italy?" Claire asks, and I nod.

"So this painting has a history?" Gisela says at the same time that Beau responds with, "What am I missing?"

"When I was working at the construction site in Castel Gandolfo, Signore Zangari, who owns the property and adjacent villa, said I looked like this painting when I was staring out at the lake one morning." I touch the painting as I look at it again. Even with the layers of dust that seeped through the sheet and onto the painting, I can see a happy smile playing about the woman's lips, like a beautiful memory is flickering through her mind like an old movie. The lake reflects the sun's rays, and you can almost see the breeze as the plants and flowers near her appear to be bending and swaying. "He said that the painting was believed to be smuggled to America."

I tip the painting and look for an artist's signature near the bottom. When I find it, I do a double take. "Angelo Valenti … that's the name of Ansel's dad." Then I brief the group on that story, since Joel is completely clueless. I don't often tell all my coworkers about every detail of my private life, but when I do, obviously, it involves a past life's death and a crime ring.

I never thought I would be such an interesting person!

Joel looks dumbfounded, but the rest of our group seems excited.

The thick tobacco smell wafts across my awareness, which draws me back to Mattie and her diary, and right when I'm about to piece it all together for them, Claire jumps in.

"So you think that the gang Mattie was following hid the stolen paintings here?" She gestures to the mountain of canvases before us.

"That's what I was thinking," I answer. "She saw several men going up and down the stairs into the basement, likely bringing in the mortar from a wheelbarrow she could see parked outside. After she spied on Mr. Conti, her client, she reported all of this to the mayor. Since the newspaper article mentioned that he was arrested in connection with the fire here, I'm curious if he brushed her off and then took the information back to the gang. Then maybe they made a plan to kill her and make it look like an accident. They couldn't have planned that they would get arrested for insurance fraud and involuntary manslaughter, but no plan is perfect."

"I would bet that you're right," Claire says.

"So who owns this building?" Gisela asks. When Beau raises his hand, she nods. "Would you like me to catalog these and see if there is a record of them being stolen? It's always possible that they are simply of personal value, but I suspect Morgan is right about them being stolen. It would help to know what to report to the police and be able to tell them where they all belong. Since these are likely hundred-year-old crimes, I don't know that they would have records for these, but in the antiques world, it should be easy for me to research."

Beau smiles and nods. "I would appreciate that." He sticks his thumbs in his pants pockets. "I don't want to rush you, but I'm curious how long it would take to do that research."

Gisela looks pensive for a moment. "Between my assistant and me, we should have it done next week." She points at the canvases like she's counting them. "We can take twenty apiece. And we already have a good idea for that one"—she gestures to *Tea and Reverie*, and then her voice takes on a curious tone—"*and that one.*"

When she points at the second painting, we all take a couple steps toward it for a better look. It's nothing that I would recognize. It makes sense that they didn't steal famous pieces because these would be easier to slip through unnoticed by those who aren't in the industry. This one is just as beautiful as *Tea and Reverie*.

The painting shows a home perched on a hill near a lake with some children playing in the yard and sheep grazing on a nearby hill. A trio of stark Italian pines reaches for the clouds in the foreground, and the lake and sky complement each other in two crystal blue tones. The entire painting feels tranquil. I see that the painting also has Angelo Valenti's signature in the corner.

Finally, I decide to ask, "How do you know that one?"

"I can't say right now." Gisela has a mischievous glint in her eye. "But I have a hunch that I know this painting's history."

———

After a delayed bedtime last night thanks to my overactive brain, I end up sleeping in. It was pretty exciting, discovering the paintings and putting those pieces together yesterday, but I also realized some things about myself that kept me up ruminating.

I spent a lot of my adulthood running. True, I followed love to Pittsburgh, which was a wonderful decision, but when I got here, my actual running began. I was young, and I left that marriage, and that was okay. I needed to do that. That was maturity. But it also launched me on a trajectory that kept me in a constant need to escape. The funny thing is that, with all my fear of finding the right person, of letting down my walls and allowing for perfect imperfection, I bounced back and forth in a relationship with someone who mirrored that. I don't think Aaron was ever really ready to let go and truly fall in love, since he often was the one who chose to leave as well. I hope that Charlotte will be good for him to get to that growth.

We had lessons that we needed to teach each other, of that I'm certain. For both of us, it was how to allow, how to give, and how to receive. For all my confidence in and love for myself, I had neglected the ability to go with the flow. I checked boxes. And I searched for a thrill outside of myself, when really, the greatest adventure I was looking for was sitting on a shelf, waiting to be opened and enjoyed like a fine wine that had to be aged to perfection.

It took limping through a near concussion and interference from a past life and *her* quest to finally understand my own. I was whole to begin with. I almost missed out by following my head instead of my heart.

And I think it would be a disservice to all the past I lived, especially the ashes that spurred this revolution, to continue trying to make sense and control and white-knuckle my destiny. I'm ready for what is. And I can approach it with my heart open.

Which is also why, even though it makes no sense whatsoever, I throw on my olive-green romper and a thick camel-colored cardigan and head out the door to my car. Then I jog back in and grab a protein bar and my Seattle baseball hat because I am a responsible adult who doesn't want to pass out on the sidewalk or scare people with my crazy hair.

I'm suddenly on a quest, and it feels weird to be doing this but also really, really right.

Pulling up in front of Gisela's, I get the confirmation I need: Cigarette smoke envelops me. I never thought I would smell that and feel relief. Like I'm not alone. Like I'm on the right track. Like I have a purpose. Like I am a legacy. And to feel like I have a place in history, like there is more after I'm gone, is a strange feeling, too, but today, it also gives me a sense of pride. I'm doing the right thing.

I feel a little breathless when I burst through the door of the Wunderkammer, the cabinet of wonders that is this beautiful store, so full of history and enchantment and beauty. Full of stories thick with lifetimes of meaning. And I'm a blip but also the expanse of another lifetime. And I'm finally here to get what I know I need: a nine-hundred-dollar antique desk.

Crazy? Yes, yes it is. But it's my desk.

Bypassing Mattie's tea set, fur, suitcases, and boots, I can feel the prickle of familiarity from these items now, like I have an extra sense to know what belonged to me before I was Morgan. Yet, I'm not scared. I don't shudder from the grip of my own mortality weighing on me. I just feel like I've changed form. I sense her presence all around me, and I feel a magnetic pull to the lovely rolltop desk where Mattie wrote the diary I've been reading for weeks.

My cheeks feel warm with the excitement of regaining ownership, and I lovingly trace the sparrow that graces the shelves. As I stand there feeling a little off-kilter, like I'm about to be sucked backward in time again, I suddenly notice someone's warmth beside me. When I turn, Gisela is there, wide-eyed. She meets my gaze.

"You're here to reclaim the desk, aren't you?" she says.

"Yes." I never thought I'd feel a rush of love, relief, and gratitude fill me up over a piece of furniture. And it's not just because being an adult is weird. It's the pulse of Mattie's joy forcing its way into my reality. "Can I use a card?"

That afternoon, Gisela has my desk delivered and carried up the stairs by two young men.

"Can you put it there?" I gesture to the spot I've cleared by the window. I've never had a really substantial desk before, just the cheap little some-assembly-required kind, so this is a big moment for me. It's like I'm a real grownup now, connecting with this piece of furniture across time.

When they leave, I step up to the desk that is now mine again. But my adventure isn't quite over. I examine every nook and cranny to see what I'll be working with, getting a feel for what Mattie used to love.

Finally, I get to the drawer on the left side of the desk, clear at the bottom. As I pull the drawer out, my face is near the desktop, and I notice the faint smell of perfume and tobacco that comes from the surface. I smile. But the bottom drawer has one more surprise for me.

Pulling it all the way out, I feel like there is something different here, like it's a little shorter than the drawer above it. Clear at the back, I find a false wall with a one-inch gap between that wall and the back of the drawer. My heart jumps and picks up speed as I tip my phone's light to look between the two pieces of wood. I reach in and pull out a folded piece of yellowed paper. It's a letter.

On the death of my dearest sister and best friend, Matilda Florence Conrad:

My heart has been broken into a thousand pieces by the death of my sister. She was my business partner, my best friend, my lifelong confidant. A few weeks ago, on a Sunday afternoon, she asked me to join her at the Lantern Palace Theater to watch The Cask of Amontillado. *She said that she had borrowed a collection of Edgar Allen Poe stories from Ansel and wanted to see the adaptation. I agreed, but when we arrived, I don't think that was the full truth of why she wanted to go.*

In a ruse that involved us searching for the restroom, we ended up in the basement of the building. She wouldn't tell me why we were there, but as she looked around the room, she said that she had confirmed her theory. It appeared that a wall had been repaired recently, based on the bricks and masonry equipment we saw. When an usher from the theater saw us exiting the basement, he directed us to the restrooms.

I asked her several times what was going on, and she said that she was concerned for me if she told me. I was so worried about her that I couldn't pay much attention to the film, especially when I noticed two men in the corner appearing to watch us, pointing in our direction.

When the fire started, there was a mad rush to get out, and though I tried to hold Mattie's hand as we ran, we were separated. I managed to make it to safety across the street from the theater, and I kept watching for her, but she never left the building.

After a long wait, the fire was out, so I hovered nearby and overheard the police discussing what they found. From their conversation, I believe that those men got to Mattie. When I asked about my sister and described her, the officer I spoke with frowned and said, "I'm sorry." They told me it seemed that she didn't try to leave the theater, as she was found near the seats rather than the stairwell, but I know she wouldn't have stayed in a fire.

She was determined to find something, to learn something, but I don't know what. And I'm afraid that it cost her her life. Sadly, I'm going to close this chapter and look the other way so I don't risk any repercussions on my family or our shop. Maybe later, the truth can come out, but for now, it must be my burden to bear. After reading the story in the paper today, I fear that the fire may have been set on purpose, and I wonder if Mattie's snooping had anything to do with that goal.

I collected the newspaper clippings about the fire and stored them with my sister's diary with the hopes that, someday, I may be able to piece together the truth. When it's safe. Poor Ansel joined our family to pack away all her belongings in the attic of her apartment. Ansel's family owns the building, and he agreed that we would all sort through the boxes when we were ready. For now, they shall remain a time capsule of all that Mattie loved, including her favorite china and the absurd glass Christmas ornaments she has been accumulating for years. What I wouldn't give to hear her joy again when she finds a unique one to add to her collection.

With a heavy heart, I will attempt to go on without my sister with the hopes that someday, her death won't have been in vain.

Sorrowfully,
Rosella Spurling

Utterly flattened from reading this, I wipe the tears from my eyes and fold the letter as I think about what I just read. So the fire could have been on purpose. As I thought, the mayor probably told his connections about what she had said. And they somehow planned this. Maybe they knew she was going to the theater. Maybe they overheard her talking about her plans in the shop, just as *she* had overheard *them* before.

But now ... now we had the paintings back. Mattie had led us there, and her diary helped us figure it out. And we put all the puzzle pieces together to discover Ansel's father's work had been right across the street from her shop all that time. It's hard to believe that this mystery sat patiently for over a hundred years, waiting for me to solve it. And it's hard for me to believe that I did it and that it took this long for the happy ending to come to fruition.

I text Beau a picture of the desk and brief him on the note. Now that all our walls are literally and figuratively down for us, I feel like every moment I'm not with him is too long to wait. Our rapid text thread ends with a *see you tonight* from him that makes my heart flutter.

When I lean back and allow myself to sink into the couch cushions, I feel unexpectedly overwhelmed by the past few days. Suddenly, I'm dozing.

I find myself in a white room with no shape or size, almost like it's a ... white space. It's like being inside a gallon of paint, it's so white and dimensionless. And it's so real that, even though I often know that I'm dreaming when I am, I can't tell if this is reality or just in my mind.

It feels like another plane of existence would, if I knew what that felt like.

I turn and see a woman in front of me. She's young, probably early twenties, and she's wearing an ankle-length charcoal gray dress with a blue ribbon around the high waist. Her long brown hair is wound into a simple low bun. She's pretty, but not extraordinary aside from her old-soul eyes that carry a depth I would never expect from someone her age.

As I observe her, she appears wilted, upset, with her arms crossed, head tipped down, and shoulders hunched. Haunted.

I feel compelled to hug her, so I approach and touch her arms as a request for approval. When she doesn't bristle, I wrap her in an embrace and tell her she's okay and cared for.

The faintest scent of honeysuckle and tobacco washes over me, and I know, somehow, that this is Mattie. As she relaxes, I take that as my cue to step back, and our eyes lock. In that moment, she smiles, her grip on her arms loosens, and she's standing tall, facing me. It feels like dawn is breaking over the horizon.

"You're safe and loved," I say once more.

She nods and turns, and I feel like we both finally release a pent-up breath. Then she's gone.

Chapter Thirteen

A few weeks after our discovery in the basement of the Morgan Building, we agreed to meet with Gisela at her shop because she said she has a surprise for us. Beau offered a ride to Claire and me, and we gladly accepted. Now, the three of us enter the shop with heavy anticipation. Did she get a cool shipment? What wonders does the Wunderkammer have in store for us today? And what do they have to do with us?

My nose has been attuned to picking up smells lately, and the first thing I check for when we enter the shop is a confirmation, that familiar tobacco smoke, like an old friend. But I don't pick up on her amid the scents of sage, crumbly books, dust, ancient leather, worn wood, and other faint odors dancing about.

She's still gone.

Being in the Wunderkammer feels different now. I can practically sense the layers of familiar history with layers of strangers' history and even more layers of what might have been, mixed with the comfort of being in a place with new friends. Today, it feels sort of like eating a piece of spice cake with cream cheese icing.

There is bitterness with spice cake, from the nutmeg and the cloves, as well as sweetness. And though I often was annoyed by the smell of tobacco and the cloying mystery that I had been stuck with, I do miss Mattie. Her absence is bittersweet, but the finishing touch, the icing, was a beautiful ending.

Without Mattie, I feel like my life has returned to normal but with a twist. I know things that I never expected to know about the world around me, things that I hadn't really given a thought to prior to her wedging her way into my life with her scents and her side quest. It's funny how you can discover things about a person you never knew or even knew *about* just by reading their diary. And it's even funnier how that person can become a part of you—in my case, I suppose, again—like a person is made of layers too, much like cake. Mattie connected me with a time that I hadn't given much thought to previously, and she let me see Hawthorne through her eyes. It's a gift I never knew I wanted.

I have certainly been transformed, and honestly, I like the woman I've become thanks to the experience she gave me. I never could have imagined that a diary would make my life so different.

Would I have connected with Beau again anyway? Maybe. Would I have gone off with Aaron? Maybe. I will never know the alternative, but I feel like there's a chance I wouldn't be here in Hawthorne anymore because I would have felt flightier. I wouldn't have seen the way that love really could be for me, the way that love could comfortably ground me, wrapping me in joy. I wouldn't have felt my roots digging into the ground here the same way. My connection and growth this fall made a difference for sure.

As our trio approaches the main desk, Gisela bustles in from the back, carrying a small box of tatting—lace made using a special technique that was popular during the Victorian era for collars and other decorations. When she sees us, she rushes forward, tucking stray loops of the stuff back into the box, her cheeks flushed with apparent excitement and her wild hair bouncing around her.

"Right on time!" she exclaims. "I'm so glad you all could make it."

"Me too," I say. "But why so cryptic?" I chuckle. "What did you want us to see?" I glance at Beau, and he squeezes my hand, shaking his head like he doesn't know either. Claire is watching Gisela with wide-eyed curiosity.

Just then, a woman pushes open the door to the shop, and the bell on the handle tinkles. She has a dignified but inquisitive presence, and her eyes are lit with an inner fire: a woman on a mission.

"Gisela!" she says. "You have good news for me?"

"I do. I do." Gisela motions for all of us to come closer, so we walk to the end of the desk and peer behind it. "I wanted all of you here for this." She winks at me and lifts a cloth-draped canvas from the floor, placing it on a stand.

Gently, she unwraps it and looks at the woman for a response.

The woman's deep brown eyes dart back and forth, like she's reading the canvas's story from the brushstrokes. Then, she gasps, hand to heart, and tears swell in her eyes. "You found it."

Glancing back at the painting, I realize that it's one from the collection we found in Beau's basement. This one shows a cottage near a lake, surrounded by rolling hills. Children are playing in the yard, and sheep are grazing nearby. Lots of blues and greens. Soft browns and yellows. And the stark red tile of the home's roof. It's the Valenti that Gisela recognized.

That's when I take a good look at the woman. I think she's the one Claire and I overheard talking to Gisela weeks ago about a painting she was searching for. I lock eyes with Claire, and we both smile.

"I would know that painting anywhere," the woman says. "That was my grandfather's childhood home." Her voice trembles a little as she continues, pointing out the features of the painting. "His brothers and sisters, the lake where they grew up in Italy, Lago Albano. It was all from memory. He used to sketch pictures of it while he told us about growing up there. So beautiful!" Then she looks from me to Beau to Claire and tips her head. "I searched for it for decades. Did *you* find it?"

Before any of us can respond, Gisela says, "They did. It's been across the street, hidden in a walled-off room, for the past century. I was lucky enough to be there when *Roots and Reaches* was unearthed again, and I researched it for the police. It was stolen in 1910 from the Novak Arts & Music Museum in D.C." She nods in my direction. "I think this corroborates your suspicions, Morgan, based on the timeline from the diary. The museum declined to reclaim it, and the police cleared it." Then she gives me a soft smile.

"Angela approached me for help in the search soon after I opened the shop."

"*Radici e Raggiunge*," the woman mumbles.

Gisela nods at the sound of the Italian name of the painting and then continues. "The museum wanted you to have it, Angela, to keep it in the family."

"I never thought it would be mine." Angela's hand shakes as she touches the canvas.

I peer at her for a moment as the pieces click into place in my mind. "You must be Ansel's daughter, then?"

She smiles at me, looking like a weight has been lifted. "Yes, I'm Angela Simons. Ansel Vale was my father. And my grandfather was the painter, Angelo Valenti."

I can't explain why I feel tears pool in my eyes at that moment, except to think that my curiosity about what happened to Ansel after Mattie was somewhat fulfilled, and I can only hope that he went on to love again, since he had a daughter. It's not sadness, *per se*, but more of a feeling of closure. I think Mattie would be happy that he didn't mourn her forever. The air near me grows chilly, and I suspect that Mattie has slipped in for a bonus last contact, looking at the paintings and feeling at peace.

We figured it all out! I whisper to her in my mind.

"That's amazing," is all I can manage to say aloud because I'm so overcome with emotions.

Everyone is grinning at each other now, and I'm thrilled that this story has a happy ending. "It's wonderful that you finally found it," Claire says. "I'm happy for you to have that piece of your history."

"As am I," Angela answers. Then her eyes grow distant. "My dad used to talk about Nonno's paintings when I was younger. I always liked to draw, and he would sit down with me and doodle, talking about doing the same with his dad when he was little." The deep-set crinkles around her eyes lift with the joy of the memory. "Of course, his dad could really draw, and neither of us had the gift. My granddaughter, though, is at the high school, and she works on the sets for the school plays. I think that talent made its way back through her. It's been a joy seeing her paint and connecting with these memories with her. I've been looking for that painting longer than she's been alive, and now, I can show her *Radici e Raggiunge* and her proud heritage."

"That's a beautiful story," Claire says.

"It's like a piece of both my dad and my grandfather came home," Angela responds. "I can never thank you enough." She squeezes each of our hands and nods her appreciation. Then Gisela wraps the canvas for her, and Beau offers to carry it to her car.

As we walk down the sidewalk, my mind is still spinning. It's hard to believe that I played a role in returning this painting to its rightful owners, bringing the legacy home where it belonged. It seems that so much has been restored lately, not just art, but relationships, my hope for the future. As I watch Beau gently sliding the canvas into the back seat of Angela's sedan, a little smile crosses my face. Restoration has been good to me lately. And I like it.

The chill of fall in Pittsburgh has faded into one of our famous brown and gray winters by December, soggy and grumbly, with clouds hanging so low in the sky that I imagine dozens of freshly washed charcoal sweaters draping over us, threatening to dribble everywhere. I always wish for a snowflake or two to turn the sog into a magical wonderland, but it's not often that we get much till January or February, when the big storms like to slam us.

Both of us bundled in heavy coats, Beau takes my hand as we leave the car and rush into the theater at Hawthorne High School. It's the kind of day that makes you grateful for the rush of heat when you enter a building, along with the feelings of nostalgia that bluster in with the chill. That early winter wind is half whine, half lullaby, and I always find it oddly comforting, like the city is complaining along with me.

Conversely, the whole lobby is buzzing with holiday cheer. Off to one side, I see a fun photo booth set up to look like Buddy's Candy Cane Forest, where some of the guests are already taking pictures with the fun props that are out.

I remove my beret and wave at Kenzi and Logan, who are already in the lobby, waiting for the doors to open, and then I spot Claire and her mom working their way toward us. Looks like our whole group has arrived! Beau nods at a gaggle of his coworkers—Ava, Mitch, Zoe, and Mira—who were excited to come see Zoe's brother in the show. They are clustered together with people who I assume are Zoe's family, laughing and smiling. In the distance, I spot Angela, likely here to see what her granddaughter did with the scenery, and it instantly warms me.

When we finally rush into the theater and grab seats with our friends, I have to admit that I'm bubbly: This is going to be a lot of fun. Though *Elf: The Musical* is not one of my usual macabre favorites, I know I'll enjoy the upbeat holiday feels. Plus, Vivi landed the part of Jovie, and I know she'll be amazing!

When the curtain goes up, I watch in delight as Vivi is witty, warm, and confident, and if I didn't already know that the kid cast as Buddy makes her heart sing, I never would have noticed the hint of awkwardness there when they interact on stage. She told me this week that playing opposite her crush has made the whole experience even more joyful, though it was certainly nerve-wracking for her. I love that she feels comfortable enough to confide in me now, and I'm thankful to be back in her world and Emmett's ... and especially Beau's.

As I watch her perform, I have a moment of weird introspection. It's strange how quickly the kids have grown into their own stories. How they've stepped up and out (almost). I wonder when she stopped being a kid and started being a leading lady, and that little clench in my heart happens again. I will it to let go, recalling that I'm here, now, and so ready to help with the next chapter.

When the show is over, everyone stands and applauds, not just because it was mostly family and friends but because they really did an amazing job! When we leave the theater, our whole group snakes through the reception line to congratulate Vivi. Beau says hi to a couple kids who call him "Mr. Blackwell," and I refrain from elbowing him in the ribs and calling him that too. I chuckle internally, though. So formal! Although I remember when being called Mrs. Blackwell melted my heart.

As that thought crosses my mind, I smile a little and check out Beau's profile as he waits his turn to talk to the star of the show. Maybe someday, again. And I feel oddly peaceful with that thought. I never thought I'd be here, never thought it would even be an option.

Finally, we swarm our favorite elf in a four-way hug that somehow leaves Beau out. Claire, Kenzi, and I all wrap our arms around her and squeeze while she laughs exuberantly and we overwhelm her with compliments. I look back at Beau again as we join her laughter, and he's just shaking his head, arms thrown out to the sides.

"Sorry, *Mr. Blackwell*." I peel myself off his niece, and my friends do too. Then I gesture for him to take a turn.

When he does, he wraps her in a huge bear hug. "I'm so proud of you!" I hear him say amid all the noise of the lobby. Again, he's going to make me cry.

A moment later, we're being swept along, but Vivi grabs our arms. "Stick around? I want to show you something."

After we pass through the line, we wait for Vivi, enjoying the reactions of all the audience members when they get to her. "She's going to have such a big head," I laugh.

"A little confidence never hurt anyone," Beau chuckles. Don't I know it.

Finally, the crowd has dispersed, and Vivi practically floats over to us and drags us to the photo booth where Emmett joins us, still dressed in all black from his time in the sound booth. We all hold up giant candy props and pose in front of the striped trees and glitter snow. Amid the laughter, I tap Vivi and whisper, "Should we grab Buddy for a couple pictures?" I tip my head toward the wiry teen wearing an elf's costume, his curly wig crooked on his head. He's surrounded by his family and a couple high school boys in street clothes.

When I look back at Vivi, her eyes go round. She grabs my arm and implores, "*No!*" I cackle in response. But I also notice that Buddy keeps glancing over at her, like he's trying to catch her eye. Too cute.

"This way," Vivi says suddenly. "I wanted to show you this." She pulls a key out of her pocket and leads us through the lobby to a hallway. We pass the main office and a restroom, but she stops in front of a pair of double doors after this and puts the key in the lock. We cluster around her.

"Are we allowed to go in there?" I look around for an idea of what *there* is, but I'm in the middle of the group and can't see any signs.

"Yes." She smiles. "I'm an assistant first period in the library, so I have a key in case the librarian isn't here when I get here. She drops her son off at daycare on her way in."

"Nice, but as much as I love a good library, why did you want us to see it?" I ask.

"Oh!" Vivi gently moves Beau out of the way so everyone can read the plaque beside the door.

Ansel Vale Library

"That's ..." I can't even express what I'm feeling right now. "Why is his name on the library?"

Vivi smiles. "Mr. Vale taught here for a few years before pursuing law. When he died, he left an endowment for the library's upkeep. The story is that something happened to a donor he had secured, and he always wanted to do something to make up for it. He wanted to make sure that our school library always had plenty of funds."

"That's a beautiful end to Mattie's story," Claire says softly. I recall some of the notes in her diary about Ansel and the donor that likely fell through. Then I tear up.

"There's more, though," Vivi says. She gestures through the doorway, and all of us file in.

It's quiet and dimly lit as we wait for the compact fluorescent bulbs to flare to their full brilliance. I look around at the stacks and breathe in the familiar smells. The overall energy is that of a peaceful place, a safe space for research and for dreaming.

Once the room is fully lit, Vivi motions for us to follow her again. "It's back here."

I round the corner, and suddenly, the back wall is in full view. There in the middle is a small framed quilt. Even with the distortion of light reflecting on the glass, though, I know it. Our group instinctively hushes as we take it in.

Approaching the quilt, my eyes trace the familiar sparrow, the fall colors of the background, the words painstakingly embroidered in crooked stitches, uneven but honest—like love itself. It's Ansel and Mattie's engagement quilt, now hanging in Ansel's library for all to see.

I touch the glass, moved by the continuity of love and memory, and I feel my heart swell with pride. *Mattie.* Beside the quilt is a plaque.

This quilt was handmade by Ansel Vale for his first love, Matilda Conrad, who tragically lost her life in Hawthorne's Lantern Palace Theater Fire in 1911. The son of a painter, Italian immigrant Angelo Valenti, Vale worked his entire life to ensure that the schools in our community were supported. An advocate of literacy and kindness, his love for Hawthorne and the children here lasted long after he left the halls as a teacher. An endowment was set up for the school library upon his death in 1991 to ensure that there would never be a shortage of books or funds to care for this part of the community's education. He would have wanted this quilt that meant so much to him to be on display in the school where he was able to change lives. This display is dedicated to Vale, whose life taught us that love endures long after we are gone. Donated by his daughter Angela Vale Simons.

"They put this up last week," Vivi adds with a soft smile.

"I wonder if finding her grandfather's painting prompted her to donate the quilt," Beau says.

I nod, still a little too overcome to risk saying anything. It's funny how stories—painted, stitched, and performed—carry us forward. I was right when I told Aaron the last time I saw him that the best stories have that forward momentum. And even though the story of me and Beau started long ago, I don't feel like it's the past. It is absolutely full-force forging the future.

And that's a tongue-twister, even in my head.

A chill passes over me, and I sense that Mattie has popped in to say hi, sans her favorite scents, just to reassure me that this is what she wanted for the ending of their love story. Now it's a memory that will outlast us all. A flicker of the lights tells me that she's not the only Lanternite here, making sure we don't forget them and watching over the next generation.

Chills dance around us as our group walks back to the cars afterward, the last ones to leave the school before it's locked up by the staff. We watch Vivi and Emmett hop in an old Honda Civic with a couple other friends to go get some grub at Medianoche Taco, our local late-night Mexican place. I sigh as I watch them. I guess growing up means eating tacos at a responsible time of night, but I'm okay with not going.

I look back at Beau and smile dreamily. I'm a dork. And I embrace it. In the moonlight, he has this otherworldly look with the shadows cast across half his face. He squeezes my hand, and I realize he caught me staring. Then he leans against my car door and pulls me to him.

"This was a really good night." He strokes my back and gazes into my eyes. He looks happy, and I'm so glad. The cold on my cheeks is no match for the internal simmer of falling in love with him again.

Then, the unthinkable happens. It starts as a whisper and then a brush, and suddenly, it's snowing big fluffy flakes like the sky cracked open from the force of holding in all that joy for so long, and it just has to share it with us in our moment here in the quiet parking lot.

A gentle laugh escapes my lips, and then I stroke his beard and lean in for a kiss.

"What is this now?" Beau says, pulling back and laughing. "You think I'm easy?"

"*Mr. Blackwell*," I begin, "this has been one of the hardest-fought victories of my life. I'm taking my prize." Then I smother his laughter with my lips, and we kiss like a couple of high schoolers—hello PDA—soft and slow, right there as the snow falls like feathers from a pillow around us.

Epilogue

Three years later ...

It couldn't be a more perfect morning. The sun has been up for a couple hours, but so have I. It was nice to have some quiet time to read the latest Margot Ashford novel while swaying on the porch swing, the salty breeze wafting over me. Everyone left me alone and went about their own business, heading to the beach, the kitchen, the coffee shop down the street ... whatever lit them up today, and I'm good with that.

"'Sisters, sisters,'" Rhiannon sings. She does a little twirl and flops onto the weathered porch swing beside me, lounging against the beach-themed pillows. Her long dark hair is twisted and held in place with a claw, and little wisps that escaped dance in the breeze. She swats at a long thread from her cutoffs dangling down her leg.

I cock my eyebrow at her and sip from my mug.

"Maybe I'll go sing to Aura," she says. "I'm sure she would appreciate Auntie's songs, no matter what they were about."

"You know, she asked me to sing a song about dirt the other day, so I'm not sure about her taste in music." I laugh, and Rhiannon sticks her tongue out at me. I gaze fondly at the toddler frolicking in the sand with Emmett and Vivi. Rhiannon's son Silas spikes a beach ball at them. When the little one catches me watching, she waves with both hands, more of an air grab than a wave, but then she runs after the ball, her little dark curls bouncing.

I never thought I would have children. Growing up, I didn't really have that mothering instinct. I mean, I wasn't exactly great with Haley and Lacey when they were little, scaring them all the time, using them for my own entertainment. When Beau and I got married the first time, we were both up-in-the-air about it. It wasn't important to us. We had tons of time. Maybe down the road. It was a decision we figured we could make ten years later.

Yeah, it ended up being a little longer than that. But when we were finally back together, steady, stable, I realized something I hadn't when I was younger. I wanted legacy, and I think the fact that we had lost his sister cemented that for me. Seeing Emmett and Vivi and thinking about how they carried on their mother's line actually made me want the same thing. I wanted to be part of that long line of females stretching back to the beginning of the human race that was all strung together by one common thread that continued on into the future.

I lost the ability to do that in my previous lifetime, Mattie's lifetime. It was taken away. And the more I thought about it, the more I knew that I wanted my soul journey and my current-life journey to keep going.

Younger Morgan would likely scoff at me because so many people think women still need a family to be whole, happy, and complete, but I know that I was already that before I added Beau to the picture. He and Aura just make the whole, happy, and completeness that much sweeter. And despite the fact that having a baby is scarier than jumping out of an airplane, she is definitely one of the sweet cherries of my life.

When I look back at Rhiannon, I see that she's watching her too. "She's a cutie," she says.

I smile. "I'm glad we could get everyone together to do this." I redo the tie on my oversized tee and flop back against the cushions again. "I haven't been to the beach in ages, and I love that she gets some time with her cousins."

"Sorrel Island is beautiful," Rhiannon says. "I'm glad your friend suggested it."

I hum in response. "We'll have to go to Bottle Beach tomorrow. She said it's practically covered in sea glass. Miles and miles of it."

"I bet it's magical." Rhiannon says. Then her eyes take on a faraway look. "I'm also glad you and I have been spending more time talking lately. But I feel like we missed a lot of partnership before we had that discussion a few years ago. I always felt like you were too grown up and headstrong for your own good, but I think you landed on your feet." Then she smirks. "Even without me over-guiding you."

I wrap my arms around her and squeeze hard. Her hair tickles my nose, and it smells like lemons and sunshine. "I fought pretty hard to be seen. I'm glad you see me now."

She gives into the hug and tips her head against mine, wrapping her hands around my arms. "Me too." We swing for a couple minutes in peace.

"Mom?" Silas exits the beach house and finds us cuddling on the swing, but he doesn't seem to judge us. He has my sister Haley's kids with him and is laden down with an armload of sand toys. "I'm taking them to the beach. Haley and Ty went to breakfast."

"Do you want help with ... oh." I can't help but laugh at the streaks of sunscreen all over little Hudson's and Sienna's exposed skin. "Come here, guys." I motion them over, and Rhiannon and I finish rubbing it in. "Points for thinking to do the sunscreen, though, Silas."

He nods and shifts the toys in his arms patiently.

"I'll get the umbrella and chairs," Rhiannon says to Silas. "I can meet you on the beach. Just give me a minute." Then she turns to me. "You stay here for a bit, mama. Make good use of all the babysitters and rest up."

I sip from my mug again and suddenly, I'm flashing back to the moment I stood on the porch in Castel Gandolfo, gazing out at the lake and wondering about my happily ever after. Or my happily right now. The moment that I became the *Tea and Reverie* print and kicked off the most bizarre story of my life.

As my thoughts float back to the present, I realize that this is a good chai latte. Vivi made it for me this morning, after her years of training at Lyon's. It's funny how she and Emmett have grown up, and Beau and I decided to start over.

My musing turns to my family as my sisters appear on the beach with their own families. Haley and Ty must have just returned from breakfast. Lacey is trying to drown her husband Colin ... at least that's what it would look like if they weren't laughing so hard. And Fallon is with her clan, building a sandcastle. This is the first time the whole family is vacationing together and the past few days have created a patchwork of noisy breakfasts, beach bonfires, and shared stories. Funny enough, I'm enjoying the chaos instead of bracing against it.

Since we reconnected a few years ago, Beau and I have been enjoying our new chapter. It's strange to have peaceful confidence in a relationship, and I still marvel at it from time to time. To know that this is permanent, rooted. To know that our emotional steadiness and my deeper sense of self has built a beautiful life for us ... and for our daughter. I never expected all of this, but here we are.

I was nervous about adding to our family initially. I wondered how Emmett and Vivi would take it, if they would feel replaced. But I couldn't have asked for a better set of older siblings for Aurelia. We've been really lucky in that respect. And they were happy to hear that we would honor their mom with her name.

I'm jolted from my daydream by the little munchkin I was just thinking about, as she throws her arms around my hips and lays her head on my lap. Immediately, I scoop her up and pull her close, sticky with sunscreen and saltwater like a sea nymph.

"Mama swing?" She peers up at me with her angelic face, those famous Blackwell brows arched high with her question.

"Mama swings," I answer. "You want to swing too?" When she nods, I hold her tight and push off. "Whoosh!" She erupts into giggles.

Then Aura leans forward. "Dada!"

I look up to see that Beau has entered the porch with a box that looks suspiciously like it contains pastries.

"Dada has a treat?" Aura slides off my lap and wraps her arms around Beau's leg, stopping him mid-stride.

"Oof. Yes, Dada has treats." He musses her hair and then scoops her up with one arm. "I got these at the Salty Mermaid Bakery Café." Then he turns to me. "You know what's funny?" When I shrug, he continues. "The owner looks just like the lady from *Braving Borders*."

"The show? You're kidding!"

"I mentioned it, and she said that they're twins. Can you believe that?" He sets the box down on the end table and joins me on the swing with our little sweetie in the middle.

"I get treat." She starts squirming to climb over Beau before he lifts her up in the air.

"Treats are for later, love."

"No. Treat now." She shoves at his hands and stretches toward the box as we both laugh.

"Who do you think you are that you get to make the rules?" Beau lays her on his lap, her head at his knees and her legs stretched against his chest. I promptly lean over and blow on the bit of tummy exposed between her swim top and bottom because, OMG, baby bellies.

She shrieks with delight and then huffs when I move my face away. Indignant, she attempts to scramble upright, and we let her. Once she's back in control, she smacks her chest and says, "Aura Tilda. In charge."

I'm almost crying with laughter. "Aurelia Matilda, darling, you are adorable, but you are *not* in charge."

"We should have known better than to give her that name." Beau grins at me and leans in for a kiss.

I greet him eagerly and then tip my head against his shoulder and sigh. Amid the smells of salt and surf, Beau's musky aroma of cedar and allspice, and the scent of sundrenched toddler and sunscreen, I swear I catch an overlay of cigarette smoke, and it almost makes me cry. Instead, I smile.

I gaze back at our little headstrong ball of mischief, the physical manifestation of what can happen when I advocate for my heart. "I wouldn't have her any other way."

Acknowledgements

The story of a little-known tragedy in Canonsburg, Pa., inspired *Ashes*, and I have my hairdresser, Holly North, to thank for telling me about it! In 1911, there was a theater on the main drag, and one evening, someone saw a spark from the projector, thought it was a fire, and yelled for everyone to get out. Sadly, many people were trampled in the exodus, so despite the absence of an actual fire, a couple dozen people passed in this tragedy. As Holly snipped and shaped my tresses, she told me about how the shop owners on that street had noticed odd things over the years—flickering lights, radio stations randomly changing, strange sounds when no one was there—and attributed them to those who passed in the theater tragedy. On a couple of my visits to her salon, I had witnessed the lights flickering in time to the music. The shop owners thought that maybe those wandering spirits were still trying to get attention.

These activities inspired me to write about the Lanternites, including Mattie with her desire to solve the mystery of the strange activities in Hawthorne. At canonsburgoperahouse.com, you'll find information about the story of the tragedy in the theater, and if you walk through the main part of the business district, you'll find a historical marker where the incident happened on the corner of East Pike Street and Central Avenue. Coincidentally, the building in Canonsburg is also called the Morgan Building. It wasn't until I had started writing the book and already knew we would be focusing on Morgan, Lacey's sister from *Good in Theory*, that I found out the name of the building.

I struggled with horrible brain fog that made writing nearly impossible, so I'm impressed that this book came together. I would write a chapter and not remember anything I wrote. I would re-read before I started the next chapter and not remember anything I just read. I had to take notes as I went along, re-read, and ask for help. When my brain started clearing up in August, I was surprised to see that I had a mostly completed manuscript that made sense except for a few little tweaks.

I guess Morgan was really determined to get her story out!

One of the characters in this book was actually created as part of a contest to name the series. The winner, Deb Herman, suggested the Soul Sisterhood series because it blended the concept of soul sisters—female friends who are bonded by something deeper than DNA—and the idea of a group of women supporting each other. I thought that was a beautiful suggestion and asked if she would like to create a character for *Ashes and Other Inheritances* as a prize. Deb decided that Gisela would be an antique shop owner who was originally from Germany and started her shop with some of her grandmother's furniture and household items. She's entrepreneurial, brave, smart, and open to the supernatural, just as Deb suggested. Deb not only shaped Gisela but also gave her her name, the same name as Deb's grandmother. I'd like to give a special shout out to Deb for her help because Gisela became an integral part of Morgan's journey.

As the end of the Soul Sisterhood series, I was excited to give a little wrap up that brought in *Braving the Shore* and *Good in Theory*, since we already had characters from *The Treasures We Seek* appear in this book. Of course, Lacey is there with the rest of her family on the beach, but I opted to have the book end on Sorrel Island, the setting for *Braving the Shore*, rather than bringing those characters in because they would be hard to explain. The bakery from that book makes an appearance, though, as the source for Beau's doughnuts.

I have to thank all of those who supported me during the writing of *Ashes*, from my writing group to my editor. My dearest CJAMS—J.V. Hilliard, Ann Howley, Em S. A'cor, and Sarah McKnight—you kept me on track, gave me great feedback, and provided the platform that encouraged me to keep going. If I have a deadline, then I have to make it, lol! And my editor, Susan Helene Gottfried, thank you for brushing and buffing Morgan's story!

The past year has been a real whirlwind for me with my writing career. Since my kids were finally both official tweens, with all the slang language installed, not joking, they have been more independent, which makes my schedule more flexible. That means I've been at more events, meeting more readers, and connecting with some fantastic authors. With this in mind, first, I want to thank my family for being so supportive of this career. It isn't easy on anyone, but I like to think that I'm not only making my own dreams come true but also showing my daughters that even the crazy dreams are possible. My husband has done a lot of the heavy lifting, both literally and figuratively, with this endeavor, so I want to specifically thank him. When you have a supportive spouse, it makes a world of difference!

And second, I'd like to ask you, my reader, to support other authors that you love. Check out the work of indies in your area, share a post that you enjoyed, show up at the local events, whether they are at libraries or breweries (yes, those are becoming more popular!). Being a creative today is certainly roughing it, and we need all the help we can get to keep things going, so more books like this one can get out in the world.

If you enjoyed this book, or any other indie author's book especially, please share a review, whether that's on a site like Amazon, Barnes and Noble, or Goodreads or on your own social media. We live and die by people spreading the word!

Thank you for reading this far and for your support! And if you catch a little whiff of cigarette smoke mixed with perfume, tell Mattie I said hi.

Discussion Questions

1. For a woman who's not actually there, Mattie is absolutely a main character in this book. And her diary helps give her shape and leave a legacy well after her death, a hundred years later when her diary is discovered. If you were a ghost signaling someone with a scent, what would you pick? What memory would you share?
2. Morgan didn't hold back much once she realized that Mattie was directing her on an adventure, even though she didn't know the goal. Would you have done the same? Or would you have thrown out the diary once you connected it with the ghost?
3. Life is full of strange coincidences and things we can't explain. When did something in your life strike you as odd, as maybe a nudge to do something you wouldn't normally? Better yet, did you follow that nudge or stay on the beaten path?
4. What is your opinion on dating an ex? Is it a breakup because it's broken? Or is there a second chance under the right circumstances?
5. Aaron hit the nail on the head with the scavenger hunt he did for Morgan. If someone could do a grand gesture for you, what would you love to see?
6. What would you name your inner critic? Bradley and Kevin are already taken.
7. Morgan found herself in an impossible situation in her early twenties. Would you have handled it differently? Do you think she would have handled it differently if she had been older?

8. Beau's family was supportive through the difficulties that he and his sister found themselves in when they were young adults. When is a time that your support system (family or friends) stepped up and really had your back?
9. Morgan's beret symbolizes a lot for her. It's red and fancy, so it gives her a little flair and makes her noticeable. It's also almost a security blanket at times, helping her tame her hair, appear put together, or give her something to do with her hands when she's nervous. What does it mean to you as the reader? Do you have something that serves a similar purpose in your life?
10. If you went to Italy, what would your souvenirs be?
11. Haunted houses: love them or leave them? What about haunted artifacts?
12. Legacy plays an important role in this story. What is one thing you hope someone would discover when you're gone that would tell them a lot about you and what's important to you?

About the Author

Cori Wamsley is the award-winning author of the Soul Sisterhood series, best friend stories with a side of sweet romance. Her books are enchanting and witty women's fiction, woven with the magic of self-discovery, history, adventure, and falling in love. She has written twelve books.

Aside from writing books, she also runs a small publishing house, Aurora Corialis Publishing, where she helps authors write and publish their personal stories, as well as some fiction.

Cori lives in Pittsburgh, Pa., US, with her husband and two creative tween daughters. When she's not at her desk, she loves painting, crafting, playing piano, and singing. She's also into reading sweet romance and dreaming about traveling to Europe.

Follow Cori on Instagram, Threads, or TikTok @coriwamsley_author.

Learn more at www.coriwamsley.com.

Soul Sisterhood Series

For more best friend stories with a side of sweet romance, check out the other books in the Soul Sisterhood series!

www.ingramcontent.com/pod-product-compliance
Lightning Source LLC
LaVergne TN
LVHW040040080526
838202LV00045B/3420